SILENT ZONE

INDEPENDENCE DAY

Created by Dean Devlin & Roland Emmerich
Novel by Stephen Molstad

Other *Independence Day* books from HarperPrism:

Independence Day
by Dean Devlin & Roland Emmerich
and Stephen Molstad

Independence Day
from the screenplay and novelization
by Dean Devlin & Roland Emmerich
and Stephen Molstad
adapted for young readers by Dionne McNeff

Look for a new *Independence Day* novel
coming in early 1998

SILENT ZONE

ID4
INDEPENDENCE DAY

Created by Dean Devlin & Roland Emmerich
Novel by Stephen Molstad

HarperPrism

A Division of HarperCollinsPublishers

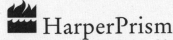 HarperPrism

A Division of HarperCollins*Publishers*
10 East 53rd Street, New York, N.Y. 10022-5299

ISBN: 0-06-105278-7

HarperCollins®, ®, and HarperPrism® are trademarks of HarperCollins*Publishers* Inc.

HarperPrism books may be purchased for educational, business, or sales promotional use. For information, please write: Special Markets Department, HarperCollins*Publishers*, 10 East 53rd Street, New York, N.Y. 10022-5299.

Printed in the United States of America

First printing: August 1997

Designed by Paul Banks

Library of Congress Cataloging in Publication data is on file with the publisher

Visit HarperPrism on the World Wide Web at
http://www.harpercollins.com

97 98 99 00 ❖ 10 9 8 7 6 5 4 3 2 1

To my science advisor,
K.R.W., and his wife.

TABLE OF CONTENTS

SILENT ZONE

ID4

INDEPENDENCE DAY

PROLOGUE

The Battle Continues

On July 5, the worldwide battle against the invaders continued. All thirty-six of the alien city destroyers had successfully been shot out of the sky, but there was no mood of celebration in the below-ground research facility referred to as Area 51. This secret lab, buried below the Nevada desert, had replaced Washington, DC, as the functioning headquarters of the United States. Inside the lab's communications and tracking room, President Thomas Whitmore, his advisors, and a crew of technicians were frantically working to coordinate a counteroffensive. Four city destroyers, along with thousands of smaller ships called attackers, had crashed to earth on American soil—many of them in the scrub desert surrounding the lab—and it was too soon to know how many survivors there might be. President Whitmore, who had first come to national prominence as a fighter pilot in the Gulf War, had personally climbed into the cockpit of an F-18 jet and led the squadron of planes which had scored the first kill against these gargantuan airships. The aliens had apparently detected the radio transmissions coming from the base and broken off another attack to fly toward the spot. They were on the verge of destroying Area 51 when Whitmore's team discovered that it only took a single AMRAAM missile detonating against the giant ship's primary weapon to cause a chain-reaction explosion powerful enough to rip the craft apart. The technicians immediately spread this news around the globe, then waited for reports to filter back.

High above the base, AWACS reconnaissance planes were circling, using their sophisticated electronic equipment to provide Area 51 with cell-phone and radio links to the remnants of America's military. From their perspective, the AWACS pilots had a clear view of the monstrous, fire-blackened hull of the destroyer lying in the desert, a smoldering shell seventeen miles wide. Also visible were the convoys of military vehicles coming from all directions to surround the destroyer. All day long, men and equipment that had survived the devastating attack poured in from military installations all across the Southwest. By midafternoon, the solid ring of soldiers and civilians surrounding the craft was thick enough to be seen from the air. On the ground, the crest of the ruined megaship was visible from as far away as Las Vegas.

Delta Company out of Fort Irwin was one of the first on the scene. This elite squad of soldiers was given the unenviable task of acting as the shock troops for the counterinvasion. They were the first ones in.

It was like storming into an impossibly large church. They entered through a two-hundred-foot break in the exterior wall, advancing quietly, twenty-five yards at a time. The size of the ship's interior spaces was stunning, incredible. Once they had secured and cleared the first thousand yards, armored vehicles, Jeeps, and hundreds of both soldiers and civilians, poured through the breach. Deeper into the ship, the rooms became a labyrinth of smaller chambers, closing down to the size of narrow hallways in some places. Delta Company pushed forward, tensely expecting to encounter hostile survivors around each corner. They began to find fragments of alien corpses ripped apart in the blast. But by the end of the first twenty-four hours, not a single survivor had been discovered.

Helicopters had entered the ship's vast central chamber through great holes that the explosion had torn through the roof. The pilots had reported "a big barrel of fish," thousands of destroyed attackers lying in a single heap three miles across. Delta Company received orders to spearhead a drive toward this central chamber, where it was thought they might find survivors and take them as prisoners.

Nolan jumped from the surface of one crashed alien attack ship, landed on the hard shell of the next, then sprinted the sixty feet to the edge of another, where he took cover and searched the vast space around him with the barrel of his assault rifle. The central chamber of the city destroyer gave him the feeling of being at the bottom of an underground lake surrounded by blackened vertical walls. He estimated the distance across the chamber to be about three miles. Gray sunlight poured in from where the explosion had torn away a large section of the roof. In the distance, he could hear the sound of a Jeep and the sporadic shouts coming from another recon team working the southern sector of the chamber. The space had obviously been some kind of portable airport, a staging area for the attacker planes, which now lay in a colossal pile, stacked ten deep in some places, after having been knocked loose from their moorings high overhead.

Nolan glanced back the way he had come and gave Simpkins the come-ahead signal. As his partner crossed the open space, Nolan covered him, tensely scanning in all directions for signs of danger. Although Delta Company hadn't heard or seen any live fire, reports had been made in other sectors of alien snipers using handheld weapons. As Simpkins made his dash, the ship under him settled slightly, groaning deeper into the pile of identical ships on which it rested. He was momentarily knocked off balance, recovering just in time to avoid being tossed over the side. Peering over the edge, he looked into the maze of narrow tunnels created by the jumble of saucers. He gulped before backing carefully away toward higher ground.

First Simpkins, then Myers, then Henderson joined Nolan under the ledge where the edge of one ship rested on another. Their objective, a cigar-shaped craft, visibly different from the others, was just on the other side of the ship they were using for cover.

Nolan spoke into his handset, "OK, Captain, we're one ship away from the target. I see some windows, but no doors. Looks like the best way in would be to shoot out one of the windows."

"Roger, team leader. Use your discretion. If you can't find a quick way in, turn around and come back down to base. Over."

"Confirmed." Nolan slipped the walkie-talkie back in his belt. Turning to the other men, he said, "Me and Simpkins go in first. As soon as we get through the windows you two advance and cover. Here we go."

And off he went. At close range, Nolan squeezed off a few

rounds from his M-15, and the armor-piercing bullets completely shattered the clear material. Up close, the surface of this long ship had a weathered look. Unlike the others, it seemed to have seen service out in the elements. And this one wasn't covered with any of the strange symbols embossed into the surfaces of the attackers. He ducked and peered through the opening. No sign of movement, but he was only looking into one, mostly empty, chamber. Using his flashlight, he could see there was a doorway leading deeper into the ship.

"Looks like an operating table," Simpkins said sourly, his own flashlight sweeping across the ceiling of the ship. Indeed, since the vehicle was upside-down, there was a weirdly contoured metallic table firmly attached to the ceiling. On what was now the floor of the vehicle, all manner of debris, including several objects that might have been surgical tools, lay in heaps.

"Sick mo' fo's," Nolan snarled to himself. "I'm going in." He fitted his flashlight into the mount at the top of his rifle, rolled through the opening, and snapped to his feet, ready to fire. Once Simpkins had joined him, he signaled toward a doorway covered with some stiff material drawn closed and obstructing the view to the back of the ship.

Communicating by gesture alone, the pair put themselves in position, then Simpkins tore back the curtain. Fingers tense against triggers, the men aimed into the next chamber. It was a narrow corridor with large shelves on both sides. These shelves had been full when the ship turned over, spilling their contents into the narrow aisle between them. Beyond the pile of debris, the space opened again.

"Nolan, check this out. What the hell were they doing in here?" Simpkins's flashlight was focused on the spilled contents of the shelves: a green nylon baseball cap with the

Quaker State logo, a prosthetic leg, hunting jackets, shoes, scarves, a rifle, photographs, all manner of human artifacts, the detritus of a thousand abductions.

"All those people who said they got kidnapped by aliens and they stuck probes up inside of them and did experiments, looks like this is where it happened. And this pile of crap is the coatroom."

". . . or the lost and found."

Nolan took four measured steps deeper into the room, crunching a pair of eyeglasses under his boot. He reached down and picked through the debris, retrieving an audiocassette. "It's in Japanese," he said, tossing it aside and picking up a piece of paper. He studied it for a second, then reached for a second sheet.

"What is it? You find something?"

"Maybe. You know how people are saying they must have had spies, humans who were helping them?"

"Yeah, I've heard that, but it's bullshit. Like they needed any help."

"Take a look." Nolan shrugged. He handed the pages over his shoulder and picked up a third. The pages had been torn from a blank book, and were full of quick-but-skillful engineering schematics of alien technology. One showed some kind of screen at the top of a wiring chart, another page labeled "aqua box" had a two-second sketch of something that looked like an Egyptian hieroglyph in a six-sided box. Surrounding the picture were equations and notes, all of them completely indecipherable to the soldiers. "There's a whole book of this crud. Let's take some of this stuff down to show the captain and come back with more men."

Simpkins relayed that plan back to Henderson and Myers, then returned to where Nolan was gathering evidence. "How convenient," he said when he noticed that his partner had found a shopping bag and was dumping items into it like this was a rummage sale. Simpkins spotted some poor slob's wallet and started flipping through it when he thought he heard Nolan say something like, *Don't worry. I won't hurt you. Be calm.* He glanced over at Nolan, who looked right back at him.

"Quit messing around, Simpkins."

Don't be afraid. Do not use your weapons. No harm will come to you. This time they were looking right at one another, and nobody's lips had moved. *Do not use your weapons,* the command repeated itself out of nowhere. Both men turned toward the back of the ship, fully expecting to see a tall alien figure step into the murky light. And a second later, that is exactly what happened.

Nolan snapped his rifle up and took aim at the thing's forehead, in the spot above its eyes where the brain was so close to the surface you could literally see it thinking. In the glare of the flashlight, the creature's glistening skin looked ghost white. Long almond-shaped lids blinked over bulging reflecting eyes the size of ripe plums.

Simpkins's first impulse was to shout "enemy in the hole," and open fire. Instead, he froze, staring down the barrel of his rifle, locked on the alien's chest. Then, almost mechanically, he felt himself change his mind. *Tell the others not to fire,* he said to himself. Then, quite aware that he was being manipulated by this bony, snot-shiny, shell-headed crawdad, he felt *the need* to tell the guys outside. Without breaking concentration on his target, he backed into the rounded room with the table on the ceiling and yelled to the others, "We got one. It's alive, but it's not dangerous! He won't attack! Hold your fire."

"It's messing with us, man," Nolan said, visibly trembling—partly from fear, partly because of the effort it took not to lay his rifle aside as the thing was urging him to do. "It's messing with my head."

In this confusing situation, Nolan and Simpkins were, quite literally, of two minds. Without losing any possession of their regular consciousness, they were "mentally listening" to the alien, who had found some way to "speak" to them. They were about to shoot anyhow, but then both men felt something like an emotion, a vibe, which assured them the alien would cooperate. It was a teletactile communication, a skillful imitation of the human feeling of friendship, a trick the creature could only have learned through previous exposure to Earthlings.

"All right, let's try to take this boy prisoner," Nolan relented. "Hands up, asswipe. Hands up." The creature awkwardly complied, lifting its slender, semi-transparent arms away from its sides. Nolan and Simpkins carefully backed into the doorway before signaling the thing forward. Slowly, clumsily, it made its way over the pile of clothing and other objects until there was nothing between it and the men's rifles.

"Hold your fire," Simpkins ordered the two men leaning in the broken window, weapons trained on the doorway. The alien stepped into the open space of the upside-down examining room, its fleshy, two-pronged feet carefully exploring the surface of the debris-littered ceiling for a secure foothold each time it advanced.

From beyond the shattered window, Henderson's voice could be heard as he spoke into his radio. "Cap, we got one. We got a prisoner. Send in some backup."

It took two full hours to march the alien prisoner back to the command post at the western extremity of the central chamber. The hard slopes created by the jumble of ships proved treacherous footing for a creature accustomed to a very different environment. At every fork in the mazelike journey, the soldiers carefully selected the path that would offer the least chance of an escape. By the time they arrived with the Extraterrestrial Biological Entity they were calling "the monster," over a hundred armed men were there, with rifles drawn to greet them.

A Jeep was brought forward to transport the alien outside. By this time, Simpkins had appointed himself the creature's bodyguard and was busy channeling the soldiers' hostilities by reminding them how valuable a prisoner would be for preventing any future attacks. The creature, doing exactly what was required in the situation, remained perfectly docile, even when Simpkins came forward with a large piece of canvas. It was draped over the alien, then tied down in a way that completely concealed its body. This was done more for the creature's security than for fear it might try to escape. Simpkins had already visualized the seven-mile journey to the outside, and foreseen the danger of an angry soldier squeezing off a few rounds in spontaneous hatred. Everyone was anxious to get some payback for what its race had done to theirs.

Bundled like a rolled-up carpet and lying passively in the back of the Jeep, shotguns leveled at its head, the creature endured the long rough road out of the destroyer without moving a muscle.

Hours later, Simpkins, Nolan, Henderson, and Myers reported to the remnants of Area 51's main hangar. Their prisoner was en route back to Fort Irwin for interrogation, and they had come to deliver the evidence they had gathered from the cigar-shaped craft to General Grey. He had requested to meet personally with these men. They were quickly coming to be known as the guys who brought the only prisoner out of

Whitmore's ship. As their story circulated, each retelling added some new detail which emphasized their bravery. In time, their story would join hundreds of others and would be told, in different forms, for many years, as part of the folklore that arose in the wake of the invasion.

While they were waiting, Nolan started thumbing through the sketchbook he'd found. He could see it was the haphazard journal of someone with very sloppy handwriting. Its pages were filled with equal parts of machinery sketches, English sentences, and mathematical equations. He turned to a watercolor painting of the desert and admired the artist's skill. The picture was signed in the bottom corner. The book had belonged to someone named Okun.

1

A New Roof for Project Smudge
1972

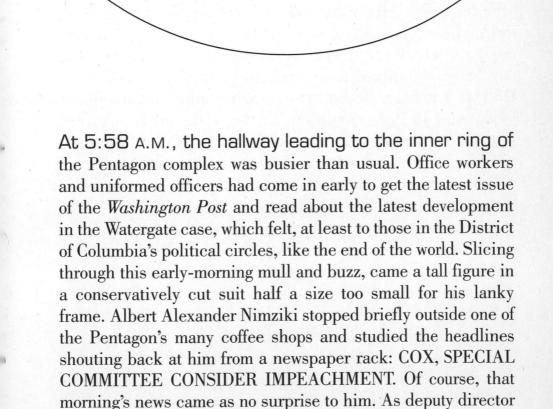

At 5:58 A.M., the hallway leading to the inner ring of the Pentagon complex was busier than usual. Office workers and uniformed officers had come in early to get the latest issue of the *Washington Post* and read about the latest development in the Watergate case, which felt, at least to those in the District of Columbia's political circles, like the end of the world. Slicing through this early-morning mull and buzz, came a tall figure in a conservatively cut suit half a size too small for his lanky frame. Albert Alexander Nimziki stopped briefly outside one of the Pentagon's many coffee shops and studied the headlines shouting back at him from a newspaper rack: COX, SPECIAL COMMITTEE CONSIDER IMPEACHMENT. Of course, that morning's news came as no surprise to him. As deputy director of the Central Intelligence Agency, it was his job to know what was going to be in the newspapers days, weeks, and sometimes years before the papers themselves knew.

Nimziki was the youngest man ever to attain the post of deputy director, but he had gotten a jump on the competition, having been a professional spook since he was sixteen years old. Nimziki grew up in Lancaster, Pennsylvania, where he internalized some of his chilliness of public demeanor from his Amish neighbors. When his agronomist father landed a job with the UN, he moved the family to New York City's Roosevelt Island, into a neighborhood crowded not only with UN diplomats but with the spies sent from around the world to keep an eye on them. Overlooking a busy, upscale intersection, the family's new apartment afforded young Albert the perfect vantage point for watching the endless game of cat and mouse. For two years it had been a spectator sport, with him spying on the spies. But one day he boldly walked downstairs and talked to one of them. Only a day later, he had a parabolic mike and telephoto lens, using them to eavesdrop on conversations transpiring at the posh outdoor café across the street. From this early training, he'd moved on to Georgetown U., where he earned a double major in criminology and international relations. Soon after joining the CIA, he proved himself to be not only a daring and talented field operative but also a highly efficient administrator, and it was this second skill which had fueled his steady rise through the agency's ranks. At only thirty-four years of age, he had aspirations to rise higher still.

He found his elevator and rode it down one floor to the building's basement. The heavy doors opened after he inserted a security card into the lock, depositing him into a bare hallway guarded by a pair of soldiers. After glancing at his ID plaque, they waved him through, and he stepped into the Tank, the most secure conference area in the entire Pentagon complex.

Inside, sitting around a long walnut conference table, were a dozen men, all of them white, all of them older than Nimziki. They were elite figures from the U.S. military and intelligence communities, men who had been entrusted, however reluctantly, with "the nation's dirtiest little secret." Collectively, they were known as Project Smudge.

After a brief round of perfunctory greetings, Nimziki sat down, and Bud Spelman, assigned to the Defense Intelligence Agency, walked to the podium at the front of the room. Serious as a bulldog, the barrel-chested Colonel Spelman had once been an Army drill instructor, and it showed in the blunt way he handled the meeting.

"Gentlemen. The purpose of this meeting is to update you on a series of possibly threatening UFO occurrences and, if warranted, to adopt an action plan. Now I trust everyone has had a chance to review the status report I sent around, so you basically know the situation, but I do want to show you a piece of radar tape shot last month by Northern Tracking Command." After pulling down a retractable white screen and dimming the lights, he moved to a projector set up at the back of the room. As the film began, the screen went black. "You're looking at the night sky over our atomic storage facility near Bangor, Maine. These are enhanced-composite radar images transferred to film to improve their quality. And here comes our visitor."

From the upper corner, an uneven blotch of white light appeared. The pulsing, indistinct shape began a slow and steady descent toward the bottom of the screen, its outline slowly coming into better focus. "In addition to the radar, we had several naked-eye witnesses on the ground who say they got a good look at it. But, as usual, their descriptions are all over the map. Some of them said the thing gave off a golden light, others called it an orange-red light, while another maintains it was bluish in color. The same with engine noise. Some people heard 'a high whine, like an electric motor' while others noted a 'complete absence of sound.' What we know for certain is that this thing hovered directly over our underground storage bunkers at an altitude of fifteen hundred feet for approximately two minutes, then—and here comes the reason for showing you the film."

All eyes were turned toward the screen. The UFO suddenly darted straight up, rising another thousand feet above the earth before commencing a series of startling zigzags across the night sky. Whatever it was, it moved with both incredible speed and astonishing agility as it executed a series of right-angle and hairpin turns without significant loss of velocity. Then, as mysteriously as it had appeared, it zipped out of view in one long streak. Spelman stopped the tape and turned to face the others.

"Looks like my wife has been giving driving lessons," an Air Force general quipped, eliciting a polite chuckle from the others.

Spelman didn't change expressions. "No aircraft known to Defense Intelligence has performance capabilities equal to what we just witnessed. After review of the tape, DIA considers it likely that what you have seen is a reconnaissance mission. And where there's smoke, there's fire. This intelligence gathering could be preparatory to some sort of attack, or, in a worst-case scenario, a full-scale invasion."

Spelman paused to let that sink in. His audience was less amazed by the tape they'd seen than by Spelman's ability to make this speech as if it were the first time he'd ever made it. Once a year, he would call a meeting such as this one to present evidence to the members of Project Smudge. And each time, he and Dr. Wells, his sole ally on the committee, would argue that the nation was exposed to a clear-and-present danger. They were the hard-liners who argued that the world was on the brink of imminent invasion by extraterrestrials. Behind their backs, they were known as the crazies, especially Dr. Wells, the only man known to have held a conversation with an intelligent life-form from another world. Eventually, Wells's desperate insistence on the need to adopt his proposals led to his banishment from Smudge. Isolated, Spelman was reluctant to call another meeting, but then had found a most unexpected ally, someone with a daring plan which might finally end the interagency bickering which had crippled the government's research into UFOs for more than a decade—Nimziki.

When it was apparent that Spelman was finished talking, Dr. Insolo of the Science and Technology Directorate was the first to raise a familiar objection, "We've been getting sightings like this for years; why is this one special?"

To Spelman, one of the true believers, the question seemed ridiculous, almost insulting. "First off, *all* of these sightings are significant. What makes this one especially threatening is that it didn't take place over the desert or the ocean. This vehicle buzzed one of our most sensitive and potentially damaging installations. We don't want all that uranium falling into the wrong hands."

Jenkins, subchief of the CIA's Domestic Collections Division, did little to disguise his feeling that this meeting was a waste of time. "Are you proposing that the committee adopt the Wells plan?" The oft-proposed and always-rejected course of action recommended by Wells called for nothing less than a full-scale preparation for war, a series of projects so large that the presence of the aliens would soon become public knowledge. The plan was always rejected by an overwhelming margin. Secrecy was priority number one, and there were two reasons for this. In the wake of every group sighting of a UFO, civilians became hysterical. There was no telling what kind of mass chaos the country would face if the government were forced to confirm the presence of these visitors. The second, related reason, was that no one wanted to take responsibility for having kept the information hidden for over twenty-five years. Secrecy begat secrecy, one denial led to another, until the participating agencies found themselves, a quarter of a century after the crash at Roswell, sitting on a full-blown conspiracy to keep the American public—and the world—in the dark. There was not a chance in hell that anyone in that room was going to commit himself to an effort like the one Wells had envisioned, especially given the present unstable political climate. No one wanted to be caught holding the bag if Congress started one of its investigations into the nation's spy agencies.

Then Nimziki unleashed his bombshell. "I've decided to support Colonel Spelman. After reading through some past reports and looking at the tape we've just seen, I think the time has come to start taking this threat seriously."

Since Nimziki had joined Smudge, he had been the most ardent critic of the Wells plan, arguing that it was a gigantic waste of time and money, that the aliens posed no significant threat. In fact, he had taken a personal dislike to Wells and had not been content with kicking him out of Smudge, but had stripped him of any security clearance and had him run out of the government altogether.

Jenkins grinned across the table. He knew Nimziki well enough to realize there must be some ulterior motive at work. "What exactly does the deputy director have in mind?"

"The plan I'm proposing takes certain elements from the one dear old Dr. Wells drew up. But, as you might expect, it's significantly more low-key. It calls for the formation of a rapid deployment alien-vehicle intercept force, a Special Weapons And Tactics squad capable of getting to one of these aircraft before it gets away. At the same time, I want to revamp and redouble our efforts at Area 51, to see if we can't get some results from the craft we already have. I have some long-term plans to get things moving out there."

"This SWAT team. What would it do?"

"The purpose of this force would be to gather better visual information on these craft, attempt to establish radio communication, and, if possible, to bring one of them down for further study and reverse-engineering purposes."

"You mean you want to shoot them down?" asked one of the Navy guys, visibly agitated by the idea.

"Is that wise?" Dr. Insolo asked. "Let's not forget, these airships are armed. They have laser cannons which, except in the Wisconsin case, they haven't used. We don't want to start a fight we're not sure we can win."

Jenkins nodded. "He's right. Besides, what good will it do to capture one of these rascals? We've already got the one that went down at Roswell, and that hasn't done us a lick of good."

One by one, the members of the committee took turns raising objections and pointing out shortcomings of the plan. Then Jim Ostrom, aka the Bishop, asked the question that was on everyone's mind.

"This is an about-face for you, Albert. I remember when Dr. Wells used to make rather similar proposals, and you'd sit there and shoot him down. What's changed? Is it this film we just watched?"

"No, it's a story I heard from your colleague at the NSA, Dr. Podsedecki." Podsedecki, a former Wells-supporter and leader of the Walker Greens, a secret society within the already hypersecret National Security Agency, was a sort of legendary cult figure in spy circles.

"It goes like this. Let's say you're out for a hike in the mountains with some old friends. You're walking down a narrow trail surrounded by tall grass. It's a beautiful day, and you're looking around enjoying the scenery when the hiker right behind you suddenly shouts RATTLER! How are you going to react? Do you stop and consider the credibility of your source? Wait for additional evidence to satisfy your threat-assessment criteria? Or would you go into immediate action, doing everything in your power to locate the threat and determine its precise nature? The tape we've witnessed this morning is one of two things: it's either a snake in the grass, or something that *appears* to be a snake in the grass. In either case, it's our responsibility to find out."

"Shoot first, ask questions later," Jenkins commented sardonically.

If the comment bothered Nimziki, he didn't show it. "There's one aspect of this plan that doesn't appear in your briefing papers. Given the political climate inside the beltway at the present moment, we all expect to see a slew of new appointees. Even if Nixon weathers this storm, his major appointments are sure to face scrutiny and possible replacement, most likely with a bunch of Midwesterners with spotless records—guys like Jim Ostrom."

Everybody who knew Jim laughed. He was a real Jimmy Stewart–type. "But unfortunately," Nimziki went on, getting to the most delicate part of his presentation, "these people aren't necessarily going to be as good at maintaining secrecy as Jim is. In other words, Project Smudge faces exposure, especially if we go ahead and adopt the proposals we're considering today. Exposure of this information to the public would, of course, be a disaster, especially now. Americans aren't sure they can trust the government at the moment, and we don't want to do anything to exacerbate that perception.

Therefore, I propose consolidating these programs under one roof."

"The question is: Whose roof?"

"Mine."

"Yours? The CIA would take control of the project?"

"Not the entire CIA," he explained, glancing at the team from Domestic Collections. "Just me. At least until things settle down."

The generals could hardly suppress their delight. This young hotshot seemed to be offering them a valuable and unexpected gift, a way out of Project Smudge. If they understood him correctly, they would all be able to wash their hands of the government's "dirtiest little secret." After a long moment of silence, Dr. Insolo spoke up.

"The Science and Technology Directorate, for one, would be extremely interested in such a proposal." Knowing that Nimziki would have a price, he went on to ask, "What would a program like this cost?"

Spelman and Nimziki took turns explaining the rather creative funding structure they had devised. It was something of a shell game that would cost each agency less than three million per year. To get out of the project, the agencies would have paid five times that price. Within a matter of minutes, the members of the committee voted unanimously for the official dissolution of Project Smudge. Then, all smiles and handshakes, they began heading out the door, anxious to get on with other business.

Bishop Jim stopped in the doorway and leaned in for a private word with Nimziki. "It's an awful risk you're taking, Albert. All it would take would be for one of these ships to buzz over Cleveland during an Indians game and . . . well, it wouldn't exactly be good for your career. But I trust you know what you're doing." What Nimziki was doing was following his instinct for accumulating power, for picking cards up off the table and tucking them up his sleeve until he needed them.

Before he went, Ostrom had one last piece of advice. "I like the idea of getting things running again out at Area 51, but be careful you don't have too much success with it too quickly. If the military finds out you've got that ship up in the air, this committee will come back to life faster than you can say the words 'Soviet Union.' You need to be careful who you select as your new lead scientist out there. Make sure it's someone you can trust."

"As a matter of fact," Nimziki replied, "I think I've already found the perfect guy for the job."

2

Recruiting Fresh Blood

Brackish Okun was a certified, bona fide, clinically tested genius. But this wasn't the opinion most people formed of the twenty-one-year-old science student upon first impression. He was often mistaken for a simpleminded hippie kid with very strange taste in clothing. It wasn't so much the bell-bottom corduroy slacks or the riot of pens, calculators, and slide rules crowding the breast pocket of his Perma-Prest shirts. Nor was it the mop of long hair that straggled down to his shoulders. The thing that most made him appear to be nothing more than a simpering blockhead was his constant nodding. Whether he was concentrating on a lecture, listening to music, or working through a thorny mathematical equation, Okun nodded. His friends teased him about it. His mother tried to get him to stop, telling him it was an obnoxious habit akin to cracking his knuckles. But Okun continued to nod. And those who spent time with him, rather than convincing him to stop, often took to nodding themselves. Although seemingly insignificant, there is a case to be made that, contained in this single quirk of character, this continuous cranial quivering, was Okun's entire orientation to life and the universe. The action signaled a positive and optimistic outlook, an ongoing acknowledgment and approval of the world around him. It was an affirmation of whatever or whomever he was focused on, especially when he nodded in conjunction with one of his favorite phrases, "groovalicious," "I dig," or "cool to the power of ten." His nodding showed him to be fascinated and intimately involved with each of the billions upon billions of details that add up to create a day. But to those who didn't know him well, it just made him look like a dimwit.

In April of '72, staring down the barrel of graduation and, beyond that, the frightening prospect of holding a real job, Okun began having second thoughts about the way he'd spent his years at Caltech. Earlier that semester, recruiting officers from major corporations like Lockheed, Hughes, and Rocketdyne had come to the campus and hired a bunch of numbskulls just because they had good grades. Okun had earned mainly As or Fs, leaving him with a dismal 2.1 grade point average. After a stellar performance in high school, where he'd won several awards and citations, crowned by the achievement of being named the winner of the nationwide Westinghouse Science Talent Search, he'd squandered his time in college. It's not that he'd stopped learning. His mind was still an unquenchable sponge thirsting for knowledge and all of that, but he'd spent way too much time applying his prodigious skills to a series of oddball projects that the school's administration had classified as pranks.

One such stunt, which Okun thought he should get course credits for, happened during Caltech's annual "Hawaii Week."

After gaining unauthorized, after-hours access to the chancellor's office, he and his friends—who called themselves "the Mothers" in honor of Frank Zappa's band—carried in a few dozen sandbags, some surplus tubing, and a giant polyvinyl tarp. They set to work constructing a small heated swimming pool right under the noses of the school's founding fathers, whose stern portraits hung on the walls of the office between its floor-to-ceiling bookcases. By the time the campus police arrived in the wee hours of the morning, the stuffy office had been transformed into a tropical paradise. Dozens of undergrads were skinny-dipping in the pool or lounging on the leather sofas sipping Mai Tais and listening to ukulele music. After a stern lecture from the chancellor, the incident was forgotten.

But the incident that was to shape the life and career of this young Einstein-with-a-mood-ring was to involve a flying saucer, and it would take place in broad daylight.

One afternoon, as students and faculty began filling Caltech's central plaza to enjoy the sun during their lunch hour, Okun and the Mothers were holding a secret meeting in the stairwell of an adjacent building that bordered the plaza. After a final check to make sure the plan was ready, they broke off in separate directions to launch the attack. Okun and a couple of other Mothers climbed the stairwell with a box of radio equipment and began setting up their command post on the roof. Peeking out between the balustrades, they could see the unsuspecting crowd below without being seen themselves.

A few moments later, precisely on schedule, a Mother named Chris Winter sauntered into the plaza carrying a nine-foot ladder under one arm and a large cardboard box in the other. Something about the way he walked through the quad announced the fact that something mischievous was afoot.

Winter set up the ladder, climbed to the top, opened the box, and removed a perfect balsa-wood replica of a flying saucer. He lifted the twenty-two-ounce vehicle over his head until he could feel it react to the invisible field of energy shooting through the air. Slowly he took his hands away, and a roar of approval erupted from the crowd. He quickly grabbed the ladder and disappeared, leaving the little saucer hovering in midair.

From his hiding place, Okun looked down on his audience and nodded in satisfaction. He tested the joystick on his remote control, and found it worked tolerably well. The radio waves sent the small ship wobbling first this way, then that. Inside the saucer, a supercharged, plate-sized magnet reacted to his command, causing the saucer to bob and skitter over a strong field of electromagnetic energy being pumped into the quad by a trio of cleverly disguised wave-particle generators the Mothers had liberated from the applied sciences building. Undergrads rushed up to get a closer look at this strange spectacle, laughing, catcalling, and looking everywhere to see who was making it fly. But the fun really started when Okun switched on his microphone and began talking to the crowd via the transistor radio speaker he'd built into the saucer.

"Greetings, Earthlings. My name is Flart. We are from the planet Crapulong. We come in peace. But we demand your cafeteria stop serving those cruddy fish sticks on Friday. This is a crime against the universe. We also demand that the one you call Professor Euben get a new toupee." It wasn't high-caliber comedy, but it put the crowd in stitches. The voice coming from the teetering saucer was distorted and full of static owing to the magnetic energy in the air, which only made Okun sound more "like an alien."

The charge in the magnet should have lasted a full hour,

but the flight was cut short when Flart made the mistake of flirting with the wrong earth girl, telling her that he, master of the universe, found her extremely desirable and would she consider spending an intimate evening with a being one-tenth her size? The crowd and the girl found all this hysterically funny, but after a while her boyfriend had had enough. He shouted to the unseen operator of the remote control vehicle to knock it off.

"Lieutenant Zarfadox," came the answer from the saucer, "prepare the anal probe. This Earthling obviously has something stuck up his ass." And so ended the flight of the alien Flart. The boyfriend hurled an apple, which struck the ship broadside just hard enough to dislodge it from the invisible net provided by the three generators. It crashed to the pavement with Flart shouting a long string of expletives. Once the generators were safely back in their labs and the Mothers had sat through a stern lecture from the chancellor, the whole incident should have been forgotten.

But the next morning, a brief account of the event appeared in the *LA Times*. Although the three-sentence article explained it had all been in good fun, it sufficiently impressed one reader, one of the CIA's army of "burrowers," who clipped it out and started a file: "Okun, Brackish (?)" In years to come, this one-page file would expand and multiply until it had become a monster, filling a cabinet all its own.

That April, the file grew considerably when the CIA came visiting. At eight in the evening during midterm week, Okun and the other Mothers had decided not to brave the crowds in the library. Instead, they'd retired to his dorm room, affectionately known as the Pad of Least Resistance, to engage in

certain herbal rites. As smoke filled the room, they engaged
in what was, for them, a rather typical conversation.

"Dude, you know what we should do?" Winter croaked,
struggling to keep from exhaling as he passed the ceramic
vase-shaped instrument back to the load-master. "We should
put up mirrors in all the halls so when you're going to class
the whole school is like a hall of mirrors at a carnival."

"Cool squared," Okun nodded. "We could invent a new prod-
uct called Mirror Paint and coat every surface in the room
with it."

The Mothers were pleased and showed their approval with
a round of silent nods. "Mirror paint. I like."

"What if everything in this room was covered in mirror
paint? The walls, the bed, the plants, all these books . . ."

"And dig this: the final step would be to dip our bodies in mirror paint so everything in the room, except your eyes, was a mirror."

"Then we could make mirror contact lenses, so we'd disappear completely and you'd have to feel your way around
the world."

More nods.

This important research discussion was interrupted by a
knock at the door. It was an official-sounding man-knuckle
rapping that sent the Mothers into immediate action. While
Okun stashed the bag, Winter opened the windows and began
fanning smoke out of the room. The knock repeated itself,
insistent.

"Just a minute," Okun yelled. "I just need to finish this
one thing." Grabbing a textbook off the bookshelf, he opened
the door a crack and saw a man in a suit standing in the hallway. He banged the door closed and mouthed the word
"NARC!" to the wide-eyed Mothers.

"Excuse me," the voice came through the door, "I'm looking for Brake-ish Okun. My name is Sam Dworkin, and I'd like to speak to him about possible employment."

After a moment of indecision, Okun opened the door six inches and slid through the gap into the hallway, a little puff of smoke trailing him outside. Once he got a good look at the man, he relaxed a little. He was about sixty-five and seemed to be alone.

"Are you Brake-ish Okun?"

"I think so. I mean, yes. It is I. I'm Brackish Okun."

"You're absolutely sure?" the guy asked, seemingly amused.

"I was just in there reading this"—he glanced down at the page—"this math book. So, you said something about a job? What company are you with?"

The gentleman quickly invented a name, then asked if they could step inside, suggesting that Okun's friends might come back another time.

"Right, good idea." But when he opened the door, he found the room empty. He crossed to the open window in time to see the last Mother jump from the trellis to the flower bed, then sprint away into the night.

"Very cool. I have a fire escape. What was your name again?"

"Dworkin. Sam Dworkin."

Okun offered him the best seat in the house, a beanbag chair, but Dworkin sat down on the unmade bed instead. He looked around the room, dismayed. The cluttered cubicle was a riot of overflowing bookshelves, home-built electronic equipment, and Okun's personal belongings. The ceiling was wallpapered with music posters and schematic drawings. The old man looked a little older once he was inside and seated on the bed. "You're not exactly who I was expecting to meet."

Okun didn't understand.

"Westinghouse Science Student of the Year, National Junior Science Foundation Merit Scholar, eight hundred in math on the SATs. I suppose I expected somebody a little more . . . square."

"I guess I don't look like my résumé." Okun chuckled.

They talked for a while about the pranks Okun and his crew had pulled off, some of the independent engineering projects he'd built—both the failures and the successes. They tossed around a few theories about how such a brainiac could be finishing college with such low grades and finally arrived at a conclusion: *Okun was most motivated when there were obstacles in his path, when what he wanted to build or find was off-limits.* Both of them made silent mental notes to remember that tidbit.

Then the guy got down to business. "Mr. Okun, do you believe in Extraterrestrial Biological Entities? Martians? UFOs?"

So that's what this is all about. Okun quickly came to the conclusion that his visitor must be some fruit loop from one of those clubs devoted to the study of flying saucers. Feeling considerably more relaxed now that he was sure the guy wasn't a narc, he explained what he believed. "It's all bull, man; it's all made up by people who haven't got anything better to do. Flying saucers, little men from distant galaxies—puleeeez, it's physically impossible. Check it out: Einstein figured out the cosmic speed limit is 286,000 miles per second, the speed of light. Nothing can move faster than that. Now, light from the nearest star where there is even a remote chance of life takes something like a hundred years to get to earth, so, even if you assume that spacemen could travel at the speed of light, which they can't, you're still looking at a trip of hundreds or even tens of thousands of years to get from Planet X to Pasadena." When he was finished with his lecture, he scrutinized his visitor. "Why? Do you?"

The guy only smiled again, asking, "Where do you see yourself working in five years?"

"I dunno. Probably in some company lab, maybe Westinghouse. I've got an interview with them next month and hopefully they'll be able to understand some of my ideas about electromagnetics and superconductivity."

"Superconductors. That's a cutting-edge field of research. They're doing some of that over at the Los Alamos labs. Do you know about the centripetal magnet accelerator? That's the kind of equipment a fellow like you should be using."

Okun, nodding, quickly imagined all the mischief he could do with a machine like that. "Of course I'd love to play around with one of those puppies, but that's all government work, so I don't feel that's realistic for me right now," he said, brushing his hair off one shoulder.

"What if I told you there was a position available with my company that would afford the right person access not only to the centripetal accelerator, but to the entire network of labs at Sandia and Los Alamos?"

"Wowwee! Who do you work for, God?"

The man chuckled. "That's actually not a bad guess. What if I could prove to you that flying saucers really do exist? Would you be interested in working on a project like that?"

Okun just grinned. This after-hours job interview was beginning to smell like a practical joke.

"What if I told you," Dworkin went on, tapping his breast pocket, "that I'm carrying photographs which show an actual flying saucer?"

"You're kidding, right? Did the Mothers put you up to this?"

The man ignored the question. "I'd like to show you these

photographs, but before I can do that, I'd need something from you."

This guy is a phenomenal actor, Okun thought. Repressing a smile, he asked what he would need.

"Your solemn commitment not to tell a soul about the photos and what they show."

Okun straightened up and looked at the man through his bloodshot eyes. Deadpan serious, he said, "I swear it."

Satisfied with this response, the man produced an envelope and handed it over to his grinning host. One look at the first photo was enough to melt the smile off Okun's face. It showed a team of scientists in lab smocks lined up for a group portrait in front of what appeared to be a badly damaged flying saucer. The ship looked to have a wingspan similar to a fighter jet's, but it was disk-shaped and looked considerably more menacing than anything he'd seen before. The photograph itself, black-and-white, seemed to be several years old.

"I'm kneeling in the front row," the old man pointed out, "third from the left." Sure enough, it was the same face fifteen or twenty years younger. The corner of an airplane hangar showed on one side of the snapshot, and a couple of uniformed soldiers patrolled the background.

The second photo showed what looked like a cockpit. A pair of tall, arching structures, chairs of some kind, were set before two windows, with an instrument panel below them. The third picture was a close-up of one of the instruments lifted out of the console by a pair of men's hands. Instead of wires, it looked like veins connecting the instrument to the console.

Dworkin waited patiently as Okun went back over the pictures, comparing them, looking, almost desperately, for some evidence that this was indeed a prank. Then, with a stunned expression on his face, Okun looked up at the man, and asked, "What is this? Where were these taken?"

With a gentle smile, Dworkin reached across and took the photos back. "I've said too much already. Of course, if you accept, everything will be explained."

"OK, I accept."

The old guy laughed. "Let's wait until you're in a more lucid frame of mind. Think it over. There are drawbacks. You'd have to leave your family and your friends, the hours are long, and you and your coworkers might not have much in common. Please remember the promise you made. Don't discuss these pictures with your friends, your professors, with your mother, with anybody."

The man got up, leaving a non-nodding Brackish in a state of confusion. As he was about to exit, Okun called after him.

"Hey, wait up a sec. How am I going to find you again?"

Dworkin couldn't resist. "Don't call us, we'll call you."

Three weeks later, Brackish was at home proudly examining his diploma alongside his mother, Saylene. His new employer had arranged for him to take his final exams a month before the semester ended, and Okun had done something he rarely did under normal circumstances: he studied for every class, not just the ones he was interested in. He'd done well on the tests, raising his grade-point average and earning himself a bachelor's degree. But there wouldn't be any time to sit around enjoying this accomplishment. His suitcases were packed and standing by the front door. A young government agent had arrived with an attaché case full of papers, legal documents whereby Okun would sign away his personal freedom in exchange for coming aboard the project. The three of them—Brackish, Saylene, and the man in the expensive suit—sat down at the kitchen table and began wading through the paperwork. Technically, he was being hired by several different entities, each requiring a separate set of applications, background information forms, insurance waivers, tax schedules, retirement plan agreements, and loyalty oaths. At first, Brackish read through each document carefully, asking questions about each one. But as they continued to materialize in thick stacks from the man's briefcase, his caution wore down. Toward the end, Brackish was John Hancocking everything the man laid in front of him without a single question.

Saylene didn't understand why everything had to be so hush-hush. All her son could tell her was that it was an engineering job with the government, and that there was a good reason why it had to be kept secret. But the one thing she understood all too clearly was that she wouldn't get to see her boy for five full years—the length of his contract. He would be allowed to phone home on the first Sunday of each month, and that was it. He was the only family she had left, and she would miss him. Her eyes were already swollen from crying, and she felt the tears rising again when the man announced they had arrived at the last document. His name was Radecker, and she had taken an instant dislike to him. He was too young, too polished, too full of himself, and he was taking her boy away from her.

"This is a copy of the Federal Espionage Act," he explained, dropping separate copies in front of each Okun as casually as if he were delivering the monthly phone bill. "Basically, all this says is that you can be prosecuted if you tell anyone about what you know about the project. You should know that the minimum penalty for violating this law is a year in a federal penitentiary."

"Heavy!" Okun sounded impressed. "What's the maximum penalty?"

"Have you ever heard of Julius and Ethel Rosenberg?"

"Oh. Heavier than I thought." Brackish gulped, hesitant to sign something that could land him in the electric chair.

"Don't worry. Just think twice before you go selling any information to the Russians." Radecker grinned.

Nodding, Okun scribbled his name at the bottom of the page.

Radecker turned to Saylene. "Whenever someone asks about your son, you tell them he's taken a job as a safety inspector with the Bechtel Corporation. This job requires him to travel around the world, so you don't know where he is at any given time. Sign here." Reluctantly, she did as she was told.

Then the agent packed up all the documents and told the family, "I'll give you a moment to say good-bye. I'll be outside in the car."

Brackish and Saylene smiled at one another, both calm on the outside, as waves of feeling crested and crashed inside. They spent their last five minutes together crying and hugging. When Radecker tooted the horn outside, Okun looked down at his mom and promised her he'd come back as soon as he could. It was a promise he would keep, however briefly.

3

Arrival at Area 51

Life got sweeter and sweeter for Okun. When Radecker told him where they were headed, he had prepared himself for a long ride in the car, but instead they went to Burbank Airport and signed in at the desk of a small cargo transport company, SwiftAir. He'd only flown twice before, once to Chicago when he'd won the Westinghouse competition, and once to New York, for a whirlwind weekend in the Big Apple.

Today they lifted off in a small twin-engine Cessna. Once they got out over the desert, the captain invited him to come up and sit in the cockpit. It was a warm spring day, and, as soon as they left LA's smog behind, the view was superb. Okun pressed his nose against the glass and imagined spotting a crashed UFO. He felt lucky. Radecker had told him they were headed for "a very important laboratory near Las Vegas." Based on what the old man had told him three weeks earlier in his dorm room, he assumed that meant one of the national labs in New Mexico. Visions of sparkling equipment and gleaming multistory buildings danced in his head.

It was a Thursday, and Okun wondered what the Mothers, sitting through Professor Frankel's theoretical physics lecture, were thinking about his sudden disappearance. He would see if there was a way to sneak a postcard out to them once he got settled.

"There she is," the pilot announced forty minutes into the flight, "Lost Wages, Nevada." Okun had only a moment to study the narrow city built up along both sides of a highway before the plane banked north. A few minutes later, the pilot turned and called back to Radecker over the noise of the engines, "We're coming up to the Nellis Range perimeter, sir."

Okun looked down and saw they were flying over a double fence, one inside the other. *I hope this isn't where we're headed.* The pilot flew over a decent-sized military base, a cluster of a hundred or so buildings and a dozen hangars, but kept going. As Okun's heart began to sink in disappointment, the pilot pointed to a sharp hill rising a thousand feet off the desert floor, and said, "Wheelbarrow Peak." At the base of this hill was a dry lake bed with a pair of landing strips that formed a big X across the cotton-colored sand. Near the center of the X stood a single airplane hangar and a few dozen small buildings. When Okun realized this was where they were going to land, he immediately marched back and piled into the seat next to Radecker.

"Man, tell me this isn't where we're going, man."

Radecker, who was just as disturbed by what he saw out the window as Okun was, said nothing. Two days ago, before leaving Washington, he'd asked around and learned that Area 51 was "a backwater facility." But the dusty collection of weathered buildings he saw from the plane didn't even deserve the name backwater. It was more like tiny-scuzzy-pond-water about nine million miles from where the action was. This wasn't a promotion; it was exile.

As the plane came in for its landing, they could see that most of the buildings were boarded-up shacks, the sleeping quarters of some long-departed army. A large 51 was painted in black on the doors of the corrugated-steel airplane hangar, before which a contingent of perhaps twenty-five people stood waiting to greet the new arrivals. A pair of antiaircraft guns stood guard over either end of this dusty little ghost town.

"Welcome, gentlemen. I'm Lieutenant Ellsworth," rasped the man who opened the plane's passenger door for them. "I'll be responsible for your security while you're here. My instructions are to escort you directly to the labs and try to answer any questions you might have." Soldiers came forward and helped unload the luggage and other cargo. Ellsworth's tough-customer face was obscured by reflective sunglasses and a baseball cap with a Groom Lake patch sewn on the front. As they marched across the warm tarmac, he explained that the base was under twenty-four-hour guard, and that someone would always be stationed at the phones in case there was any emergency. Everyone who worked in the underground lab was free to come topside whenever he wished, but, for security reasons, would the gentlemen please refrain from fraternizing with the soldiers. When they arrived at the hangar doors, they were met by a group of elderly gentlemen whom Ellsworth introduced as the scientific staff. There were four of them, all about seventy years old, dressed in lab coats and sporting beards. "This is Dr. Freiling, Dr. Cibatutto, Dr. Lenel, and I believe you already know Dr. Dworkin."

Sure enough, standing there with the same avuncular smile Okun recognized from the interview in his dorm room, was Sam Dworkin. Standing next to the sun-darkened soldiers, the quartet of aging scientists looked extremely pale. After a round of handshakes and hellos, the party moved inside.

The hangar was empty except for a few jeeps. They came to a stairwell and began to descend the stairs in silence. Four flights down, it felt like they were preparing to enter an excavated tomb, and Okun could feel himself getting claustrophobic. He took comfort in the sight of telex cables and phone lines snaking up the bare concrete walls of the stairwell. Finally, after six steep flights of steps, they came to a set of heavy steel doors. Okun and Radecker both noticed that these could be bolted closed from the outside.

Okun stopped walking and raised his hand in the air. "I have a question."

"Yes, sir?"

"Is it just me, or is this whole situation starting to feel like an Edgar Allen Poe story? You aren't planning on locking us inside those doors, are you?" Okun chuckled nervously, hoping the others would chuckle with him.

Ellsworth answered mirthlessly. "The doors are never locked, sir. The bolts are there just in case there's an emergency."

"Has there ever been one?"

"Not yet." Ellsworth handed Okun's suitcases over to him. "This is as far as I go. I'm not allowed inside the lab."

"Except in case of emergency," one of the scientists added.

Inside, each of the four elderly scientists carried a crate of new supplies that had been left by the door and led the new arrivals into a long, dimly lit room. Every few paces they moved into a pool of light cast by the lamps mounted on the ceiling. Although half of the lightbulbs had died, Okun and Radecker could see the room stretching out to the length of a football field. Other than a few hundred crates and dusty filing cabinets, it was empty.

"Don't mind this mess," Dr. Cibatutto told them in what was left of his Italian accent. "It's only a storage area for obsolete equipment and a lot of old documents nobody cares about. Someday we'll clean it up, and put in a bowlin galley."

"Put in a what?" Okun asked.

"A bowling alley," repeated Cibatutto, shortest and plumpest of the scientists, enunciating carefully.

"This way, gentlemen." Dworkin turned into one hallway, then another, leading them into the most often used room in this top-secret government lab: the kitchen. In contrast to the murky light and cobwebs of the entrance hall, this room was brightly lit and tastefully decorated. A long table with picnic benches was elegantly set for six diners.

"We take turns cooking down here and, over the years, we've developed into rather adequate chefs, but none finer than Signor Cibatutto," Dworkin told them, setting down the crate he'd carried in. "And, in honor of your arrival, he has prepared one of his most mouthwatering specialties."

Cibatutto beamed proudly. "Tonight we're gonna have a mushroom risotto with salmon and a delicious chicken cacciatore."

"Dr. Lenel and I will show you to your rooms," Dworkin said, picking up one of Okun's bags. "We'll give you a chance to relax from your journey, and then dinner will be served."

Radecker wasn't in the mood for a dinner party. "Is it just the four of you down here? Isn't there anyone else?"

All the doctors glanced at one another nervously. "No, just the four of us. Were you expecting others?"

"No, I didn't know what to expect," Radecker retorted.

"I remember now!" Freiling erupted. He'd spent the last few minutes staring at Brackish, scrutinizing him, but now he turned around toward Dworkin. "This is that hippie kid you were telling us about. I been standing here thinking it was a damned girl, but it's not. It's that hippie kid, isn't it?"

Okun grinned sourly at the old man, not nodding.

Dworkin chuckled in blithe amusement and tried to dismiss the incident. "Dr. Freiling's eyesight isn't what it once was."

"Look, gentlemen"—Radecker felt there was too much nonsense going on—"I appreciate the effort you've gone to, but Mr. Okun and I would like to get oriented right away. Why don't you give us a tour."

The old men stared at the young men, their feelings bruised. "Now, now," Dworkin said, "there will be more than enough time for a tour later on. Whenever we show the place to visitors, there are invariably a thousand questions. It takes hours. But first thing tomorrow morning, we'll be sure and—"

"Show us the vehicle!" Radecker demanded with a vehemence that surprised everyone, including himself. He was getting very nervous about the idea of being marooned in this concrete bunker for who knew how long.

The high-spirited mood in the room crashed like a tray full of fine china. The stunned scientists looked at one another. *Who is this guy?*

Dworkin led them through another set of hallways until they came to a steel door with a wheel lock, the same type found at a bulkhead in a submarine. He pulled the door open and stepped into the pitch-black room beyond. A second later, dozens of fluorescent tubes sputtered to life, illuminating the interior of a giant concrete cube, six stories deep. In the center of the room was the alien ship that had crashed at Roswell many years before. Okun's jaw fell open, and his eyes glazed over. In the photograph, the thing had looked somehow ordinary, a machine and nothing more. But now, looking it in the face, there was an animal quality to its appearance, like a great black-gray stingray sleeping peacefully at the bottom of this large concrete tank. It rested seven feet off the ground on a series of wooden trestles. A pair of windows facing the visitors seemed to stare back like sharply focused eyes. Gulp.

They stepped through the doorway and onto an observation platform, as Dr. Lenel made his way along the underside of the beast and scampered up a ladder into its belly. In a moment, lights came on inside the ship, and Lenel could be seen behind the windows standing in the cockpit.

"This," Okun said to no one in particular, "is far beyond cool." Then, nodding for the first time since he arrived at Area 51, he stepped off the observation platform. Moving closer, he examined the large projection running along the ship's backbone. "The fin," as the scientists called it, started out some six feet tall just behind the windows, then tapered gracefully to a needle-sharp point at the tail. The ship's exterior surface was composed of several armored plates which were etched with thinly cut grooves and embossed designs that looked somewhat like Egyptian hieroglyphs. "I don't recognize this material. Do you know what kind of metal it is?"

"The vehicle's carapace is composed of a very rigid material, but it isn't metal," Dr. Dworkin explained, moving past Okun to reach up and run his hand over the surface. "If you look very closely, you'll notice something curious. Can you see these very small holes? We think they're either pores or hair follicles. This armored plate was once the shell of a living animal."

"Outta sight," the younger scientist commented softly.

Lenel beckoned him even closer to the ship, pointing into the gap between two of the plates. In the crevice, Okun could see countless pieces of intricate machine tooling, tiny metallic gadgets set in place with the same extraordinary precision as the muscles in the human hand. This outstanding workmanship received a large and approving nod.

Mounted on the ship's underside were what looked like a couple of thruster rockets. One of them had been sheared away in the crash and was currently held in place by an awkward network of spot welds and metal plumber's tape.

Radecker, reluctant to move closer to the menacing ship, asked a question from the observation platform. "What about these symbols or designs?"

"They appear to have been pressed into the shells using some sort of mold. We can only speculate as to why they are there. They might be a brand, like the kind we use to identify cattle," Dworkin offered.

"Or they could be technical details for the operation of the vehicle," Freiling countered.

"I personally think they are some kinda heraldic device like the ones you find on a medieval coat of arms," Cibatutto put in.

"We did have one gentleman down here several years ago who had received some training as a cryptographer, but he was not able to decipher their meaning. In short, we don't know."

As far as Radecker was concerned, this whole experience was quickly turning into a nightmare. For the second time since they were introduced, he raised his voice to these mild-mannered scientists twice his age. "Why is this place in such bad shape?"

Cibatutto and Lenel looked at Freiling, who looked at Dworkin. "Bad shape? In what sense?"

"Don't act dumb with me," Radecker shot back. "Look at this dump. It's dark, it's dusty, and it seems like you haven't gotten diddly-squat done on the ship in the last twenty years."

Dworkin, in his refined and gentle manner, offered his new boss some background on the lab. "Since the day the cranes lowered this ship to where it is sitting, no maintenance workers have been allowed access because of legitimate concerns for security. In years past, we did whatever repair work was necessary, but as we've advanced in age, we've been less able to do this work ourselves. And then there is the unfortunate matter of Dr. Wells, who was, until fairly recently, Area 51's director of research. He was a brilliant man early in his career, but with age he became . . . oh, how shall I put this?"

"The bastard went crazy," Dr. Lenel mumbled, speaking to the new arrivals for the first time. "Went right off the deep end."

Dworkin attempted a chuckle. "That's not exactly the phrase I was searching for, but it gives you the idea. In the early years, Area 51 was quite an exciting place to work. There were over forty of us on permanent staff, and we had several visitors each year. Perhaps you noticed the old sleeping quarters outside. But then Dr. Wells and his ideas became increasingly unpopular in Washington with the very people upon whom we depend for funding. We've had our operating budget reduced every year for the last seventeen years. When Wells was removed as director four years ago, we were optimistic about getting things back up to speed, but actually conditions have become even worse. Since his departure, we have received no money whatsoever."

"So that's why you guys are so old," Okun blurted out, having put two and two together. "You haven't been able to hire anyone new."

"And that," Dworkin said magnanimously, "is why we're all so excited about your arrival. It represents a new chapter in the history of this project. We haven't seen anything concrete yet, but Colonel Spelman has given us every reason to be hopeful."

When Radecker heard their story he felt sorry he'd yelled at them. "I'll get on the phone with Colonel Spelman this afternoon and see what I can do about this situation. But let's have a look at the inside of this thing."

A steel ladder led to a hatch door twice the size of a manhole cover that lead down to the sewers. And a sewer is what it smelled like as the men climbed up into the ship. The acrid, penetrating stench of ammonia hung in the air, like old urine.

"The fumes make you crazy after a while." This time, pudgy Dr. Enrico Cibatutto led the way. They climbed the ladder and came through the floor of the small spaceship to examine the spartan interior. There wasn't much to see. The domed interior of the cabin was twenty by twenty at its widest point, and seven feet tall at its peak. The focus of attention was the command console. Two pea-pod-shaped chairs faced the windows, and, below the windows, a bank of instruments was mounted along the front wall of the cabin, in an arrangement the scientists called the dashboard. As Okun stooped over and followed the much shorter Cibatutto to the front of the ship, the scientist warned him, "Mind the pods, they're covered in a thick jelly. Like the tar of a pine, if you get it on your hands, it takes a lot of scrubbing to get off."

Okun regarded the slimy seats in the dim light. They were long arching structures, sticky hammocks connected to both floor and ceiling at forty-five-degree angles and kept in place by means of a web of solid bars. The sight of the chairs reminded the young scientist that spaceships don't crash to earth by themselves. Not sure he wanted to hear the answer, he asked Cibatutto if there had been any bodies.

"Of course. You can see them later."

"So they're, like, down here? Close by?" Goose bumps erupted over most of Okun's body.

The scientist laughed and stroked his short beard. "Don't worry. Not only are they dead, but we have them locked away in a very secure place."

Somewhat relieved, Okun returned to the subject. "I guess the pilot is supposed to sit in this chair, and the gum acts as a seat belt."

Cibatutto politely pointed out that "at several hundred miles per hour, the resin might provide some safety, but its cohesion strength is not as strong as, say, a seat belt."

"Yeah, I guess you're right."

"So, this is the instrument console." It was a mess, showing the signs of having been taken apart and reassembled many times. In an open toolbox, stray pieces of the ship mingled with hammers, soldering irons, screws, and a dozen notepads full of schematic drawings. Cibatutto seemed not to mind the clutter. Okun poked through the box for a moment, then picked up a particularly interesting fragment.

"Cool, an ankh."

"What's an ankh?"

"An ankh is the ancient Egyptian symbol of life, a hieroglyph." He held the half-inch-tall figure up to the light and realized he had been half-right. Like the ancient symbol, the thing between his fingers was composed of a central shaft with a shorter bar crossing it like a stick-man's arms and a rounded open head. But this one was 3-D. Instead of two little arms, there were four. Likewise, the hole at the top opened east–west and north–south. *Ankh cubed*, he thought. For whatever reason, it struck Okun as supremely cool, and he put it in his pocket. *It's not stealing*, he told himself. *It's not like I'm going anywhere with it.*

"Here we have the steering controls," Cibatutto continued, pointing to what looked like a tightly folded bundle of greasy bones lying on the floor. "This mechanism goes here, in front of the pilot, and we think it opens outward." It had been removed from its original position and was connected to the console by a series of thin strands that looked like roots or perhaps really hairy veins. "Dr. Lenel went to medical school, so he's the one who sews up our patient after we amputate her a little bit." Indeed, the vein-roots at the bottom of the bony mechanism had been severed and stitched back together using medical sutures. "She looks like a machine," he said, rapping very hard on the dashboard, "but she's actually alive, living tissue. Look closely, and you can see the little tiny scars."

"What does that thing do?" Okun was already on to the next instrument on the dashboard, something that looked like a shell.

Cibatutto said no one knew, but he lifted the thing out of its resting place and held it up to the windows. The yellowish shell plate was thin enough to allow light to pass through, and was laced with a network of very fine veins. There were no dials or switches. As the scientist put it, "She's a mystery."

Cibatutto went on to explain that because the ship was not functioning, it was impossible to say with certainty what the various instruments were and exactly how they worked. Nevertheless, over the course of the years, Area 51's scientists had made a number of highly educated guesses which, in time, would be discovered to have been surprisingly accurate. For Okun, Cibatutto's thumbnail overview of each instrument in the cabin was like the opening pages of a long and fascinating science-fiction novel with him as the hero. He was confident he could figure all these gizmos out. By the end of his quick tour of the interior, he had completely lost his feeling of disappointment about this place. His mind was exploding with questions, possible solutions, and experiments he could run to test his hypotheses.

Radecker couldn't get over the horrible smell of the cockpit. "Why won't this thing fly?"

The question seemed to confuse Cibatutto, and once again Dworkin assumed command of the tour. He was standing halfway up the access ladder, so that only his head and shoulders protruded into the cabin. "Ah, the thorniest problem of them all—the power supply! If you'll follow me, I can show you the aqua-box."

"Here is the main culprit," he said a few moments later, pointing up to it. "Our most insoluble problem, the ship's generator." Dworkin was standing five feet behind the main hatchway, looking up into a square recess in one of the armored plates. The cover, he explained, had been torn loose in the crash, leaving the possibility that the device inside had been damaged or that something had fallen out. Lenel, grumbling about something under his breath, came forward with a flashlight to show Okun and Radecker what was inside. Six dark green walls formed an open hexagon three feet across which tapered slightly toward the top. These walls were the color of dirty jade and appeared to be just as solid. Connecting the six sides were thousands upon thousands of ultrafine strands, thinner than human hairs. They looked like cobwebs pulled taut to form a complex geometric pattern that hugged the walls and left an open space in the center of the hexagon. As the flashlight played over these extrusive threads, it was refracted and splintered, causing tiny dots of light to bounce around the inside of the chamber. *The Mothers would dig this*, Okun thought with a nod.

Dworkin blew a puff of air into the chamber, and, to the visitors' surprise, the rock walls of the hexagon reacted, fluttering like the paper walls of a Chinese lantern.

"No way," Okun said, wide-eyed. "Do that again." Dworkin obliged, and as the long-haired young scientist watched the gossamer walls shudder under the swirl of light dancing through the threads, a word popped out of his mouth, "Fragility."

"Seemingly," Dworkin allowed, "but watch this." He stepped away to give Dr. Lenel center stage. Lenel turned the flashlight around in his hand, reached up into the chamber, and began clanging and smashing it against the walls. Radecker and Okun were horrified, positive Lenel was doing irreparable damage to the device. But a second later the gruff old man showed them no damage had been done. The walls swayed back and forth as serenely as they had before. Dworkin's voice came over their shoulders. "We've tried for years to cut off a sample of this material so we could have it analyzed. Believe me, as delicate as it might appear, it is extremely tough."

"You should see what that sucker does when we pump some juice through the system. It's beautiful," Freiling put in.

Radecker's ears perked up. "What's he talking about? Does that mean you can make it work?"

"Not exactly." Dworkin told them about an experiment Dr. Wells had organized some years earlier, in which the ship was bombarded with a controlled ray of electromagnetic energy. "When we pointed the beam into the aqua-box, we were able to bring the ship's system to temporary life. The instrumentation lit up, and the generator here—we sometimes call it the aqua-box—produced a faint whirring sound. However, the power was purged from the system just as fast as it could be fed in."

"Sounds like your circuit isn't closed," Okun mused. "Maybe there's a wire you didn't connect right and the power's leaching out."

"Exactly." The old man sighed. "We've been searching for that missed connection for years, but because we don't have any blueprints or another ship in working order, we're having to do a lot of guesswork. It's rather like searching for a needle in a haystack with the lights out."

Radecker interrupted. "Wait a second. Let's back up so I can get this straight. You guys brought some kind of generator down here and pumped power into the ship and it *worked* for a second?" He didn't wait for an answer. "Well, I'm not a scientist, but why don't we just get a *bigger* generator and pump in *more* power?"

"Because our power isn't like theirs." This time Lenel answered. "The most we can do is raise a spark. Even for that we have to use so damn much energy we overheat the circuits and the ship gets hot as an oven. If we gave it more charge, we'd just burn her up."

Okun listened to the explanation, wagging his head deeply. "And I bet you guys tested a whole range of levels."

"Yes, of course. The minimum application of EM radiation required to wake up the system is five thousand volts. We tested up to two hundred thousand volts and found no difference other than the resulting temperature of the ship."

"I see your problem," Okun said, stroking his beardless chin. "That's a toughie, a definite toughie."

Everyone fell silent for a moment. The tour had led Okun through the labyrinth of what was known only to drop him off here at this dead end.

"Another question." Okun's hand was up in the air again. "Aren't we missing something here? Something more important than whether we can get this ship to work. The so-called *bigger picture*?"

"What question are you thinking of?"

"Are there more aliens out there, and are they going to come back?"

4

The Y

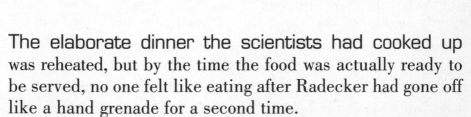

The elaborate dinner the scientists had cooked up was reheated, but by the time the food was actually ready to be served, no one felt like eating after Radecker had gone off like a hand grenade for a second time.

He'd gone down to the director's office to nose around in his new digs and found something that made him very, very unhappy. In fact, after a few minutes of examining the lab's accounting ledgers, he was furious. Everyone in the kitchen stopped what they were doing and listened to the shouts bouncing off the walls. He came storming down the hallway and stopped in the doorway. In his hand he had a stack of receipts. On his face he had an indignant expression, which he focused on Dworkin. "Were you guys thinking I wouldn't turn you in when I found out about this? Have you all gone crazy from living down here so long?"

I can't really believe Spelman has given this barbarous

hothead any real power, Dworkin thought, knowing he would have to defend himself against this uppity technocrat.

It hadn't taken Radecker very long to discover some of the creative bookkeeping procedures the scientists had developed to help them through the lean years of underfunding. Among other things, he'd checked the active personnel roster. According to this document, there were supposedly nine old men working at the below-ground facility—one of them 103 years old. Every month, a government paycheck came in for every name on that list. Radecker wanted an explanation. "What happens to the extra paychecks?" he demanded. Cibatutto suddenly remembered an urgent errand over near the oven, so the task of explaining fell to Dworkin.

"We cash them," he explained.

The scheme had been in operation for several years. When it became clear that the flow of money for the project was slowly being choked down to a trickle, the staff had either resigned in protest or received transfers to other places. A hard-core group of twelve refused to leave. They all felt the questions surrounding these visitors were too urgent, too important, to let the lab die. So they dedicated not only their energy, but very often their personal savings as well to the effort. They had pooled their money to pay for new equipment and services such as the chemical tests they'd had done on several alien materials. When the members of this fraternity began to die off, their purchasing power declined as well. They couldn't get at the money in their retirement accounts, so they created a new one. They'd found a small bank in Las Vegas, Parducci Savings, that was known for asking very few questions, and they opened a joint account. Every month the checks were endorsed and deposited.

"I knew something was wrong when I saw all that new equipment in the other room."

"Sam," Freiling whispered loudly across the table, "this young man is angry with us. Who is he?"

"And this is ridiculous!" Radecker blew up again, pointing at Freiling. "The man is senile, totally unfit to be working here. The only reason you're keeping him down here is so you can collect his money. He's leaving on the next cargo plane."

"Mr. Radecker, please. We have maintained very detailed records, which I would be glad to have you examine. They show how every penny of the money was used to further our research efforts. Take a look around the labs, and you'll see we haven't used these funds on any extravagances for ourselves. We have dedicated our entire lives to the task of repairing and studying this vehicle. Area 51 is our home. It's been Dr. Freiling's home since 1951. He has nowhere else to go. We are his family now."

Radecker stood in the doorway, shaking his head at the ceiling. Dworkin's speech seemed to soften his stance, but only slightly. "Do you understand how much trouble you could get into for this? How am I going to explain this to Spelman? I suppose you want me to hide it from him and hang my own ass out on the line." He waved the papers in the air once more. "This is corruption, gentlemen. This is theft, this is tax fraud, this is . . ." An idea suddenly occurred to him. With a sickened expression on his face, he gazed at Dworkin. "Tell me these dead guys aren't buried down here."

"No, no. We own a group plot at a cemetery outside of Las Vegas."

Disgusted, Radecker marched away back to his office.

"Sam"—Freiling looked up at Dworkin—"don't let him send me away."

•   •   •

Brackish's room was a former office suite on the same corridor with the other scientists. It came with its own bathroom and a plain steel bed with a lumpy mattress. He stretched out in bed that night and told himself he should think about everything that had happened on this, the most extraordinary day of his life. But he found he couldn't stop thinking about the generator on the ship. He hadn't gotten a chance to ask them why they called it the aqua-box despite its decidedly non-aqua color.

On the one hand, it seemed so simple: the ship's power system wasn't holding a charge. There must be a rupture in the circuitry. In that case, it was merely a matter of locating the broken line and stitching it together as Cibatutto had shown him. On the other hand, it could be some other problem, something totally unrelated to the circuitry, something so exotic no human being could even conceive of its existence. The first possibility was, as Dworkin said, like looking for a needle in a haystack. The second offered even lower chances of success.

Nevertheless, he decided to center on the second possibility. His instincts told him to trust the work the scientists had done over the past twenty-odd years. Not only that. He didn't want to be down there for twenty years himself duplicating their efforts. He decided to assume that the scientists had reassembled every piece of the ship correctly and that it was "good as new." He found himself thinking about the little balsa-wood-and-magnet saucer he'd caused to fly over Caltech. If someone had come along and found that saucer on the ground and started looking for its power source, they could put it together ten million ways and never figure it out. The power wasn't inside the ship. It was in the electromagnetic cannons strapped to the walls. Could the aliens have space-based generators? Of course, they wouldn't be EMFs, or we'd have picked that up as radio and television distortion. He smiled at the ludicrous picture in his head of megamonster power stations circling the earth and beaming power down to the UFOs. But if the power wasn't inside the ship and wasn't being "beamed in" from the outside, there wasn't any place left except for . . . That was it! In a flash, Okun hit upon an idea that would obsess him for years to come. The power must somehow exist *between* the ships. Maybe the reason the system wouldn't hold a charge was that it had been designed *not* to. Hadn't Dworkin said something about the energy being drained out of the ship? "Purged" was the word he had used. If the power was being intentionally drained from the system, where did the energy go once the ship spit it out? It had to go to another ship, which would spit it right back. He had a vision of the stingray ships flying in groups, most likely arranged in rigid geometrical patterns. If this was a warship of some kind, it would make perfect sense from a tactical point of view. If every ship were continuously powering all the others, a squadron could maintain the power of its ships even if some of them were lost. There was only one problem: the idea contradicted something Radecker had told him about the so-called bigger picture.

Out in the hall he heard whispering. He got up and went to the door. Three of the scientists were out there holding a conference. As soon as they saw Okun standing in the doorway, they quickly said good night and broke their huddle.

"Pssst, hey, you guys. I think I figured out the power problem."

The men didn't seem to be at all interested and retreated toward their rooms. As Dworkin moved past him, Okun stepped out into the hall. "Sam, I was thinking about the power supply. What if—"

"Young man, I've had a very difficult evening, and I need

some time alone with my thoughts." Not only was Dworkin upset about his confrontation with his new boss, he knew from long experience that newly arrived visitors to Area 51 invariably had a middle-of-the-night epiphany that would miraculously answer, once and for all, all the mysteries surrounding the ship. Right now he was in no mood to listen to the uneducated guesses of this enthusiastic post-adolescent. It didn't help that Okun was standing there in nothing more than his Jockey shorts and a pair of mismatched socks when the long-established decorum of the labs called for robes to be worn when using the common areas at bedtime. "We can talk tomorrow."

Dworkin disappeared into his room. When Okun turned around, both Lenel and Cibatutto were shutting their doors as well. He considered going to see Radecker, but thought better of it. If there was going to be a conflict between the misfit employees and the tight-ass management, Okun knew which side he wanted to be on. It looked like his theories would have to wait for the morning.

He had just resigned himself to going back to bed when old Dr. Freiling came shuffling around the corner. It took Okun about five minutes to explain the idea he'd hit on. When he was done, the old man looked up at him and asked him to say the whole thing again. Even though he thought it was hopeless, Okun knew he wouldn't be able to sleep anyway, so he went through the idea once more. When he was almost finished, Freiling surprised him by saying, "That's a pretty darn good idea. If it were true, it'd explain a lot. But there's a problem."

"I know," Okun said, beating him to the punch. "This ship came alone on a one-time exploration mission."

"That's a bunch of nonsense. Who told you that?" the old man demanded, even though he'd been standing right there when Radecker had explained this to Okun. "Don't start making things up, young man. It's tempting, I know. There are so many questions and so few answers, but you can't start assuming things you have no proof for. We don't know whether this ship came alone or was part of a group."

"But Mr. Dworkin gave me the idea that—"

"Bah! Don't trust everything Sam tells you." The old man leaned forward and looked over the top of his bifocals. "Like the rest of us, he's not getting any younger and, just between you and me, I think some of his screws are coming loose. No, the problem with your idea is proving it. If you think the ships work in groups, you'll have to get another ship down here to see if you're right."

"Oh, yeah."

"Unless . . ."

"Unless what?" Okun asked. Freiling had gone into a long blank stare. It was hard to tell if he was thinking something through or had fallen asleep with his eyes open. But suddenly, the old-timer snapped out of his trance and began explaining a complicated set of procedures for testing the multi-ship theory. Once he had explained the whole idea, Okun glanced at him sideways, and said, "Can you say that whole thing again?"

Half an hour later, Freiling had rustled up the other scientists and herded them into his room. They listened first to Okun explain his ideas, then Freiling told them the experiment he'd come up with. The others were not as convinced as Freiling, but liked it nonetheless. Besides, they were desperate to show Radecker some progress before he had a chance to start shipping them out. Once they had all signed on, they shuffled down the hall to see the boss.

They found Radecker still awake, and, once the ideas were explained to him, surprisingly cooperative. So cooperative, in fact, that he didn't even bother to think through the implications of what his science team was telling him. It was all mumbo jumbo to him. It didn't seem to bother him that the whole idea contradicted the one-ship-one-time theory he'd been so insistent about earlier that evening.

It was near midnight when Radecker picked up the phone and got through to a supply depot officer in Colorado Springs. It was a chance for him to flex his muscles and feel like he could actually get something done. By the time he'd finished the conversation, the supply sergeant on the other end had been sufficiently intimidated to promise the equipment would be flown to Nevada the very next morning.

Temporarily a functioning and coherent team, the men of Area 51 said good night and went to bed.

It took two days to set the experiment up. The electromagnetic cannon was brought out of storage and given an overhaul while Okun, using mountain-climbing gear lent to him by Lieutenant Ellsworth, dangled from the sheer concrete cliffs of the bunker affixing dozens of sensors to the walls with duct tape. If his theory was correct, these sensors would give him valuable information about how the ships flew together—their positioning and distance. When everything was ready to go, the alien airship was hooked up to more machines than a patient about to undergo brain surgery.

Everyone had a job. Dworkin would monitor the input/output meters while Lenel operated the cannon. Freiling tracked the energy levels reaching the sensors, and Cibatutto stood ready to give the cutoff signal when the ship's temperature climbed past 140 degrees. That left Okun and Radecker with their hands free to watch the show. A mirror was positioned at an angle below the generator to let them see how it worked. Special prismatic crystal goggles were distributed. If everything worked like it was supposed to, they would allow the team to watch the energy surge spit out of the ship and travel through the room. When everything seemed to be in order, Okun gave the final go-ahead.

"Okey-dokey, boys, let's get it on."

Lenel was standing on the operator's platform of the cannon, a device that looked like a dentist's X-ray machine built to battleship-sized proportions. He adjusted his goggles, then threw the switch. Everything happened at once. The cannon sent a beam of arcing electrical power through the air, penetrating the walls of the ship and coursing into the generator. A tremendous crack ripped through the bunker, and the ship seemed to explode into flames of blue light. The glass on the instrument panel in front of Dworkin shattered, and Okun was sure he'd ruined the ship forever. But Lenel continued to fire. A firestorm of hazy blue light flared out of the ship in all directions, stabbing into the air in a zigzag dance of truly alarming speed, like a thousand ghosts looking for a way out of a pillowcase at the speed of light. When Cibatutto directed his attention to the generator at the bottom of the ship, Okun instantly knew why they called it the aqua-box: green light was spilling out of the opening and, on the surface of the mirror, Okun could see energy racing around the inside of the generator chamber like a waterspout, a cyclone of crystal green water. Then Cibatutto waved his arms, Lenel killed the power, and it all came to a dead stop. The room echoed with silence except for the frazzled sputter coming from one of the lighting fixtures, which popped and died. The whole thing had taken less than ten seconds.

The scientists all looked at Okun, who pulled off his goggles and stared wide-eyed at the ship. "That was pretty trippy." It was a few moments before the young genius realized what had happened. He had been proved right. The energy wasn't simply leaching out of the ship; it was being forced out, purged, by the ship's design. And the aqua-box, as he had predicted, seemed to function as some sort of capacitor, a device which multiplied the energy before passing it back to the system. It had more than quadrupled the power input from the cannon, overwhelming the meters on Dworkin's output monitors and sending them into meltdown.

"Nicely done, young man, nicely done indeed! We haven't made this much progress in years." Dworkin and the others were jubilant. Even Lenel was smiling.

They began checking the registers on the meters wired to the sensors on the walls. Despite all the visual fireworks, Okun was surprised that they hadn't burned up along with Dworkin's voltmeter. In fact, the numbers were rather low. Very little energy had reached the sensors up near the ceiling. That, he realized immediately, spelled trouble for his theory. The energy was dissipating much more quickly than he guessed it would. Then again, the violent, flailing, spasmodic way the energy had shot around the room could indicate a mistake in the way the scientists had put things back together.

Dworkin was already calling for a bottle of champagne. He was busy extolling this advance in their knowledge to Radecker when Okun called across the room, "Something's not right." He came and explained the sensor readouts to the others. "It means these alien ships would have to fly wingtip to wingtip in order to keep their communal energy supply alive."

"Still," Dworkin countered, "you have proved that the ship is designed to take energy in, magnify it, and pump it back out. Perhaps the presence of other ships would attract or draw the energy from this one."

Okun screwed up his face and shook his head no. "I don't buy it."

Lenel joined them and was characteristically blunt. "Of course this means we've spent twenty-five years screwing around down here for nothing. But at least now we know."

"Know what?" Radecker asked.

"The kid just proved this hunk of alien junk can't fly by itself. If we're ever gonna get it to fly, we'll need another ship just like it." When no one backed him up, Lenel asked, "Isn't that right, fellas?"

"That would seem to be the logical conclusion," Dworkin agreed. "Didn't we mention that part?"

"No! No one mentioned that," Radecker yelled. "Did I mention the fact that I can't leave until we get this thing to fly?" Radecker reached up and began massaging his temples. Obviously, he hadn't understood the full implications of the test until that moment. When he felt the impulse to grab the first seventy-year-old he could lay his hands on and begin choking him to death, he reminded himself to breathe deeply.

Okun wanted to run the test again at a slightly higher input level and see if he could get a different reading on the sensors. And an hour later, when the ship had cooled down, the scientists agreed. After carefully setting the levels on the energy input cannon, Okun asked the others to tell him if the flaring aura of light behaved any differently, then headed off toward the center of the ship.

"Where are you going?"

"Um, inside. I noticed last time that some of the gizmos inside the cockpit lit up, and I want to check out what's going on in there."

Dworkin chuckled. "Mr. Okun, I'm afraid that's impossible. I believe I've already mentioned to you that the energy levels we're using overheat the circuits and generate intolerably high temperatures."

Freiling concurred. "He's right, Breakfast."

"Brackish. My name is Brackish."

Freiling didn't seem to listen. "The inside of the cockpit gets hotter than a skillet. If you touch it, you'll get burned."

"Look, guys, I'm young, I'm nimble, I'm a natural athlete. Don't worry. When it starts getting hot, I'll get out quick."

"I won't allow it." Dworkin put his foot down. "Mr. Radecker, as director of the lab, would you please forbid this young man from going through with this foolish idea. The temperature inside the craft quickly rises to more than two hundred degrees. He'll roast. Dr. Lenel, come down off that gun. The experiment is canceled."

"Stay where you are, Doctor." Radecker thought about it: *No more Okun, no more five-year contract*. Without their boy genius, Spelman would have to pull the plug on the project, or at least reorganize. "Mr. Okun, do you honestly think you can get out of there in time?"

Okun's mind made another odd connection. "Have any of you guys ever seen that show called *Thrillseekers*? Where these guys crash cars and jump motorcycles over things? Anyways, I saw this one where a guy, a stuntman, walks into a house, a little fake house they built for the stunt, dig? He's got his crash helmet and these fire-retarding overalls on. So, he waves to the crowd and goes inside. Then these other guys come and set fire to the shack and then throw this honkin' bundle of dynamite inside. A couple of seconds later, kablooey! The whole thing blows sky-high, and you see the stuntman come flying through the air—Aaaaagh!—in this perfect swan dive, and he lands on this big air mattress. For a minute he just lies there—*I might be dead*—but then he jumps up and takes a bow."

"I think I saw that one," Freiling shouted. "It was at a race-track."

"If you have a point to make, why don't you get to it?" Radecker snapped.

"Are you dense?" Freiling demanded, wheeling around and looking at Radecker like he was the crazy one. "The boy is asking for some safety equipment. He needs a crash helmet and something to land on."

And fifteen minutes later, that is what he had. Cibatutto had taken a colander from the kitchen, lined the inside with foam padding, and attached a chin strap. By the time this makeshift headgear was ready, Okun and Radecker had created a landing pad by stacking mattresses under the hatchway of the alien ship. Okun strapped on the helmet, climbed the ladder, and practiced diving to safety. It was fun, it was simple, they were ready to go.

When he saw they meant to go through with it, Dworkin announced that he refused to participate and started to leave the hangar.

"Dr. Dworkin," Radecker called across the room. "I wouldn't do that if I were you. Have you already forgotten our deal?" The tall gaunt scientist stood there for a moment while his conscience wrestled with his sense of self-preservation. Finally, he turned around and returned a few steps closer to the ship. "How would the director like me to assist?"

"That's OK, you can just stand there and watch. Dr. Lenel, why don't you show me how to work this contraption. I'd like to operate it, if that's okay with our stuntman."

Okun realized Radecker was blackmailing the men, holding their embezzlement over their heads like a hatchet. And while it made him sad to see the regal old Dworkin having to kowtow to a man of half his years and a quarter of his IQ, he figured there was nothing he could do about it. Looking completely ridiculous standing next to the spaceship with the big stainless-steel strainer strapped to his head, he offered Radecker a manly thumbs-up, then, after a few deep breaths, climbed the ladder and disappeared into the dark mass of the alien vehicle.

Lenel turned the power dial a tad lower than Okun had requested, then showed Radecker how to activate the power by means of a simple switch. As he turned and stepped off the operator's platform, Radecker quickly reached down and cranked the power regulator up a full twist to the right. *That ought to do the job.*

Inside, Okun looked around uncertainly. This was starting to seem like a very bad idea. It wasn't the power surge that would rip through the ship in a moment; it was the dark interior. Being in there alone, he suddenly felt how foreign, how otherworldly this claustrophobic environment was. There was just enough light seeping through the cabin windows to cast dim shadows across the rounded walls, which were dripping with creepy, semiorganic technology. It felt more like a mausoleum than a flying machine. He was on the verge of chickening out, but instead he pulled on his goggles and yelled down through the hatch that he was ready.

As soon as the power switched on, the same loud crack ripped through the ship, knocking Okun slightly off-balance. He reached out to steady himself on the wall. All across the instrument panel lights snapped on, including the shell screen Cibatutto had shown him. He jerked his hand away from the wall when he felt it swell to life under his palm. Unfortunately, the momentum of his arm combined with the uncertainty of his feet to cause the natural athlete to trip once over his left foot, then immediately again over his right, all of it taking him farther away from the escape door. His stumbling landed him flat-ass on the floor directly in front of the shell screen, where he saw something that scared the bejesus out of him. A picture filled the vein-laced screen, a fuzzy, distorted image of a giant Y rising straight out of the ground. The alien technology gave this image a visual texture unlike any Okun had seen before. The picture spoke to him. Not with words, but in emotional terms. For reasons he would never fully understand, this simple image communicated a deep emotional sensation that hit him like a punch in the gut. It seemed like the loneliest, most desolate thing he'd ever seen in his life. He got the sense this great Y-shape was somehow an instrument of torture, an enemy. But at the same time, it was beckoning Okun, urgently calling for him to come. His plan to check the other instruments completely forgotten, Okun sat on the floor, mesmerized by the picture and his strong emotional response to it. Later he would be able to joke about the moment, likening it to reading a travel brochure for Hell written by Samuel Beckett, but at the moment he was in trouble. The temperature inside the ship was rising fast. Fortunately, something nearby started moving. The steering controls, that neatly folded stack of bones, opened itself and twitched to life like a pair of giant lobster legs. This distraction saved his life, occurring as it did just as a butt-bubbling wave of heat suddenly rose in the floor. In one giant stride, Okun crossed the cockpit and dived through the hatch, landing facefirst on the mattress.

Radecker switched off the power.

The scientists looked at the long-haired daredevil stunt-man—cum—lab worker and waited for a sign that he would live. His exit from the ship could not fairly be called a swan dive, but it was pretty close, especially for a beginner, so the gentlemen were expecting him to leap up any moment and take a bow.

"Mr. Okun?. . . Mr. Okun?. . ."

5

Into the Stacks

Standing on a chair with his pants around his ankles and his ass toward the bathroom mirror, Okun examined his burns. The doctor who examined him upstairs in the hangar had assured him they weren't serious. But they were painful enough to keep him from sitting down for a few days. He gingerly pulled up his trousers, then examined his new piece of jewelry. He'd attached the ankh-shaped gizmo he'd found in the ship to a piece of leather string to make himself a necklace. He admired his new treasure in the mirror. "Groovy," he nodded. Then, feeling hungry, he went looking for food.

"Howdy, hot pants," Lenel barked out for the benefit of the other scientists when Okun wandered into the kitchen. The young man ignored the comment. He grabbed a box of cereal and lay down, belly first, on the daybed they'd brought in for him.

Cibatutto couldn't resist cracking a joke of his own. "We were going to have hot dogs for lunch," he sniggered, "but we can't seem to find any toasted buns!" The old men howled with laughter.

"Fortunately," Dworkin added, "it looks as though there's plenty of rump roast." This witticism brought on yet another round of guffaws.

When they were finished, Okun turned a jaundiced eye on them and tried out a one-liner of his own. "Hardy har har. You guys are so hilarious, you should work in Vegas. Call yourselves 'Jerry's kids'—Jerry Atrics, that is." The scientists didn't get it. "As in Geriatrics? Oh, forget it." The men had been in the hole too long to know anything about the telethon.

For the next ten minutes, these distinguished gentlemen of science devoted their attention to the creation of one butt joke after another. The wisecracks were their way of welcoming Okun into their clique. He'd passed a major test the day before. Although he hadn't exactly spilled blood for the good of the project, he'd brought it to the surface of his skin, and that was close enough.

Freiling called for everyone's attention. "OK, Brecklish, I got one for you." He smiled devilishly. "I made it up myself."

"Brackish. The name is Brackish."

Freiling seemed to blank out for a moment. "Now I forgot the damn joke! No, wait, I got it. Why did the newspaper editor call the lobster?"

Brackish knew he was supposed to ask why. The Y! "Oh my God," he burst out, "I didn't tell you guys what I saw inside the ship!" He turned to Cibatutto. "You know that yellowy shell instrument deal with the all the little whatchamacallits running through it?"

Cibatutto nodded.

"When the energy came through the ship, it had a *picture* on it, and—I don't want you guys to think I'm a complete weirdo for telling you this, but—it was giving off feelings, emotions. Seriously, it was like the visual image was only one part of a larger message. There was another layer of communication going on, something meant to be *felt*—desperation, doom, abandonment, something like that. Now that I think about it, it might have been some kind of SOS, a distress call."

This announcement dramatically changed the mood in the kitchen. "That would fit nicely with your second-ship theory," Dworkin pointed out, skeptical.

"Did this image look like anything in particular?" Lenel inquired.

"You bet. It looked like a Y. Like a big old honkin' letter Y standing out in the middle of nowhere." His audience reacted strangely to this last bit of information, exchanging wide-eyed looks. "What's the matter? Did I say something wrong?"

Before anyone could answer, Radecker's footsteps came clacking down the hallway. Dworkin looked quickly across the table and put his index finger to his lips, telling Okun to keep this news quiet.

"It took all day, but I finally got Spelman on the phone," Radecker announced, marching straight to the fridge and fishing out a soda.

"And?"

"Well, I didn't explain all the particulars. I just told him we'd proved beyond any shadow of a doubt that the ship can't fly."

"And?"

"I don't think he believed me. He said, '*Your assignment is to get that ship to fly.*' So I said, 'I'm telling you it cannot and will not fly.' '*Well, sir, I don't know what to tell you. You're assigned to the project for a five-year term or until such time as blah blah blah.'* So I asked him what he would like for us to be doing out here. And you know what the son of a female dog says to me? He goes, *'You've got four years, eleven months, and twenty-six days to figure that one out for yourselves. Stay in touch.'"* Radecker sat down with the others at the table and drowned his sorrows in a long slug of soda.

"Did you happen to mention the matter of our finances?" Dworkin inquired gingerly.

"Not yet," he said, with a look which suggested he still might. Glancing over his shoulder, he noticed Okun across the room, preoccupied with a reexamination of his burns. Radecker leaned in and whispered to the scientists, "I might be able to keep you guys off the hook. It didn't sound like Spelman plans to come out here for a visit anytime soon, so we might be able to just start killing off the other names on the payroll one by one. Every couple of months, we'll call the Treasury Department and say another one has died. By the way, I saw your life insurance policy. Cute trick naming one another beneficiaries. How did you ever get a policy like that?"

"Our banking friends in Las Vegas are very flexible."

"Also, it sounds like you guys can get everything you want in the way of materials and equipment—as long as Boy Wonder over there approves it."

"I don't understand," Dworkin whispered back. "Our appropriations have to be approved by Mr. Okun?"

Radecker rolled his eyes as if to agree that the idea was ludicrous. "Spelman was pretty clear. Whatever Okun needs in the way of research materials will be automatically OKed."

Lenel asked, "So why do you say *we* can get anything we want?"

"Oh, please," Radecker said dismissively. "Look at this punk. He'll do whatever I tell him to, and if he doesn't obey, I'll make his life miserable." An idea occurred to him. "Now, listen up. I respect you guys, and I think we can work together. I'll try to help you out with hiding the names of these dead guys. And I want just one thing in exchange." The CIA operative leaned in even closer and explained what he expected of the gray-haired men. When he was finished, he looked them in the eyes, one by one. "Are we all agreed on that?"

"What are you guys talking about?" Okun called from his daybed. No one answered, so he asked again. Finally Radecker turned around.

"We're discussing how we're going to get this ship to fly. I just talked to my boss, and he's convinced you can do it."

"I can," Okun replied. "Just have your boss send us another ship exactly like the one we've got, and our problems will be solved."

"There aren't any other ships."

"Well"—Okun grimaced as he rolled onto his side—"there *are* other ships. We might not *have* any of them, but there must be other ships. Otherwise, the aliens couldn't have come to Earth."

"Sorry, pal. That's not the way it works. I can't tell you how I know, but I have it on very good authority that this ship came here alone."

Okun snorted. "Right. Who's your authority, some palm reader?"

"Military intelligence," Radecker fired back, not liking the younger man's tone.

"Military intelligence?" Okun asked. "Isn't that a contradiction in terms? Who are you going to believe, a bunch of Army dudes or what you saw with your own eyes? Our experiment showed the ship can't fly without other ships just like it. It's proved."

Radecker shrugged as he stood up. "All I know is what they tell me. And they tell me there was no second ship. From now on our official position is that there are no additional ships." With that he left the room.

Okun wasn't finished with the discussion. He threw his legs over the side of the bed and was about to follow Radecker down the hall when he realized he was sitting on his burns. His face contorted into a silent howl as he lifted his buns away from the blanket. When his posterior pain subsided, he appealed to his senior coworkers. "There's got to be a second ship, right? In fact, there must have been at least *three* ships at Roswell. If there were only two, both of them would have gone down. When this one crashed, it would have broken the power relay and knocked the other one down. Besides, what about all these people that say they've seen UFOs? Don't they all describe something that looks remarkably similar to the one we've got?"

Okun was angry and started pacing the kitchen as he talked. It was a side of himself he hadn't shown the others until that moment. It wasn't Radecker's ignorance of technical matters that bothered him. It was being told what he could and could not think. The idea that future research on the spacecraft would be limited by some anonymous panel of military experts really chapped his ass, so to speak. And then there was that phrase Radecker had used, *I can't tell you how I know*. "There's some kind of government conspiracy going on," he burst out. "It's the man, the establishment, the system. See what I'm saying?"

None of the scientists knew quite how to respond to their companion's ranting. "In fact," Dworkin said, "except for our latest experiment, there is little evidence to support your multi-ship theory."

"But that's all the evidence we need! . . . Isn't it?" He could see the scientists were avoiding making eye contact with him. "You said it yourself yesterday: this ship cannot fly without the presence of another."

Dworkin hesitated, then finally replied. "It's possible that we've misinterpreted the results."

"OK, what's going on here?" Okun stood over the elderly gentlemen like an impatient schoolmaster who'd caught them hiding something. "This is about those paychecks for the dead men, isn't it. Radecker's holding it over your heads." Of course, that was exactly what was happening. But none of them would admit it out loud.

Lenel was fed up with the whole idiotic situation. "You want to look for a second ship? Follow me." He marched out of the room, and, after a moment of hesitation, Okun followed him. The grizzled scientist led the way through the maze of halls toward the steel doors to the outside, muttering under his breath the whole while. Instead of turning toward the exit, however, Lenel stopped in the long hallway that the scientists used for storage and gestured toward the crates and filing cabinets pushed against the walls.

"We call this mess the stacks. In these boxes you'll find every government document associated with our research. You name it, it's in there. That means every scientific report, every position paper from DC, every memo, every police report on sightings, reported abductions, strange dreams, everything. Anything and everything that has to do with extraterrestrial life-forms."

Nodding, Okun surveyed the room. He did a quick calculation and guesstimated there were two hundred crates full of documents, each one holding about twenty reams of paper. At five hundred sheets per ream that meant there were about two million pieces of paper. Adding in the filing cabinets would bring that number closer to three million. "You might want to change the name from the stacks to something like *the piles*. Does anyone actually read this stuff?"

"Some of it. We get a new shipment every first Monday of the month. We look through the box and pull out anything that looks interesting, but mostly it just gets dumped out here. Years ago, there was a fellow named Pike who had everything organized. If you needed to see a particular report, you'd go ask Pike. When the new reports came in, he'd make sure they got into the right hands. After he quit, I took over the job."

From the looks of things, Lenel hadn't been doing a very good job. Okun pulled open the top drawer of a file cabinet and looked inside. A few thousand pages of yellowing paper were strewn around in heaps. They had been stuffed carelessly into the drawer, with no regard for organization. "What kind of filing system are you using here?"

"There is no system. The whole place is a damned mess now on account of Wells. That man was always in such a hurry. He'd come in here and take out a hundred files to find the one he was looking for. He never put anything back, and I got tired of doing his work for him. So I quit. I've had nothing to do with the stacks for the last ten years or so. Still, if there's anything in particular you need, I can probably help you find it."

Until then, Okun hadn't understood why he was being introduced to this ancient collection of worthless paper. He didn't know what was going on in Lenel's head, but apparently the old grump was expecting him to start reading this stuff.

"I should warn you," he went on, "that 99.9 percent of what's in these reports is a bunch of hooey. First you've got your crackpots who make up stories to get themselves noticed. Then you've got your little old ladies who see a spark on a telephone pole and wet their pants because they're sure it was men from Mars. But you've also got something that's harder to spot."

"What's that?"

"Reports started leaking out about what we had down here. Since there was no way to keep the files completely hidden, the geniuses at the CIA and the Pentagon started something they call disinformation. As if there weren't enough bogus reports of sightings and encounters already, they started making up new ones by the hundreds. Some of the most convincing stories were written by some hack sitting in an office making the whole thing up. They deliberately buried false leads, stories that seem like they'll lead somewhere, but then the trail goes cold, and you're back where you started from."

Finally, Okun had to ask. "Dr. Lenel, why are you showing me all this stuff?"

"If you're convinced there's a second alien ship, this is the best place to go looking for it."

It was three weeks before Okun made his first independent foray into the stacks. Life in the labs was beginning to settle into a comfortable routine. His elderly cohort continued with their repairs on the alien vehicle and, once his rear end had healed sufficiently, Okun joined them. Even though he was convinced they were wasting their time, they made pleasant company, and he assisted them as they puttered through repairs to the wiring system and damaged fuselage.

The atmosphere underground improved considerably once Radecker began spending his days at the Officers' Club. Groom Lake, the flat salt bed under which Area 51 was buried, was only a tiny fraction of the enormous Nellis

Weapons Testing Range. At roughly five thousand square miles in area, the range was as large as a small European country. At its southern edge, near Frenchman Lake, was a cluster of buildings which, with their manicured lawns, swimming pool, and tennis courts could, from the air, easily be mistaken for a luxury hotel. It was a gathering spot for high-ranking officials from all areas of the base, a place to hold meetings or simply relax in the air-conditioned comfort of the bar. Radecker quickly discovered that a convoy of Jeeps traveled between Groom and Frenchman lakes twice a day, when a new group of soldiers came on duty. From six in the morning until six in the evening, his phone calls were rerouted to the lounge of the Officers' Club.

On one particular Friday, Okun was in the labs by himself. Dworkin and the others had left for their once-a-week excursion into Las Vegas. The previous two Fridays, the men had convinced Okun to join them. He was shocked by what he learned. After taking care of their banking business and other errands, the four old timers headed for the casinos, where they played high-stakes poker. They seemed to be on a first-name basis with nearly every dealer and pit boss they ran into. Apparently, they had been eighty-sixed from many of the major houses on the Strip because, although no one could prove it, they cheated at cards and always took home much more than they lost, often several hundred dollars between them. It was one more way they had found to end-run the funding restrictions imposed on them by the Pentagon.

It was spooky being down there by himself, so he didn't linger in the long dim hallway that housed the stacks. After a quick look around, he found the sloppiest box of all, the one that looked like it had been organized by a madman. He lifted out the first two hundred pages and took them back to his room, locking the door behind him—a habit he'd gotten himself into after the scientists showed him the corpses of the alien astronauts. Even though they were very very dead and floating in steel-reinforced tanks of formaldehyde, this extra precaution of locking his door provided the young man with the last little bit of psychological reassurance he needed to sleep peacefully. He put the documents on his desk and began to sort through them. He had intentionally selected the most disorganized set of files on the assumption that it would contain the last papers this mysterious Dr. Wells had been reading before they carried him away. He didn't expect these pages to lead him anywhere. But if they did turn out to be Wells's last readings, well, that would be pretty cool. Most of the pages were single-sheet memos concerning mundane topics like equipment orders, travel arrangements, and test results. He put these aside and turned his attention to one of the thicker documents. It was a report entitled "National Security Briefing Paper on Project Aquarius/B. Jones, Subject." At the bottom of the title page, there was a typed note:

> WARNING! This is a TOP SECRET—EYES ONLY document containing compartmentalized information essential to the national security of the United States. EYES ONLY ACCESS to the material herein is strictly limited to those possessing Project Aquarius clearance level. Reproduction in any form or the taking of written or mechanically transcribed notes is strictly forbidden.

Bridget Jones was an unpopular, pudgy twelve-year-old from a well-to-do family living in a farming community about thirty minutes outside Cleveland, Ohio. She was a notorious liar, with a specialty for inserting herself into factual events. Whenever something newsworthy occurred, Bridget was there. When, for example, the Farlin brothers totaled their GTO into the front wall of the high school, Bridget told everyone she'd been riding in the backseat. When a half dozen sheep turned up missing from a farm a few miles down the road, Bridget filed a police report, complete with her own pencil sketches of the suspects. She claimed to have been out on a walk when she noticed four men loading the animals into the back of a Volkswagen. So when Bridget found a tiny artifact left behind after a close encounter with an alien spaceship, no one was prepared to believe her story.

About 9 P.M. on a Sunday evening she had been in the garage listening to her father's brand-new police scanner radio—just another one of dad's electronic toys—when she heard a voice she recognized and two words that caught her attention: flying saucer. The voice belonged to her neighbor, County Sheriff Jon Varner.

"Looks like we got a plane on fire out here, repeat, there's a plane coming in low, and it's on fire," she heard him yelling into his radio. "I'm on Brooderman Road, near the old Chalmers place. It seems to be flying level to the ground. My God! It's not a plane. It's a flying saucer!"

"Jon, what are you seeing out there?" the female dispatcher's voice broke in.

"About the size of a two-story house. Orange light, it's glowing, I guess it's red and gold, but it's hard to make out. Now it's halfway between the railroad tracks and Brooderman Road. It's getting closer."

"Jon, are you all right?"

"Jeannie, you should see this thing, it's unbelievable. It's going to fly right over me. It looks like there are some windows. I can see light coming from inside. I think it's—"

The patrol car's radio died. There was panic in the dispatcher's voice. "Jon? Officer Varner, are you all right? Can you hear me!"

Bridget switched off the radio, grabbed the flashlight off the shelf above the washing machine and jumped on her bike. The Chalmers place wasn't more than a mile and a half from her house. She tore down the driveway, then turned onto the main road. It was the fastest she'd ever gone on a bike, and she nearly lost control more than once as she scanned the sky for signs of the UFO. The warm breezy night and darkness of the road made her feel like she was racing through a dream. She turned onto Brooderman and saw the headlights of Varner's car far ahead. When she came within seventy-five feet, she got a bad feeling—like she was being watched—and slowed down, turning her head sideways to get the wind off her ears. She listened for footsteps, a murmur of conversation, anything that might signal this was a trap. But the only sound was the purr of the police car's idling motor, so she rode cautiously forward. The driver's door was open, and Varner was laid across the front seat flat on his back. Bridget pulled up, grabbed his foot, and gave it a shake.

"Mr. Varner, are you all right?" The officer stirred slightly, so she gave him another shake, harder this time. "Mr. Varner, wake up."

She heard someone behind her and spun around. A tall stooped figure stepped onto the road. "Is that Jon Varner in that car?" he said, cinching up his housecoat. He was an older guy she'd seen in town before. "What's the matter with him?"

"I don't know," Bridget said. "I think a flying saucer got him. I heard it on my dad's radio."

The old man stepped past her and pulled the officer into a sitting position. Varner woke up but had no recollection of what had happened to him. The last thing he remembered was standing on the pavement watching the saucer moving overhead. "Didn't you see it?" Varner asked when he learned the man's house was close by. "It lit up the field like it was noon."

The man swore he hadn't seen or heard anything unusual. He'd been inside watching television when he got a call from Jeannie down at the station house asking him to come outside and check.

A few minutes later, two more police cars arrived with sirens wailing. The noise attracted more neighbors into the street. Passing motorists stopped to find out what was going on, and soon there were two dozen folks standing in the middle of the road listening to the officer tell and retell his story. Bridget joined a group of people who started searching the edges of the road for clues. She wandered several feet into the waist-high field of wheat and came across something strange, a depression in the grass. It looked like somebody had been lying in the spot only a few minutes before. She could see the tall grass untangling itself and trying to stand back up. Like a good detective, she made sure to check for footprints. There were none. There was no pathway leading to or from the place where the person had been lying. She turned and saw that her own path into the field was clearly marked by the trail of trampled grass.

"Hey, people, I found something! Come and look!"

Before anyone got there, she looked down and noticed something metal near the head of the body-shaped depression. She reached down and picked up the shiny object, which looked like a BB pellet.

"Honey, you shouldn't be knocking down that man's wheat," a woman's voice called out. "What did you find?"

"Mrs. Milch? It's me, Bridget. Come and look at this; I think it's important."

If the woman was reluctant to step onto the damp soil before, she was doubly so now that she knew who was asking her to come. Everyone knew about Bridget's little problem with telling the truth. But this was an urgent situation, so she followed Bridget's trail out to the spot. "OK, what is it?"

"Look, this is where the aliens probably held Mr. Varner down."

The woman didn't believe her. She said the depression in the grass was too small to have been made by a man. That it looked more like a little girl had made it. She asked why there wasn't another set of man-sized tracks between there and the road. When the girl protested that this time she was telling the truth, Mrs. Milch shook her head and pointed out the grass on the girl's knees. Bridget explained to the woman about having bent down to pick up the BB and tried to show it to her, but Mrs. Milch walked away.

Bridget had never felt so insulted in her entire life. She jammed the BB into her pocket, got on her bike, and rode away. When she got home and examined it under brighter light, she noticed that the object was covered with tiny bristles. Even with the help of a magnifying glass, these spiky projections were difficult to see. But she could feel them when she squeezed the object hard. The bristles felt like electricity under her fingertips.

News traveled fast. By the time she got to school the next morning, all the kids had heard there had been a UFO sighting the night before. Bridget made sure everyone in the school knew of the central role she had played in the drama. She stuck to the facts for the most part, but couldn't resist adding a few small wrinkles of her own. During the nutrition break, she told her classmates how she had driven the spaceship away by pulling the gun from the unconscious officer's holster and using some choice language to scare "the Martians" off. By lunch, she had made eye contact with one of the blobbish creatures through the spacecraft's windows and flipped him the bird. By the end of the day, no one believed a word. Just before the bell rang, Bridget raised her hand and asked whether there could be show-and-tell the next day. She promised to bring in the "Martian BB" she'd found. Her classmates jeered their disbelief, but Ms. Sandoval, her favorite teacher of all time, said it was a good idea.

The next morning Bridget smelled another trap. A black-and-white was parked in front of the school next to another, suspiciously official-looking car. A policeman and a man in a dark suit were standing outside of her room talking to Ms. Sandoval. When she walked up, she knew from their smiles that they were not to be trusted. The man in the suit asked her about the BB. She admitted that she had it, and offered to let them see it, on one condition. She made both men promise they wouldn't take it away from her, that they wouldn't even touch it. The men agreed. Bridget opened up her lunch bag and started rummaging through it. Suddenly the policeman snatched the bag out of her hands. "Here, lemme help you look for it."

"You big liars!" she screamed in anger. "Taking advantage of a little kid! You're disgusting!" When the cop had emptied the sack out completely and determined there was nothing unusual inside, the men turned once more toward the girl. The chubby sixth-grader was smirking like a jack-o'-lantern, holding the BB between her fingers. "Ha-ha, I fooled you." Before either man could get to her, she popped the fuzzy little pill into her mouth and swallowed it.

•   •   •

She was rushed to Merciful Redeemer Hospital and admitted to the Intensive Care Unit. After vomiting several times, she'd gone into a sustained fit of dry heaves. Covered with sweat and moaning between gagging spells, she was like an overweight kitten trying to pass a large hair ball. In addition to her nausea, she complained of dizziness and a ringing in her ears. The doctors took X-rays but could find no sign of the foreign object. A toxicologist ran several blood tests but could find no poison. None of the experts could find anything physically wrong with her. Her mysterious illness became more mysterious still when it suddenly disappeared without a trace moments before her parents arrived. When her mother and father accused her of making the whole thing up, the man in the dark suit who'd driven her to the hospital stepped forward.

"Mr. and Mrs. Jones, my name is Bradley Kepnik. I'm with the Central Intelligence Agency." He flashed them his credentials. "I was there when the girl swallowed the object, and I'm positive she's not making this up. Could I have a word with the two of you in private?"

Bridget spent that night at home in her own bed. Agent Kepnik was there with her, sleeping on a cot in the hallway. He'd installed a lock on the outside of the bathroom door, which only he could open. They were going to wait this thing out. In the morning, the girl defecated into a shallow plastic tub which it was Kepnik's job to search. To her delight, Bridget learned she wouldn't be going to school for the next day or two. She spent the day raiding the icebox and watching soap operas. About three o'clock, under the watchful eye of her chaperone, she went outside to play handball against the garage door in the driveway. Despite her many invitations, Kepnik declined to join her, claiming old football injuries. Bridget stopped playing when a large passenger plane flew overhead. She watched it intently for a minute.

"What's the matter?" the fed asked.

"The guy who's driving that plane is named Cassella. He's the pilot. The copilot is named . . . I can't read it, Tenashi, Tanashawsee, something like that. They're eating potato chips. And there's another guy sitting behind them with headphones on."

"I see," Kepnik said smoothly. By now he knew all about the girl's mythomania. "And what's his name?"

"I don't know," she hissed back at him, annoyed. She knew when she was being treated as a child. "He doesn't have a jacket on, so there's no name tag. If you don't believe me call the airport. The company's name is Hartford Air. It's written on the backs of the seats."

Kepnik was beginning to get interested. By now the plane was nearly out of view. "Where's the plane going to land? And where's it coming from?"

"Well of course it's going to land in Cleveland, the airport's right over that way. But where are they coming from?" She closed her eyes and concentrated as if she were hunting around the cockpit. "Denver. And they took off at 11:45. This is neato. I can see inside the plane. Let's call the airport and find out if I'm right."

Kepnik phoned the Hartford Air arrivals desk and discovered there was indeed an 11:45 from Denver. He confirmed that the pilot's name was Mark Cassella and the copilot was Peter Tanashian. He didn't ask about the potato chips.

●   ●   ●

Accompanied by her mother and Agent Kepnik, Bridget was flown to Arlington, Virginia, and taken to the offices of Project Aquarius. Aquarius, its critics said, was proof that the Army had too much money and free time on its hands. It brought together psychics, astrologers, mediums, and other practitioners of the paranormal arts and tried to channel their talents toward military goals. Twelve-year-old Bridget was what the people in the office complex referred to as an RV. This was not a reference to her weight. RV stood for Remote Visualizer, and the Army had six people with this special talent under full-time contract.

The first step was to test her powers. She was introduced to one of the project's researchers, a forty-year-old woman with huge blue eyes, Dr. Joan Sachville-West, who did everything she could to put the girl at ease.

"We're going to try a simple experiment with these cards," she explained. "They're called Zener cards, and each one has a design on it. There are five different designs," she said, showing the icons to the girl, "and I would like for you to concentrate and try to guess which design is on the back of the card I hold up. Simple?"

"Wavy lines!" the girl shouted the second Sachville-West lifted the first card off the deck.

"Very good. You're right."

"Star."

"Right again."

"Circle."

"Excellent."

When Bridget had gone fifteen for fifteen, the woman took her hands away and asked what the next card was.

"I can't see it until you pick it up."

"Guess."

"That's not how it works," she whined. "I have to be able to see it."

"Give it a try. Just for fun."

Unhappily, Bridget guessed. "Another wavy lines card?"

Sachville-West turned it over: star.

"See! I told you!" Angry that the researcher's insistence had ruined her perfect streak, she retaliated by telling everyone what color underwear the scientist was wearing.

The woman only crossed her legs under the table and smiled. "You've got quite a gift."

The rest of the afternoon was devoted to giving the girl a crash course in geography. When her attention waned, and she refused to cooperate, her mother came to the rescue by opening her purse and pulling out a bag of candy bars. "My emergency kit," she explained with an embarrassed smile.

When Bridget had mastered the names of the seven continents and several bodies of water, the real work of Project Aquarius began. She was shown an aerial photograph of a Soviet Wolf-class submarine.

"Young lady," a man in an Army uniform began, "there are two submarines like this one in the water right now. Let's see if you can tell me where they are." The USSR had a total of four of these nuclear-powered subs. Two of them were in dry dock at that moment for repairs. One had been picked up on radar overnight off the Oregon coast and one was unaccounted for.

Bridget, working over a wad of chocolate, studied the globe sitting on the desk beside her. This whole thing was starting to bore her. She plunked one finger down in the Pacific Ocean near the Oregon coastline, then pointed to the waters off Cuba's southern shore. "Cienfuegos," she read the tiny print on the globe through a buildup of chocolate saliva.

"That's amazing," said the man in the uniform.

"Don't speak with your mouth full," said her mother.

For the next six days, Bridget Jones was the most powerful weapon in the United States military's arsenal. She located and described dozens of enemy positions around the world, many of them previously unknown. The girl loved being the center of attention, and she worked for peanuts—literally. Because of her penchant for prevaricating, each morning began with a series of new test questions. The researchers would ask her to remote-visualize locations they knew she had never visited, such as the Statue of Liberty, then ask her to count the windows in the observation deck. On the morning of her seventh day in Arlington, when asked about the leaning tower of Pisa, she answered that it was three stories tall. When asked what color socks the interviewer was wearing, she tried to sneak a look under the table. The experiment with the Zener cards was repeated. Her score was five out of twenty-five, the statistical average. Although she protested, it appeared that she had lost her powers. This seemed to be confirmed when Agent Kepnik came into the room holding a clear plastic evidence bag. A search of the young lady's morning stool had turned up a small metallic object.

Confronted with this evidence, Bridget told the truth. Her powers had deserted her. The BB, she said, looked different than it had when she swallowed it: it was half the size and was now completely bald, the fuzz of small bristles having apparently been eaten away by her digestive fluids. "So what happens to me now?"

There was a period of waiting while the proper officials reviewed the case. Eventually, they decided to follow a little-known government protocol, MJ—1949-O4W/82. The family was relocated to an undisclosed location in France, where they were housed in a luxury villa owned by friends of the U.S. government and guaranteed an income of approximately $100,000 per year in exchange for their cooperation in keeping the matter silent.

Unfortunately, six months after moving to France, just as she was learning the language, Bridget and her family were killed when their car collided with a truck owned by the French postal authority.

Until he came to the ending, Okun found the story amusing. Remembering Dr. Lenel's warning, he wondered how much of it was true. But more interesting to him than the story of the girl, were the handwritten notes jotted in the margins of the report. They seemed to have been written at great speed and most of them were absolutely illegible. Only two were carefully printed, and both of them startled the young researcher. The first one read: "obj housed at AF Acad Colo Sprgs, evid #PE—8323-MJ—1949-acc21,21a." Evidence number? Okun wondered if there really were, somewhere in a warehouse at the Air Force Academy, a small plastic bag holding a metallic pea recovered from the excrement of a bratty twelve-year-old.

The other piece of noteworthy marginalia was a doodled picture. On the last page of the report, someone had drawn a three-dimensional figure of the letter Y.

6

Roswell

Every time Okun had tried to discuss the mysterious and troubling image of the Y, the scientists—normally so talkative, so eager to kick around ideas—would merely shrug their shoulders, agree it was very interesting, then go on to say they had no idea what to do with the information. After that, they changed the subject as quickly as possible. Up to that point, Okun had let them get away with it. But now that he'd seen the same image penciled into the margin of the Bridget Jones report, he was ready for a confrontation. His intuition told him the old men were hiding something, and he was determined to find out what it was.

The next morning, he came into the kitchen and found Freiling counting money. Vegas had been kind to them once more, this time to the tune of $675. Dworkin was studying a copy of the *Los Angeles Times* he'd picked up in town.

"Ahem." The young man cleared his throat. "Where's Radecker?"

"Working on his tennis game, I suspect. He didn't come back last night."

"Then we can talk."

Dworkin peered over the top of his newspaper. "Talk?"

"You guys are holding out on me. There's something you're not telling me."

Dworkin feigned indignation. He began to rattle on about the ethics men of ideas must adhere to, but Okun cut him short by tossing the Jones report onto the table. "What's this?" Dworkin asked.

"Something I found in the stacks. It's about a girl who swallowed an object she found in the grass after a close encounter with a UFO." Dworkin thumbed through the pages. He seemed more interested in the handwritten notes than in the report itself. Noticing this, Okun asked if he recognized the handwriting. After a moment of beard-stroking indecision, the old man admitted that he did.

"This seems to be the chaotic penmanship of our dear friend Dr. Wells. Have I told you the interesting story of how he came to be named Director of Research for this project?"

Okun wasn't going to let himself be sidetracked again. "Check the last page."

Sensing he would find something unpleasant there, Dworkin reluctantly obliged. The sight of the block-perspective sketch of the Y seemed to startle him slightly. His mind scrambled to find a cover story. If only his long-haired coinvestigator had confronted him with this evidence during a poker game! In that situation, Dworkin was a different man, capable of saying whatever the situation required. He would have been able to make something up on the spot. But in matters of work, he was accustomed to always speaking the truth. He crumpled toward the tabletop like a house of cards under Okun's stern glare.

"Brickman, some stones are better left unturned," Freiling broke in. "None of us knows anything about that darn Y message."

But it was too late to back out now, and Dworkin knew it. He braced himself with a sip of tea, then explained. "Dr. Wells had a long obsession with this form, this shape. He claimed it was communicated to him by the alien shortly after the crash at Roswell. Like you, he said there was a feeling of urgent desperation associated with the transmission of the image. I believe you used the words 'doom' and 'abandoned' to describe it. In his last years he became more and more obsessed with deciphering the meaning of the symbol, until it got to the point of blocking out other thoughts. It drove him to insanity. As this mania progressed, he neglected more and more of his duties as director. We were able to mask the situation for several months, hoping he would make a recovery, but then he was called away to meetings in Washington. Apparently he behaved himself quite poorly and was not allowed to return to Area 51."

"Poor dude."

"Yes, indeed. The disintegration of his personality was a difficult thing to watch."

"Let's be honest," Freiling said. "The man was loopy to begin with. Slightly off-kilter."

"So what did he figure out about the Y?"

"Nothing."

"Nothing?" Okun asked, suspicious again. "He must have made *some* progress on it if he worked for years. Didn't he even have a theory?"

With a worried look on his face, the old man finally came completely clean. "Wells suspected a second ship. He believed that the Y was a signal, the alien equivalent of our SOS. There! Now you know."

Okun nodded with satisfaction. Once more, his gut instincts had proved to be correct—or, at least, he wasn't completely alone in having them. Someone else had arrived independently at the same conclusion, even if that someone was a mental case. There had to be a second ship.

"But Mr. Okun, I must ask you in the strongest possible terms to keep this information secret, especially from Mr. Radecker. As unsavory as this might sound, I promised him I wouldn't tell you."

"We all did," Freiling added. "If we didn't, he threatened to tell his bosses about the extra paychecks we've been collecting. Next thing you know, we'd all be doing twenty years at Leavenworth."

Without endorsing that last comment, Dworkin admitted, "Mr. Radecker has found our soft spot. None of us wants to leave Area 51 at this late date. I hope you can understand that."

Again, Okun's head bobbed up and down. He knew how scared the old men were and realized he'd never be able to betray them. Still, thinking ahead to his next encounter with Radecker, he could feel the urge to lay the whole matter on the table. "Why doesn't Radecker want me to know about the stupid Y?"

"We made a deal with him. We're not to give you any information which might support your theory of a second ship. In fact, we're supposed to try and talk you out of it."

"But why?"

Freiling and Dworkin shrugged their shoulders simultaneously. "That's all the man wanted, so we agreed."

"It's especially curious," Dworkin added, "when you consider that there really *isn't* much evidence to support such a theory. It's rather far-fetched in light of the accumulated evidence."

Okun narrowed his eyes. "Are you trying to talk me out of it?"

"Don't take my word for it. Ask Dr. Wells."

"What the hell are you doing in here?" Radecker asked, poking his head into the vault.

Okun responded with his Bela Lugosi imitation. "I have come to the crypt to visit my long-lost friends." He had developed a morbid fascination with the alien bodies and came into the secured room every couple of days to watch them floating in their tanks. "It's like having an aquarium full of really strange dead fish."

"Well, I've got the information you wanted. If you want to hear it, come outside. This place gives me the creeps."

Okun stepped into the hallway and fastened the thick steel dead bolt, locking the bodies inside. He'd asked Radecker for help in finding the whereabouts of Dr. Wells. None of the scientists knew what had become of him after he failed to return from his trip to the capital. There had been a phone call from Dr. Insolo of the Science and Technology Directorate saying that Wells was being held for psychiatric observation and that Dr. Dworkin should take over his responsibilities as director during the interim. That had been four years ago.

"The good news is I found a copy of the report you asked for, the one Wells wrote in '47. That should be interesting. It's in Washington, but they're going to send us a copy. The bad news is he's dead." Radecker feigned disappointment. "The story I got from headquarters was he was in a meeting back in DC when he snapped. Just went berserk. Started shouting and throwing things at people. They took him to Seabury Psychiatric Hospital, where he was diagnosed as schizophrenic. Then about six months later, he was transferred to Glenhaven Home in Richmond. That's where he died about two and a half years ago."

Masking a wave of authentic disappointment, Okun shrugged. "No biggie. Thanks for checking it out."

"Just doing my job. I'll tell you when the report comes in."

Brackish smiled pleasantly until Radecker disappeared around the corner. Then he kicked the wall and used language his mother wouldn't have approved of. He was sure Wells, demented or not, could have given him information about other ships. He had already imagined the scene a dozen times: him walking down the deserted institutional corridors with all the windows heavily barred, a pair of bodybuilder orderlies unlocking a heavy steel door and pulling it open to reveal the insane scientist, hair standing on end as if he'd recently been struck by lightning, eyes bulging wide as he struggled to escape from his straitjacket. Oh, well. Lenel had warned him about promising trails suddenly going cold. After a moment of consideration, he realized he had no other choice: he headed back to the stacks.

This time, he was looking for something in particular. And even with Freiling's help, it took the next twenty-four hours to find it. Realizing it would take the rest of his life to read through the anarchic accumulation of archives in the stacks, Okun needed to limit the scope of his search. There had to be a way of separating the genuine reports from the rest. He had no idea how to do it, but reasoned that the logical place to begin would be with the one alien encounter he knew for sure had taken place: the one at Roswell.

•   •   •

The incident actually began two days before the crash. On July 2, 1947, radar screens scanning the skies above the White Sands Proving Grounds in New Mexico picked up an unsteady blip wandering back and forth. It appeared to pulse larger, then smaller, every few seconds, and the crew in the tracking room suspected an equipment malfunction. They called two other facilities, one in Albuquerque, the other in Roswell, and asked if they could confirm the sighting. Within hours, they had. There was no doubt that something was up there. All three tracking stations went on alert as Intelligence Officer Ian Leigh boarded a plane in Washington, DC. If the same phenomenon had occurred in another part of the state, there would have been less concern. But White Sands was a highly restricted area. Besides the secret rocket and missile tests being conducted there, White Sands had been the site, a couple of years before, of the world's first nuclear explosion. The Manhattan Project, led by Robert Oppenheimer, had caused a "controlled detonation" near Alamogordo in a quiet valley once called Jornada de los Muertos, or Trek of the Dead.

On the Fourth of July, the blip returned at approximately ten-thirty. This time it didn't wander across the radar screen; it tore across. According to those most familiar with the tracking technology, it reached speeds of better than a thousand miles per hour. What made these speeds all the more amazing was that the plane—or whatever it was—seemed to accelerate, then come to a dead stop, then accelerate again, racing helter-skelter over the southeastern part of the state. At 11:20, the blip flared into a wide splotch of light and vanished from the screens. After communication between the various tracking stations, they decided the ship had gone down somewhere north of Roswell. The search began at dawn.

●   ●   ●

Caesar "Corky" Riddle slammed the door of his pickup and started the engine. He was frustrated, more frustrated than his kids were, and now all of them were soaking wet. For a month, he'd been promising his three daughters a big fireworks show on the Fourth. He'd driven all the way to Albuquerque and spent a fortune at the Red Devil stand. Then he'd put up with the girls' impatience all day, telling them to wait until dark. But by the time evening began to fall over the desert, a storm had blown in. Thirty- and forty-mile-per-hour winds were gusting, pushing a thunderstorm up from the Gulf of Mexico. The Riddle family gathered on their front porch and watched the situation grow worse. Finally, about ten-thirty, the winds died down. The girls wanted to light the fireworks out on the road in front of the house, but Corky insisted on sticking to the original plan. So they piled into the truck and raced toward the park in downtown Roswell. As long as they had all that gunpowder, Corky figured, they ought to put on a show for the whole town. But at nearly 11 P.M. on a stormy night, the streets were deserted, and the park was empty. As soon as they were ready to start lighting fuses, the winds picked up again, knocking the blast cones on their sides. They kept at it anyhow, trying various ways of anchoring them to the ground. Then the rain came out of nowhere—it poured down in sheets—drenching the Riddles and their stockpile of fireworks.

They rode home in silence, driving north along 268. A bright flash behind the truck cast shadows of the family across the dashboard. Corky assumed it was another flash of lightning, but then a bright streak came over the top of the truck and shot away into the distance. A bright sizzle of white light, tearing through the night like a meteor. But it wasn't like any meteor they'd ever seen. For one thing, it wasn't falling. It was traveling parallel to the ground. And instead of a smooth stroke of light, this one was scattering blue-and-green energy. It reminded Corky of the shower of sparks created by a welder's torch. As it sank behind the hills and disappeared from view, he pulled onto the shoulder of the road and told the girls to stay inside. He got out and climbed onto the front bumper, expecting whatever it was to explode on impact. He cupped his hands behind his ears and waited. But everything stayed quiet.

He climbed back inside feeling a little better. His fireworks show had turned out to be a disaster, but at least they'd seen something unusual. The girls were excited again. They said it was God playing with a sparkler and talked about it all the way home.

Grant Weston had spent the afternoon hunting for fossils. He was the leader of a group of seven archaeologists, vertebrate paleontologists to be exact, who had hiked into the desert and set up camp for the three-day holiday weekend. The sudden rain had nearly extinguished their campfire, and he was adding dry kindling to it when the sky lit up above his head. He looked up and watched the hissing fireball flash past. A few seconds after it disappeared behind the trees, the group heard two crashing noises in quick succession. The first was a hollow thud, while the second was a sharp echoing crack.

"What the hell was that?" everyone wanted to know.

One of the graduate students initiated a brief panic by proclaiming they had just witnessed the crash of a flying saucer. But Weston proposed a more plausible theory. Familiar with that part of New Mexico, he explained that nearby Roswell Field was a testing site for the Army's new and experimental aircraft. Residents of the area, he said, had grown accustomed to seeing strange-looking planes in the sky. That calmed the nerves of his fellow campers. They discussed setting out immediately to look for the wreckage, but decided it was too dangerous. Judging from the trajectory of the streaking light and the sound of the crash, they estimated the craft had gone down about five miles north of their location. The moon was new, and the terrain could be treacherous even in daylight. There was nothing they could do until daybreak.

In all probability, Weston knew, there would be no survivors. But all night the possibility of a wounded survivor tangled in the wreckage haunted him. He couldn't sleep, and he wasn't the only one. Well before dawn, the archaeologists were sipping coffee, waiting for first light. They had packed up the first-aid kit and enough food and water for the day. As soon as they could see the edges of their campsite, they set out.

Progress was slow. The land was a mixture of rock, loose sand, and thorny scrub. Flash floods had cut steep ravines between the rolling hills, forcing the group to double back and find a new path every few minutes. About the time the sun began to rise, they noticed a spotter plane searching the area, a welcome sign. Within half an hour, the plane was circling over a spot about a mile east of them.

"They must have found the crash site," Weston reasoned. "Let's head in that direction."

A set of steep hills separated them from where the plane was circling. They followed a path between two peaks and came into an arroyo. A few hundred yards to their left, they noticed the tail of the craft. As they moved farther into the dry riverbed, the archaeologists, who had spent their lives studying earth's ancient past, stepped forward to meet its future.

"That doesn't look like an Army plane to me, experimental or not."

"It looks like a fat airplane without any wings."

Skilled in the reconstruction of events, Weston deduced what had happened the night before. "See those flattened bushes on the crest of that ridge? The plane must have bottomed out there—that was the thud we heard—and then bounced up and come down here." The black, roughly circular ship had plowed nose first into a sheer cliff. For the amount of rock it had shattered, Weston was surprised it wasn't in worse shape. He headed up the incline for a closer look.

When Betty Kagayama saw what he meant to do, she yelled after him. "Grant, what are you doing? Please don't go near it! Let's wait for help." She and Professor Weston had developed a relationship that was something more than platonic. "I don't care what you say; that thing isn't from earth."

"I've got to check to see if anyone's still alive. Here, take this." He handed her his field camera. "I'll climb up there and pose like a big-game hunter. We'll laugh about it later." Over Betty's protests, he jogged up the hill.

As he got closer, he knew she was right. The black ship hadn't been built by humans. He stopped a few feet from the tail section and examined the small markings cut into the surface. "Looks like hieroglyphics," he called down the slope. There was a hole torn open along the side of the ship. He squatted down and looked up into it. "Hello? Anybody in there?" He could see sunlight on the interior walls of the vessel. He considered squeezing through the gap, but the foul, acrid smell coming out of it drove him away. He walked around to the front of the ship and saw there were windows. To get to them, he began clambering up the pile of debris caused by the crash.

"Grant, someone's coming! Over there."

He looked in the direction Betty was pointing. Two black sedans followed by a dozen military trucks were cutting cross-country toward the site. He started to come back down the slope, but curiosity got the better of him. He knew how the military was. They'd shoo him away, and he'd never get to see what was inside. So he climbed high enough onto the slope so that he could step onto the edge of the disk-shaped craft, then carefully walked across the surface and peered in the windows. A pair of blunt, bony faces was staring back at him through the window. They looked like large death masks fashioned out of living tissue, gristle, and tendon. Horrified and repulsed, Weston fell backwards off the ship, then ran down the slope. Before he had rejoined the group, the first black sedan pulled up. The man who stepped out introduced himself as Special Agent Ian Leigh.

He talked with the archaeologists for a moment. He asked Professor Weston to sit in the sedan and directed the others to wait in a group off to the side. He then jogged back to the head of the military convoy and called a huddle with the commanding officers. One of them asked if he should take the civilians into custody.

"They seem like a cooperative group. We'll worry about them later. Right now our problem is these soldiers; they've already seen too much." The group turned and noticed six troop transport vehicles, each one loaded to the brim with gawking enlisted men. Like everyone else, they were transfixed by the sight of the wreckage. Leigh thought for a minute before coming up with a plan. "Here's what we'll do. We'll use these men to establish a cordon. Nobody comes in or out without my approval. Tell the men to walk back out of this ravine the same way we drove in. Put four or five guys up on the cliff above the ship and fan the rest of them out in a circle. Make sure they're far enough away to where they can't see what's going on."

"Why don't we just have them turn their backs?"

"Good idea. As soon as they're in position, you guys drive the trucks down close to the wreck, and we'll use them to create a screen. OK, get busy." Leigh moved around the crash site with impressive efficiency. It was as if he'd done all of this before. "Steiger, let's go; this is your big moment, kid. You're elected to be our welcoming committee," he called across the gravel to one of the men he'd brought in from DC. "Put on that protective gear. You're going in first." Steiger, a rail-thin man who stood well over six feet, popped open the trunk of the first sedan. A minute later, covered head to toe in a rubbery, lead-lined suit, he was moving toward the fallen spacecraft. He carried a Geiger counter. He moved around the outside of the ship for several minutes, sampling radiation levels, and found nothing abnormal. Very carefully, he approached the breach in the wall and reached in with the Geiger counter. Finding all levels normal again, he poked his head through the gap and cautiously climbed inside.

A few hours later, the work was finished. Every square inch of the impact area had been carefully photographed. The three large bodies found inside had been sealed in lead-lined body bags, lowered through the opening, and piled into the back of an ambulance, which took them to the base hospital. After a loading crane had hoisted the ship onto the back of a flatbed truck, it was buried under a collection of tarps and poles meant to disguise the vehicle's shape. Before turning the archaeologists loose, Leigh had sworn them to secrecy. He reminded them that they were the only ones outside the military who knew about the ship, and he had cataloged a short list of accidents that might befall anyone who broke the silence. The next morning he would return to the site with a hundred soldiers, MPs with reputations for being able to keep their mouths shut gathered from six different bases across three states. After cleaning the area once by hand, they used industrial vacuum cleaners to remove every last shred of evidence. At that point, Leigh was convinced he had succeeded in making the whole situation disappear.

But that same morning, a man walked into the Chaves County Sheriff's Headquarters carrying a crate full of a strange, lightweight material he'd found scattered over a large area of his ranch. His name was Mac Brazel. He was one of those leather-skinned, scuffed-up cowboys who eked out a living by keeping cattle and sheep herds up in the hardscrabble mountains.

On the night of July 4, he'd heard a loud crashing sound, one that didn't sound like thunder. He'd forgotten about it completely until he found the field of shiny material. Initially he seemed angry. His sheep wouldn't go near the stuff and he wanted to know who was going to come out there and clean it up. But then he asked if his discovery might lead to him collecting some of the reward money that magazines had been offering to anyone who could prove the existence of flying saucers. Until he arrived at the sheriff's office, he'd heard none of the rumors concerning the craft that had gone down north of town.

The sheriff, George Wilcox, came out of his office and examined the material. It was unlike anything he'd seen before. It seemed to be some kind of metal. Although it was as light as balsa wood, none of the men in the office could bend it. They tried hammering on it with a stapler and burning it with their lighters, all to no avail.

Wilcox was angry with the way the Army had pushed him out of the investigation of the crashed ship, refusing him access to the site. Nevertheless, he called Roswell Field to report Brazel's find. He spoke with Major Jesse Marcel, who said he'd come into town right away. Thinking the Army would shunt him aside once more, Wilcox dispatched two of his deputies to the Brazel ranch to look for the debris field. As soon as they left, the phone rang. It was Walt Wasserman, the owner of local radio station KGFL, calling to see if there had been any new developments in the investigation of the crash. Wilcox put Brazel on the phone and, after the two men talked for several minutes, Wasserman was given directions to the rancher's home.

Major Marcel arrived with a plainclothes counterintelligence officer, Sheridan Cavitt. After they had inspected the debris that Mac Brazel had brought to town, they instructed Sheriff Wilcox to lock it in a secure office, then made plans to follow Brazel out to his ranch. Moments after they left, the two deputies returned from the ranch. Instead of finding the field of debris, they'd come across a large circular burn mark in the grass. It was their opinion that something hot had landed in the spot, scorching the grass and baking the earth to a hard clay beneath it. They had come back to get a camera before it got dark.

Brazel led the two military officers, each of them driving separate vehicles, across his rocky property to a wide-open field of sand and knee-high dead grass. They were about twelve miles from the site of the downed saucer. Scattered over an area three-quarters of a mile long and two hundred feet wide, were thousands of pieces of the mysterious light-weight material. Most of them were very small, the size of a fingernail and just as thin; others were almost three feet long. After a short examination of the site, the officers agreed with Brazel that "something had exploded in the air while flying south by southeast." Brazel left when the sun began to set, telling the men that he had agreed to give an interview to KGFL. Cavitt and Marcel loaded their cars with as much of the debris as they could pack up before darkness fell. Cavitt drove straight back to the base, but Marcel was so impressed with the strange material, he stopped at his house to show it to his wife and son.

That night, station-owner Wasserman drove out to the Brazel property, picked him up, and drove him into town, where they made a recording of the rancher's story. By the time they were finished, the station was ready to sign off for the night. So they scheduled it for the next afternoon.

But the recording would never be aired. Much to Wasserman's surprise, he got an early-morning phone call from the Federal Communications Commission. He was ordered not to broadcast the interview. "If you do," the man warned, "you'd better start looking for another line of work because you'll be out of the radio business permanently within twenty-four hours."

Wasserman tried to get in touch with Brazel but learned a squad of soldiers had come to his house in the middle of the night and taken him somewhere.

Marcel spent about an hour at home. He brought in one of the boxes he'd filled that afternoon and spread the contents out on the kitchen floor. The family tried to fit the pieces together, but had no luck. They experimented with pliers, attempting to bend the paper-thin substance out of shape. They realized that there was more than one kind of material. While most of it was amazingly rigid, other pieces could be folded easily between their fingers. Whichever way this second material was folded or bent, it retained the shape.

"Look at this one, it has signs on it," Jesse, Jr., said.

His mother said the writing looked like hieroglyphics. The piece in question looked like a very small I-beam. It was about four inches long and appeared undamaged. The writing was a dull purple color etched onto the gray surface of the beam. Eleven-year-old Jesse, Jr., had seen hieroglyphs in schoolbooks, and knew these were different. They were geometric shapes, including circles and one pattern that looked like a leaf. The family couldn't tell if the images were meant to be read; they were evenly spaced up and down the flat surfaces of the beam.

The son asked the father if he could keep some of the pieces as souvenirs. Marcel said he would ask his commanding officer about it, but that night he made sure all the pieces were put back in the box, which he then delivered to the base.

The next morning, First Lieutenant Walter Haut, the information officer for the 509th Bomb Group, held a series of discussions with people who had information concerning the strange goings-on. He learned from Marcel about the debris scattered around Brazel's ranch and spoke with a few of the soldiers who had been out to the site of the crashed ship. Haut had received hundreds of telegrams and phone calls from all over the country asking him to confirm or deny the rumors coming out of the area. After gathering what he felt was a sufficient amount of information, he sat down at his typewriter and composed a brief, not very accurate press release. He then drove into town to deliver it. His first stop was KGFL.

Not wanting to be hounded with a lot of questions he didn't have answers for, he handed a copy of the statement to the receptionist and slipped out the door while she was reading through it. He did the same thing at KSWS, the town's other radio station. Next, he drove to the newspaper offices of the *Roswell Daily Record*, stopping to chat with one of the reporters for a few minutes. By the time he came to his final stop, the *Roswell Morning Dispatch*, their phones had already started ringing off the hooks. As soon as the story had gone out on the wire, news editors from all forty-eight states had picked up their phones to confirm the story. While Haut was standing in the office, a call came in from Hong Kong. He didn't even know where Hong Kong was. There was certainly more interest in the story than he had anticipated. It was about noon, so he walked down the street to a hamburger stand and had lunch by himself, an extra copy of the press release sitting on the counter soaking up water and grease:

> Roswell, N.M.—The many rumors regarding flying disks became a reality yesterday when the Intelligence Office of the 509th Bomb Group of the Eighth Air Force, Roswell Air Field, was fortunate enough to gain possession of a crashed flying object of extraterrestrial origin through the cooperation of one of the local ranchers and the sheriff's office of Chaves County.
>
> Action was taken immediately and the disk was picked up at the rancher's home and taken to the Roswell Air Base. Following examination by Major Jesse A. Marcel of the 509th Intelligence Office, the disk was flown by intelligence officers in a B-29 superfortress to an undisclosed "Higher Headquarters."

Residents near the ranch on which the disk was found reported seeing a strange blue light several days ago about three o'clock in the morning.

J. Bond Johnson was a reporter and photographer for the *Fort Worth Star-Telegram*. At four o'clock, he was on the phone researching a local political story when his editor walked in, took the receiver away from him, and calmly put it in the cradle. He'd been on the phone himself and had arranged for Johnson to get in on something more interesting. "If it pans out," the editor said, "it'll be the story of the century." He told Johnson about the press release from Roswell, which had been dominating the wire services all afternoon. He'd been trying to get through to Roswell, but all the lines were jammed. Then, out of the blue, he'd gotten a call from General Ramey's office. They were bringing the saucer from New Mexico to the Fort Worth Army Air Field. He told Johnson to grab his camera and get over there before Ramey called anyone else.

Thirty minutes later, Johnson pulled up to the front gates, expecting to check in with the Public Affairs Liaison. To his surprise, the guard directed him straight to Ramey's office. He was shown in immediately. Laid out on the floor were big sheets of butcher paper upon which rested a gnarled combination of rubber, steel cable, balsa wood, and something that looked like dirty aluminum foil.

"This is what all the damn excitement's about," Ramey said, shaking his head. "There's nothing to it. It's a rawin high-altitude sounding device. I must have seen a dozen of these in the Pacific. The Japanese launched them all the time from Okinawa. My instructions were to examine it, then send it on to Wright Field. But the minute I laid eyes on it I knew what it was, and now I'm not going to bother." The general was, however, quite anxious to put a stop to the rumors about spaceships and men from the moon. He had Johnson snap a dozen photos of the balloon, then sent him speeding back to the office to develop them.

At one minute before midnight, one of Johnson's photos was sent out on the Associated Press news wire. The caption read: "Brigadier General Roger M. Ramey, Commanding General of the 8th Air Force, identifies metallic fragments found near Roswell N. Mex. as a rawin high-altitude sounding device used by air force and weather bureau to determine wind velocity and direction and not a flying disk. Photo by J. Bond Johnson."

The next morning, the story was dead. Newspapers across the country and many overseas ran tongue-in-cheek articles about Major Marcel, who had apparently leaped to cosmic conclusions. None of the writers bothered to learn that the major had previously been assigned to a meteorology station and had extensive familiarity with both weather balloons and high-atmosphere balloon bombs. Marcel was angry and humiliated.

But Ramey wasn't done with him yet. He ordered the major to fly to Fort Worth, which he did the following day. Before he came, he stopped by the sheriff's office and retrieved a few pieces of the debris still locked up there. Marcel brought the fragments into Ramey's office and demonstrated some of the material's exotic properties. The only logical conclusion, as far as Marcel was concerned, was that the stuff had not come from earth. The men left the material behind as they went to a map room to try and pinpoint the exact location of the craft. When they returned, the material was gone. Instead, a ruined weather balloon had been brought in and laid out on the floor. On the general's orders, Marcel knelt beside the balloon to have his picture taken. Then, a few hours later, a dozen reporters were invited into the office for a good look at the "flying disk" Marcel had discovered. The newsmen wanted to ask the major questions, but Ramey had given him strict orders not to utter a single word. He was going to be the goat, the overexcitable idiot who had caused all this fuss, and Ramey was going to play the role of his benevolent commanding officer, speaking to the reporters on his behalf to spare him any further embarrassment.

Back in Roswell, Mac Brazel was also speaking to the press. A few of the local newspeople had gathered outside KGFL's audio room to watch Wasserman interview the craggy old rancher. An unmarked car with two intelligence officers inside had dropped him off and was waiting to take him away as soon as the interview was completed. Mac had spent the last two days in a guesthouse on the Army base. During that time, a large group of MPs had invaded his ranch, allowing no one to enter the property. Before they were ordered away at gunpoint, his neighbors had caught glimpses of soldiers working on hands and knees in the debris field.

Brazel told Wasserman a different story than he had during their first interview. He had been out inspecting his herds with his wife and son when he had come across the debris, he said. It was scattered over an area of about two hundred feet and seemed to be composed mainly of a rubbery gray material. Smaller pieces of heavy-duty tinfoil were strewn around the central hunk of the wreckage. He had noticed pieces of Scotch tape attached to it, as well as tape of another sort with little flowers on it.

He spoke softly the whole time and kept his eyes anchored to the ground. Before he was finished, Wasserman switched off the microphone. "This is all a load of bull,

Mac, and you know it. These Army guys got you to change your story, didn't they?" Wasserman continued to pester Brazel for an explanation as he headed back outside. When they were out of earshot of the others, Brazel pleaded with the man, whispering, "Don't make me talk about it. It'll go hard on me and my family."

He got back in the car with the intelligence officers and drove away. He refused to speak of the matter ever again— not with Marcel, not with Wilcox, not even with his wife.

7

Interview with an Alien

One morning about a week after starting his Roswell research, Okun stumbled out of bed at about eight o'clock. He was trying to remember his dream. It had something to do with him being a roadie for Frank Zappa and having to chase a grizzly bear away from the backstage area during a concert out in the forest. He had repeatedly yelled at the animal that it didn't have a pass. Without a pass it could not go backstage and would have to move away.

He put on the robe and slippers the other scientists had given him, unlocked the door, and started off toward the bathroom when he stepped on something lying outside his door. It was a thick yellow envelope which had been sealed with masking tape. He knew what it must be and tossed it on his bed. About twenty minutes later, he returned with a cup of coffee and tore the package open. He was right. It was the report Wells had written immediately after his so-called conversation with the creature from outer space.

On the night of July 5, 1947, Colonel William Blanchard phoned the Los Alamos Laboratories and asked to speak with Dr. Robert Oppenheimer, head of the Manhattan Project. He said it was an emergency situation with implications for the national security of the United States. Immanuel Wells, the mid-level scientist who had answered the phone, heard the urgency in the colonel's voice, but explained that all of the senior staff were traveling and could not be reached.

Blanchard was desperate to get some "scientific backup" and ended up telling Wells that three bodies had been recovered from a crashed airship. Wells asked what made that a special situation. After a moment of hesitation, Blanchard told him the ship was of extraterrestrial origin and the bodies were unlike anything his medical staff had ever seen. He and the examining doctors both wanted as much help as they could get without going outside New Mexico's large population of high-level security-cleared personnel. Wells left immediately, arriving at Roswell Field's small base hospital about nine in the evening, a few hours after the three bodies had been delivered from the crash site. Soldiers posted outside informed him the entire building was under a Stage Four Quarantine. If he chose to enter, he would not be allowed out until the base commander lifted the order. Wells didn't hesitate for a second. He knew he had been presented with a rare opportunity and was determined to get a look at these cadavers from outer space.

Inside, the lobby was deserted except for a handful of soldiers and a distraught nurse. When Wells walked up and put a hand on her shoulder, she jumped halfway out of her skin.

Something had shaken her up pretty badly. She told him everyone had gone into the observation area because the doctors were just beginning the autopsy on the first "eebie." She had just come from another room, where she was helping prepare the other two bodies to be embalmed and airlifted away, but the sight of them had been too much for her, and she'd come into the lobby to get some air. When Wells asked what an "eebie" was, she explained it stood for EBE or Extraterrestrial Biological Entity.

The observation area was a darkened, L-shaped corridor with windows looking into the hospital's primary operating room. Wells could see the medical team hovering around a bulky shape lying on the table. At first glance, it looked like something dredged up from the depths of the ocean: an enormous clamshell surrounded by a mop of limp tentacles. Wells paced the length of the enclosure and studied the cadaver behind the glass partition. He soon became impressed with how similar, morphologically speaking, the creature was to humans. It was seven or eight feet tall and looked as if it might be capable of standing erect. The majority of its weight was contained in a very large head-chest region, which, even at close range, with its flared design and scalloped ridges, reminded him of a mollusk shell. This main shell was composed of two symmetrical halves which came together at the front, so that the seam between them created a long scar running from the crest of the head, down the center of the face, all the way to the pointed, coccyxlike projection at the bottom of the chest. The face itself was nothing more than a blunt slab of bone and ligament, with four short feeler-tentacles hanging off the sides. The eyes were hidden deep in narrow black sockets that looked like long gashes chopped into the surface of a rock. The creature could not be laid on its back owing to the presence of six rounded appendages, eight-foot-long tentacles, which sprouted from the back of the shell in the area of the shoulder blades. In contrast to the rigid exoskeleton, which protected the rest of the body, these long tentacles looked soft and pulpy, like thick ropes of flesh.

It was a menacing sight to behold. Apart from the obvious fact that it was unlike any creature found on earth, it appeared that it might also be *stronger* than any creature on earth. Though slender, its limbs showed a highly developed musculature. Even the muscles in its foot-long hands were visibly well defined. If the thing had lived and had proved to be hostile, Wells thought, it would have made a formidable opponent—especially in a forest or a jungle environment where its profusion of limbs would allow it to climb with ease.

The autopsy was conducted by Army surgeon Dr. Daniel Solomon and three assistants. His first step was to drag a large scalpel down the long seam connecting the halves of the skull, slicing into the cartilage tissue which filled the gap. When the incision was complete, efforts were made to pry open the large shell. This took some time and was finally accomplished by driving a large spike into the crevice. Piercing ammonium fumes poured into the air out of the head-chest cavity, forcing the medical team to back away from the body, their eyes watering. When the air cleared enough for work to resume, the four men positioned themselves on either side of the creature, twisted the snout toward the ceiling, then pulled hard in opposite directions. The shell cracked open, and Solomon's team made a gruesome discovery. Where they had expected to find the creature's entrails, they found instead another being, fully formed, tucked inside under a thick membrane of clear gel. The soldiers posted inside the operating room took aim at the ghoulish, glistening biomass. When it showed no signs of life, Solomon gathered his courage to come forward again. He reached in and prodded the figure with the blunt end of his scalpel several times. Eventually, he used a towel to wipe away some of the thick gelatin ooze and examined the thing more closely. He soon determined that it, too, was dead. Unclear whether this was a fully developed embryo or some sort of parasite, the medical technicians carefully lifted the smaller creature out from its hiding place, the gelatinous substance causing a loud slurping smack as it finally pulled free. Two puzzling discoveries were made. First, the smaller alien appeared to be of a completely different species than its host. Second, the larger animal appeared to have been gutted; there was a complete absence of anything the doctors recognized as internal organs.

While they were discussing these new revelations, someone standing near Wells in the observation hall called through the glass to Dr. Solomon, asking about the other two creatures. Immediately, the medical team went to the room where the other bodies were being prepared for shipment. Solomon put a stethoscope against the hard chest of the exoskeleton and, after listening for a moment, looked up and announced, "This one's still alive."

It was during the exhumation of the second alien that Wells became centrally involved. The second exoskeleton remained lifeless as it was lifted onto a gurney and wheeled into the operating room. But when Solomon inserted his scalpel into the seam and began slicing away the ligament holding the skull halves together, the tentacle-arms lifted weakly off the ground and tried to push the doctor away from the table. Suddenly Solomon understood the relationship between the two types of alien beings, explaining to his crew and the onlookers that the EBE inside seemed to be manipulating the larger body, which was being used as a biological suit of armor. Intent on reaching the hidden creature before it died, he called for help from the observation gallery. He wanted volunteers to restrain the extremities while he split open the torso. Wells was among the volunteers. He was given a pair of gloves and assigned the task of holding a tentacle against the tabletop. He grasped the serpentine appendage in two places, sinking his fingers deeply into its spongy flesh. As Solomon resumed work with his scalpel, Wells could feel the thing writhing weakly beneath his hands—a sensation which caused him to grow increasingly light-headed. He was on the verge of fainting when the ammonia vapors lifted into the room and momentarily cleared his head. The creature inside began to struggle harder. There was a loud sound of cracking bone as the shell was fully retracted. Wells glanced at the tabletop and saw the goo-slathered alien wriggling around the chest cavity of its host animal. He felt his fingers losing their strength and his knees beginning to buckle. Fighting to maintain control, he focused his eyes on the edge of the table and began to hum the first melody that came into his head. Concentrating on his song, he kept himself conscious long enough for the medical crew to begin lifting the smaller body out of the larger one. Taking a deep breath, he raised his eyes to watch this part of the operation.

"Don't stop, keep on humming," Solomon commanded. "It's keeping it calm."

So, the physicist from the atom-bomb project continued to hum. When he heard the slurping noise that signaled the separation of the two animals, he looked up and found himself face-to-face with the goop-slathered body. The creature's enormous eyes, like reflecting pools of mercury, were open and looking straight at him. When a pair of heavy eyelids closed slowly over these quicksilver orbs, Wells felt as if a heavy curtain were being lowered over him as well. The room lost its shape, and he felt himself sinking toward the floor.

He came to the next morning, Dr. Solomon by his side.

"Welcome back. You got a little squeamish on us last night and passed out."

Wells sat up and accepted a cup of coffee, but as he brought it toward his lips, the smell of it struck him as repulsive, and he set it aside.

"I wanted to thank you," Solomon continued. "It was a brilliant idea you had, humming to the eebie like that. I guess music really is the universal language."

"I was just trying not to faint," Wells admitted, "but I'm glad I could help. Is it still alive?" As quickly as he asked this question, Wells realized he already knew the answer.

"Yes it is, but I don't know how long that will last. We can't figure out how to help it. It's been dropping in and out of consciousness all night. We've offered it food and water, but it hasn't accepted anything yet. We aren't even sure how it eats yet. If it doesn't die from its internal injuries, it's going to starve to death."

"That would be good news, wouldn't it?" Wells asked.

"You're quick." Solomon smiled. Like Wells, he was in his early forties, but looked much older this morning after missing a night of sleep. "The military is overjoyed to hear it won't eat anything. They think it proves the alien can't survive here, but I'm not convinced of that. The thing is badly wounded—of course it has no appetite."

Although Solomon's idea had a great deal of common sense to it, Wells somehow got the idea that it was wrong. He sat staring into space wondering about this idea until Solomon spoke again.

"I'm off to try and get some sleep myself. They're in there questioning the eebie now. You might want to get some breakfast, then go in and watch." With that, he left the room.

Wells dressed himself and went into the lobby. A large buffet table had been set up with food passed through the quarantine perimeter. Although he had not eaten anything for well over twelve hours, he found he was not hungry. In fact, the food smelled rotten and repulsive to him, and he quickly made his way to the observation room in order to escape the odors.

The frail creature lying passively on the operating table was awake. Its eyes were open but turned blankly toward the ceiling. Standing at what they felt was a safe distance, a pair of agents from Army Intelligence were trying every-thing they could think of to initiate communication with the alien. Wells sat down and watched them work for the next six hours. They asked it questions in several languages, waved their hands, snapped, drew simple pictures on a tablet, then set the writing instruments beside the creature. They played music on a tape machine, then made a whole series of ridiculous noises with their mouths and hands, hoping something would catch the thing's attention and elicit a response. They showed it newly developed pho-tographs of the crashed spaceship but got no reaction. When they had tried everything they could think of, they made way for another team. Wells, still sitting comfortably in the same spot, watched for another six hours as a second set of questioners went through a similar routine and achieved similar results. Eventually people began to notice this man who had not left his chair to use the bathroom, have a drink of water, or merely stretch his legs all day long.

The matter was mentioned to Dr. Solomon, who came into

the observation room and took the chair next to Wells, who barely noticed his arrival.

"Fascinating, isn't it?" Solomon said in reference to the alien. Wells knew why he had come, but said nothing, felt nothing. "Dr. Wells, you've been sitting here an awfully long time. Why don't you come out into the lobby and have something to eat?"

"Not hungry," Wells said matter-of-factly. It reminded the doctor that the EBE still had taken no food or drink. They had offered it lettuce, sugar, milk, bread, sliced peaches, and various meats, both raw and cooked. So far, these offerings had brought the only intelligible reaction from the patient— it had waved them away with a limp hand.

"It won't eat anything," Wells said. "It's made up its mind not to eat anything."

Solomon cast a long sideways glance at his companion. "What does that mean, *made up its mind*?"

"The injuries aren't enough to kill it. It's going to starve itself to death."

"What leads you to that conclusion?"

"I don't know. I just feel it. And the longer I sit here, the more convinced I am." For the first time in half a day, Wells broke his concentration on the alien to look Solomon in the eyes. "I can tell what it's thinking. It could eat the food if it wanted to, it's not a matter of it being poisonous. It wants to eat, but it is forbidden. And these interrogators aren't going to get anywhere. The thing communicates telepathically. You ought to try getting a psychic or a mind reader in here."

"Dr. Wells," Solomon whispered to avoid embarrassing his companion, "all of us are running on jangled nerves in here. Several people have noticed that you've been sitting here for—"

"Wait!" Wells's attention was once more riveted on the EBE. "It recognizes something." Solomon looked through the glass and saw the alien in the same position he'd been in for hours. A man inside the room was holding yet another piece of paper in its line of vision. He was about to go on to the next sheet when the creature lifted an arm and seemed to grasp at the image. The man walked the paper back and forth across the room and the creature turned its head, struggling to keep its eyes on the picture. There was an audible reaction in the observation area. Finally something had worked. The agent turned around and showed them what had caught the alien's attention: a block letter "Y."

Solomon looked toward Wells. "I think it's time we had a chat with Blanchard. Please follow me."

An hour later, Wells went inside the observation room a second time. His clothes were wrinkled, his eyes were red around the rims, and he needed a shave. Without hesitating, he quietly brought a chair across the floor and set it close to the alien's bedside. Unlike the interrogators before him, he took a seat, folded his hands in his lap, and merely sat there.

"Where are you from?" he whispered softly. He wasn't asking a question, just listening to the words. He knew he had to translate them into a language this creature from another galaxy could understand. *Where are you from?* he asked again, trying to push the idea out of his head and into the space separating their bodies. Where are you from? over and over, as if it were a matter of will, a matter of concentrating hard enough to find and flex those mental muscles mind readers must have. His instinct, or whatever was leading him, told him the creature communicated by ESP, which turned out to be pretty close, as close as his earthbound imagination could have taken him.

The creature rolled its head to look at him. Behind the almost-human face, the cranium was a thick, translucent plate extending straight back. Through the walls of the skull, Wells traced the lacy pattern of veins and watched small clots of tissue contract, then release. The way the eyelids closed over the surface of the moist mirror-black eyes, the way it had turned its head, and manipulated its fingers, everything indicated that this exotic creature possessed an intelligence similar to our own.

Wells decided on another approach. He tried sending eidetic imagery or mental pictures. But how to translate the question *Where are you from?* into images? He worked at it for a few minutes but found himself trying to mentally broadcast pictures of stick-figure bodies, simple houses, a question mark. He knew it was wrong, that his logic was too abstract, too human. Then, all at once, it hit him. He knew how to ask the question.

He thought of his own home, the two-story structure he shared with his wife in the hills outside of Santa Fe. He meditated on this idea for some time, leading the alien on a tour of the house. He concentrated not only on what the place looked like, but also his feelings for it. Exploring his own heart, Wells lingered on the comfort he felt in this place and his strong sense of possession for it. He moved into the living room, empty now but still echoing with the warmth and laughter of visiting friends, and sat down in his favorite chair, remembering the feel of the upholstery under his hands. Without warning, this meditation was ended as his mind was abruptly plunged into a completely new reality. The frail creature on the table took the scientist on a tour of its own.

•   •   •

Even before he recognized that there was no light, he could feel the heat. Blast-furnace heat, the limit of what his body could withstand, came at him from all directions. And it was getting hotter the deeper he went. It was a cave, and he sensed the presence of other bodies moving around him, with him, hundreds of them. They were deep below the surface of a ruined planet, miles deep already, and following the sloped floor of the cave deeper still and closer to the center. This tunnel connected to others, which branched into others. The entire mantle of the planet was perforated by a great system of these caves, from ruined crust to molten core, and was home to billions like him. Long before, they had lived above ground in a lush infinite garden. Now everything was gone, dead, and they lived here. The rocky ground burned his feet, but instead of turning back, the pain only made him increase his speed. Running blind through the dark, he felt the space around him open up and knew they had come into a large cavern. He smelled the walls thick with food, lush carpets of a plant that felt like moss or lichen in his hands as he tore a heavy sheet of it free from the scalding rock wall, then immediately dragged it tugging and stumbling back into the passageway. Up one slope, then another, towing his heavy treasure closer to the surface. When the heat grew less intense, so did his urgency. The number of bodies around him grew, a dense crowd of them swarmed in like piranha from every direction and began ripping into the carpet of lichen. He stopped pulling and joined the fierce scramble, kicking and pushing his way deeper into the orgy until he found an open space and dived toward it, his mouth open wide, and sucked in a mouthful of the still-warm vegetation.

•　　　　　•　　　　　•

Wells found himself once more looking into the eyes of the visitor. He felt his scalp damp with sweat and his heart pounding. His first impulse was to recoil, to run from the troubling vision he'd been shown. But he fought it down. He could barely believe that the serene and noble creature before him could have come from such a repulsive place. Despite the troubling vision he had just seen, Wells smiled. He had broken through and established communication.

Later, his report to the military staff went poorly. The officers were only mildly interested in what Wells had learned and angry that he hadn't asked the questions they had previously agreed upon. Although the vision of the EBE's home planet might prove to be useful at some future date, it did not address the burning question of *why*. Why had these creatures come to earth and what did they want? To make matters worse, the scientist's behavior during the session was erratic. He rambled in his descriptions, became emotional, and frequently lost his train of thought. This led the soldiers to suspect his trance-vision was nothing more than his own hallucination.

Solomon intervened and explained his suspicion that Wells was suffering from dehydration. He had taken no food or water for almost forty-eight hours. Still, when someone brought him a glass of water, he adamantly refused it. By the end of the thirty-minute meeting, Wells had lost the confidence of those in charge. The decision was made to keep him away from the creature until his mental state improved. Others could use the same techniques to communicate with the EBE.

Others did try. They worked for days, without success.

On the afternoon of the fourth day, as Wells slept in one of the unused rooms, Solomon entered quietly, followed by a team of assistants. Wells bolted out of his sleep, knowing why they had come. Before he could get to his feet, the men grabbed him and pinned him down while Solomon used a hypodermic needle to inject a sedative into his arm. When he woke up twenty hours later, he was in a new room strapped down tight to the bed with a drip IV stuck into his forearm. When Dr. Solomon came in, he found Wells feeling rested and alert. Although he still refused to eat anything, the fluids in his system had brought him back to his senses.

"No one else has had any luck," the doctor told him. "And the creature seems to be getting weaker. If you're feeling up to it, the generals want you to go back inside."

As soon as he stepped inside the glass room, Wells could feel how close to death the alien was. He brought a glass of water to the creature's side and, still struggling to control his own hydrophobia, held it in front of the huge black eyes, mentally imploring the creature to drink.

He felt the thing's response: it was a command to take the liquid away. Wells complied, handing the glass to one of the soldiers behind him. Although he knew the frail body before him needed water, he empathized with its refusal. But the tone of the command was troubling. Wells got the sense of being "spoken to" as an underling, an inferior being, as if the scrawny half-dead form on the table were a delirious lord barking orders to a serf.

Following the script prepared for him, he got down to the business of asking the questions to which the Army needed to know the answers. He queried the creature about why it had come, about the chain of command among its species, about its military capabilities and whether other ships had entered earth's atmosphere. But the only answer Wells received was a vision of something that looked like an enormous Y. Perhaps owing to the visitor's weakened physical state, the vision had none of the power of its previous communication. It was a blurred mental image of a branching structure in the middle of a barren landscape. The blinding light of a sun washed the vision out, causing the scientist to squint. He assumed the place was somewhere on the ruined surface of the planet he had been shown before. He could feel the alien's desire to travel to this place, but that was all the information he could gather. And it wasn't what he was after.

He returned to the question of why the creature and its companions had come to earth. Having found the *window* or *channel* which allowed him to interact with the foreign being, he began to move more quickly, with more confidence. He sensed the alien understood his questions, but was too weak to answer. Wells sat back in his chair and contemplated the possibility that it was too late, that the creature had passed the point of being able to communicate. Although he was quickly learning how to share the creature's thoughts, he couldn't *feel* them with the same intensity he had previously. Then he had another idea, one he wasn't particularly anxious to try out. He looked at the hand resting on the table. It had two plump, opposable fingers, each about six inches in length. The hand was still covered with the piss-smelling goop that lined the chest cavity of the larger, tentacled, exoskeletal suit. Wells drew a deep breath, reached out, and laid his hand over one of the alien's fingers. He squeezed it gently, feeling the resinous substance squish into the gaps between his own fingers. A moment later, the second finger closed around Wells's hand, gripping it with the strength of a small child.

Why have you come here? Who are your leaders? What do you want? The questions traveled through one body and into the other. For two full hours, they sat motionless and in outward silence while the observers behind the glass looked on. Then the creature opened its hand and took it away. Wells whispered something to it, then came out of the room.

"Our friend," as Wells began calling the EBE, was a scientist-explorer, as were the other beings who had died in the crash. They had stumbled upon our planet during what seems to have been a random search through the universe. They somehow picked up energy, possibly radio waves, emanating from earth and came to investigate. One thing had been made perfectly clear—these aliens wished only to observe. They had taken great care to avoid being noticed and, although they did not seem to fear humans, wanted no interaction with them. They seemed to be just as interested in other animals and even plant life. "As a matter of fact," as Wells said, "I got the sense that our good friend found me physically repulsive. It was as strange for it to touch me as it was for me to touch it."

When he'd asked about the alien's social structure and chain of command, he was shown the image of a very tall alien, considerably larger than the others, which was some kind of leader or commander. There was a strong sense of benevolence associated with this tall creature. It was a protector of some sort, although it wasn't clear whom it was protecting. Wells had the most difficulty understanding the creature's reply to his questions about additional ships. He was shown a vision of the sixty-foot craft traveling through deep space. When Wells asked why there were no provisions on board and communicated the military's belief that the ship was only a short-range vehicle, the interview ended.

The scientist openly expressed his admiration for the space voyager, discussing the bravery it must have taken to embark upon a dangerous journey of the sort his friend had taken.

•   •   •

That evening Wells was standing in the hospital's lobby chatting with a group of officers. He was trying to describe the physical sensation involved in reading the alien's thoughts when he suddenly broke off in mid-sentence, complaining of dizziness. Reaching out, he grabbed one of the men by the arm, struggling to stay on his feet, then collapsed to the floor before anyone could catch him.

Both he and the alien had lapsed into a shared coma, one that would last for the next nine days. Solomon became convinced that the EBE and Wells had developed a sympathetic bond. It was, he argued, related to the phenomenon sometimes observed in human twins, where one can feel the pain of the other. He cited the Metcheck case, where a sister in Dallas called police in Connecticut to report a traffic accident. She claimed to have visualized her twin sister's car sliding off an icy road and plunging down an embankment. Although she had never visited Connecticut, she was able to describe several landmarks along the road and the exact place where the car had broken through a retaining wall. When the police investigated, they found the injured twin exactly where they had been told to look. Solomon feared the alien might be trying to take Wells with it, and won permission for the scientist to be moved away from the quarantine area. He was transported to Wright-Patterson Air Force Base, where he remained until the EBE died.

When he woke up, he had permanently lost the use of both his legs, and movement in his upper body was impaired. After that, Dr. Wells no longer referred to the alien survivor as his friend.

8

The Bikini Connection

After reading the Wells report, Okun opened his door and began wandering the hallways, lost in contemplation. He ended up pacing the corridor outside the vault room and decided to pay the dead aliens a visit.

The tanks lay side by side on the floor, a trio of steel-reinforced glass coffins filled with murky liquid. He squatted, put his nose inches from the glass, and sent a telepathic message to wake up. Each time he played this game, some part of him actually expected to see the twitch of a muscle, the blink of an eye, a sign of life that would send him racing through the halls hollering, "They're alive! They're alive!" But the pasty white corpses continued to float tranquilly in their formaldehyde graves. They looked as peaceful in death as the Wells report had described them in life. Their wide open eyes gave them a startled, innocent expression which almost made it possible to believe they had come here for the sake of pure science, that they had no ulterior motives.

But Okun wasn't convinced. Although he proudly considered himself a peacenik, he was also a realistic scientist. The creatures might be from a different galaxy, but they were still animals, with instincts and drives. If they were anything like humans, he doubted they could be as selfless as Wells made them out to be.

He thought back to a story he'd heard at Caltech about the emperor Napoleon Bonaparte. As he was preparing to invade Egypt, he was approached by a group of France's most famous philosophers and historians. Sensing this would be a historic moment, they wanted to witness and record the campaign firsthand. They appealed to Napoleon's ego, promising to write a book glorifying his exploits, one that would assure the general's place in history. He agreed, but only on the condition the academics stay to the rear of the march where they belonged, "with the whores and the cooking wagons." The professor who told Brackish this story said it illustrated the typical relationship between science and the military. "Where there is science," she said, "there is war. And the idea of pure science is nothing more than a myth. There is always another motive lurking beneath the surface."

At the time, Okun hadn't taken her too seriously, but here he was only a couple of years later working, basically, for the military. Sure, he had shoulder length hair, wore an ankh necklace, and had a "War is Unhealthy for Children and Other Living Creatures" poster taped to the wall in his room, but he, too, was marching at the rear of the caravan.

If he could have spoken with the dead aliens, he would have asked them about their biomechanical suits. The doctors present at the autopsy had concluded the two animals were of different species. Although the idea hadn't occurred to any of the medical examiners in '47, Okun wondered if perhaps the beings came from different *planets*. If so, it would indicate the creatures floating in the tank were members of a conquering race, one that had used the alien bodies in much the same way humans used, say, cattle. Either way, it made him want to become a vegetarian. The exoskeletal suits were, unfortunately, long gone. They were unintentionally destroyed when, to prevent the spread of otherworldly bacteria, they were sprayed with the insecticide DDT. The spray triggered a chemical reaction that reduced the shells to thick liquid paste.

Okun sat down on the nearest coffin, thinking about the question of a second ship. "Am I being paranoid," he asked the extraterrestrial life-form below him, "or does my government know about more of your guys' ships? Maybe there's even an Area *52* someplace. Otherwise, why would they be trying to discourage me from investigating that possibility?"

The aliens didn't say it was all part of a plan to keep the young genius motivated.

"Just the man I've been waiting to see."

"I don't like the sound of that. What's up?" Radecker, no longer trying to disguise the fact that he was on a five-year vacation, was dressed in tennis whites. A covered racket protruded from his small suitcase. He'd just returned from thirty-six hours of fun and sun on the shores of Frenchman Lake.

"Been playing tennis?"

"Yes, I have. You getting ready to head off to Woodstock?" the boss shot back defensively. Okun was wearing open-toed sandals and a grungy old T-shirt with Jimi Hendrix's silhouette on it.

"That Wells report was pretty interesting. Did you read any of it?"

"Glanced at it. Why? Is there something I should know?"

Okun scrutinized him for signs he was lying and thought he saw them. "It's just that the table of contents on the front page lists an addendum added a couple of years later, a section called 'Revision of Preliminary Conclusions.' But it's not there. Those pages are missing."

"And you think I took them?"

"I didn't say that." Okun tried to maintain a poker face, but failed. Radecker knew from the cocked head and the narrowed eyes that he was being accused.

"Look, you asked me for the report, and I got it for you. Why would I go to the trouble of having it sent here and then not show you the whole thing?"

Both of them knew the answer to that question. Because there might be information in those pages concerning additional ships. Brackish opened his mouth to say something, but stopped when he remembered the promise he'd made to Dworkin. He couldn't let Radecker know what the old men had told him.

"I'm not saying you removed the pages, but it looks like somebody did. Maybe somebody in DC wants to keep us in the dark about something."

"If that's true, there's really nothing we can do about it, is there?" He went off to his room to unpack.

Okun shook his head. He wondered if Colonel Spelman knew how Radecker was spending his time in Nevada. He knew from things the agent had said during their first days in the lab that he was ambitious, that he wanted to climb the career ladder at the CIA. But he appeared to possess only moderate intelligence and didn't seem to be a very diligent worker. For the first time, the idea occurred to Okun that perhaps Radecker wasn't a good CIA man. Maybe they'd chosen him because he was mediocre, expendable. But without a doubt, Radecker was right about one thing. If the Pentagon and the CIA didn't want them to know something, they had the power to keep the men of Area 51 in the dark.

Okun followed the labyrinth of hallways toward the exit doors and turned on the long row of lights that illuminated the stacks. Somewhere in that welter of printed material, he sensed, was the clue he needed. But where? Since his introduction to this wildly disorganized library, he had finished reading over forty reports. He pulled a pen out of his shirt pocket and used the palm of his hand as scratch paper. At his present rate of speed, he calculated it would take him 513 years to read every document in the room.

Suddenly dejected, he switched off the lights. It would be nearly a year before he turned them on again.

A month to the day after the arrival of the Wells report, Radecker came dancing into the kitchen waving a telegram in the air. "Pack your bags, gentlemen, we're taking this show out on the road! This just came in from Spelman," he announced, dropping the printout on the table in front of a gloomy Okun. "They've approved your proposal!"

"You must be kidding. I wasn't serious about that." After being depressed and listless for two weeks, Brackish had realized he had to do something, *anything*, to stay busy. With the help of his colleagues, he'd written a half-demented proposal to retrofit the alien spacecraft with human-built technology—half of which would need to be invented. The men had laughed at their ideas, realizing how ludicrous most of them were. For Okun, it had been just like sitting around brainstorming with the Mothers in his dorm room—except his new group would have been called the Grandpas of Invention.

One of the minor ideas called for in the proposal turned out to be astonishingly prophetic once the secrets of the alien technology were revealed years later. Although there was no particular need for it from an engineering standpoint, he decided to base the steering and velocity controls on telekinetic energy. Okun recalled Dr. Solomon's theory on how the aliens controlled their biomechanical suits through acts of will. Based on their fetus-like riding position inside the chest cavity and the fact that the visitors had no tentacles, Solomon had ruled out the possibility of the suits responding mimetically to the physical actions of the wearer. It must have been done through mental signals. Okun wanted to apply similar principles to the operation of the ship. Years before there was any such thing as Virtual Reality, he conceived of a "sensory suit" to be worn by pilots which would read their slightest physical impulses and translate them into a series of commands intelligible to the ship's control system. In his proposal, he'd called this function the "Look, Ma, No Hands Interface," explaining that it would "significantly reduce pilot reaction time."

Dworkin was struck dumb that the document had been taken seriously. He had urged his junior colleague not to submit it, warning that it would damage his credibility with the powers-that-be. After he read the telegram, he turned to Okun and raised his eyebrows. "Somebody up there likes you."

Spelman thought the plan was ridiculous. It showed how little serious work was being done at the secret labs. As soon as he was finished reading the document, he phoned CIA headquarters and asked to be put through to the Office of the Deputy Director. "Al, I'm worried about our boy. I think he may be losing his marbles. He just sent me this proposal to rebuild the blackbird with conventional technology. There are so many weird ideas in this thing my first thought was, 'uh-oh, we've got another Manny Wells on our hands.'"

"What does he want to do?" Nimziki sounded like he was busy doing something else, not really paying attention. Spelman ran through the basic outlines of the plan, making sure to mention some of its nuttier aspects.

"And get this," he quoted from the report. "'In order to accomplish these goals, we will need to spend time at the following research institutions: the Los Alamos National Labs, the Massachusetts Institute of Technology, the Lawrence Livermore Labs, the University of California at Berkeley, Oak Ridge' . . . There are about twenty-five places they want to go to."

"Let them go, it can't hurt."

The colonel couldn't believe what he was hearing. "In my opinion, it would be faster and easier simply to feed him some more clues. Radecker's obviously doing a better job than you'd anticipated."

"Not yet," Nimziki snapped. "I have my sources, and everything's going along fine out there. The kid needs a vacation is all. He's been down there long enough. Let's send them out. You take care of it."

Reluctantly, Spelman agreed, but not before chopping back the proposed itinerary to just a pair of sites: Los Alamos and JPL. He also arranged special security procedures. Dworkin and the others, he knew, could be trusted not to reveal any information about Area 51, but Okun was untested. Although Spelman had never met him face-to-face, everything he knew about the young man suggested he would be a major security risk. He assigned two of his crafti-est agents the task of getting Okun to divulge sensitive infor-mation.

Radecker and his staff were away from their labs for ten months. Seven of them were spent at the prestigious Los Alamos National Laboratories, where the group enjoyed full access to the knowledgeable technical staff and the ultramod-ern equipment, before moving on to a shorter stay at the Jet Propulsion Labs in Pasadena, Okun's old stomping grounds. Twice a day, he glimpsed his alma mater from behind the tinted windows of the van that shuttled the crew between the labs and their hotel. Since they received the red carpet treat-ment everywhere they went, the trip turned out to be relaxing and enjoyable for everyone except Okun. Since he had never studied many of the subjects that the engineers around him—even Freiling—knew like the backs of their hands, he was forced to play catch-up. He spent most of the year with his nose buried in books about rocketry, aerodynamics, or the newly emerging field of computer science. It was his graduate school. Under the patient tutelage of his elderly companions, he crammed three years of study into ten months. Without revealing why they needed the information, the scientists were able to learn many things that would help them repair the ship once they returned—everything from advanced, sol-derless welding techniques to the design of microcircuitry. As for security concerns, Spelman's worries proved unnecessary. Okun was far too busy to sit around gabbing with strangers. Besides, both facilities were staffed by very normal, very responsible, people, who had reached their positions by fol-lowing the rules. They dressed, spoke, and wore their hair in the manner they felt was expected of them. When these squares saw Okun trucking toward them in a hallway, they dipped into nearby doorways to avoid him. He caused a small panic among a group of secretaries one morning when he came in wearing his security clearance card pinned to a happy face T-shirt worn over a brand-new pair of plaid pants which revealed—and this was what horrified them—he wasn't wearing any socks under his EARTH SHOES. He had about as much chance of conversing about national security issues with these employees as if he had been a leader of the Black Panther Party. Spelman's spies never got close to him.

They began their trip "home" on a warm spring morning. Okun persuaded Radecker to let him pay his mother a quick surprise visit. But when the van pulled up in the driveway, a neighbor told Radecker that Saylene had gone shopping. On the long drive back to the desert, Okun found himself thinking about his mom and his friends. But then something triggered another memory. This one concerned a film he'd seen at Los Alamos months before. It was a dull old documentary about the work of the labs—the Manhattan Project, rocket experiments, and the history of the U.S. nuclear program. In one clip, Brackish got his first look at Dr. Wells. He appeared in the background of a scene at the laboratory. But the footage that kept replaying itself in his mind had been shot in the South Pacific. It was a bald and awkward moment of military propaganda that featured a Navy officer speaking to a group of coyly grinning native islanders. They were being moved off the Bikini atoll, part of the Marshall Islands Group, in preparation for a test of the newly built hydrogen bomb. The officer made it annoyingly clear these simple people were leaving of their own free will and had plenty of other islands to go to. A disturbing moment of history caught on film, but Okun couldn't figure out why he kept thinking about it. It seemed important somehow.

The moment he walked into his room and saw the Wells report sitting on his desk exactly where he'd left it, he knew. He stood stock-still staring at the pages, still holding his luggage. Very slowly he began to nod.

The next morning, after a phone call to Los Alamos, he gathered everyone for a meeting. "Remember that movie they showed us about Oppenheimer and von Braun? And there were all those scenes about the rocket tests they conducted around the time of the H-bomb?"

"Yes, what about it?"

"There was that one rocket that exploded, remember? It blew up after it left the atmosphere, and nobody could figure out why. This morning I called the labs and had them check the date of that footage for me. The explosion happened at 4:30 P.M. on July 5, 1947."

"So?"

"That means," Okun announced proudly, "it was 10:30 P.M. on July 4 in New Mexico. Which in turn means . . ."

". . . it was just before our alien vehicle crashed," Cibatutto finished the sentence.

"Yup."

"And you think there's a connection between the two events?"

Freiling interjected. "That test was halfway around the world in the Southern Hemisphere. How would that affect something in the skies over New Mexico?"

"I have no idea," Okun lied, "but it's too much of a coincidence not to investigate."

Dworkin glanced at Lenel, and said, "I seem to recall seeing a report on that rocket's failure."

"Of course there's a report," Lenel groused. "Anytime you

blow up several million dollars' worth of government equipment, you end up writing a report. Finding it is going to be a different matter."

Okun gestured grandly in the direction of the stacks. "After you, gentlemen." The old men let out a collective groan, realizing they would spend the rest of the day thumbing through old documents. Reluctantly, they allowed themselves to be herded toward the stacks.

A day and a half later, they found what they were looking for. The staff members opened a bag of pretzels and passed them around the kitchen table as Okun read from the report.

"We have returned to the Garden of Eden with the intention of blowing it up. The beauty of this tropical island is so astonishing one senses everywhere the hand of God in its creation. We can only pray He will forgive us." So wrote an English electrician of the Bikini atoll. He was one of over two hundred men employed by the Manhattan Project for a series of rocket and bomb tests to be conducted in the Marshall Islands. Although the tests were classified experiments conducted by the United States, half of the conversations took place in German. A large contingent of technicians who had been working for the Nazis a year earlier now formed the backbone of the U.S. rocket program. In the closing days of the war, Wernher von Braun and his crew had been ordered to return from the northern island of Peenemünde to a country inn near Berlin. Hitler, determined to prevent them from joining the allies, sent a team of SS agents to execute them all. By sheer luck, a cousin of von Braun's learned of the assassination plot and led the engineers into American-held territory, where they surrendered. Within weeks, these talented scientists were reunited at the White Sands Proving Grounds in New Mexico.

During the war, they had developed the deadly V-2 rocket, the world's first ballistic missile, which was capable of reaching altitudes of seventy-five miles. But the new rocket they were preparing to test at Bikini, the first of the Redstone weapons, would reach higher still. It would soar three hundred miles above the earth before making a controlled reentry and exploding a small bomb in its nose cone on the nearby island of Kwajelin. The film crews and reporters who had come to the island ignored the Germans, focusing instead on the upcoming test of the first hydrogen bomb. Nevertheless, these engineers felt their experiments were just as significant as those being conducted by Oppenheimer and company. If the launch was successful, it would mark the beginning of the space program.

State-of-the-art equipment had been brought to Bikini in order to monitor the rocket's flight. High-speed cameras with newly improved telephoto capacity, ultrasensitive radar equipment along with infrared and radio tracking systems were set up under thatch huts not far from the launchpad. After a final check of all systems, the countdown began. Liftoff occurred without complications at 4:18 P.M. local time. With an earsplitting roar, the forty-ton assembly lifted into the cloudless sky, leaving the graceful arch of a contrail in its wake. The ground crew watched it rise until it disappeared from view, then gathered around the banks of monitors. Without warning, the rocket disintegrated at 185 miles. Until that moment, everything had gone exactly according to plan—a rarity in highly complex tests of this kind.

Radar watchers reported seeing something in the rocket's vicinity flash across the screen a split second before the blast. The "ghost" had appeared out of nowhere and vanished just as suddenly. The consensus among the technicians was that it had been a false reading caused by energy related to the explosion. There was just one troubling aspect to the way the shape had moved. It seemed to *accelerate*. As one of the observers put it: "It was like a fish resting in the sand that darts away a moment before you step on it."

The report advanced several explanations for the cause of the explosion. One of these concerned "a layer of radiation in the atmosphere at an altitude of 185 miles." The authors of the report were puzzled and somewhat alarmed by the discovery of this layer. Okun would have read right past this section if Cibatutto hadn't interrupted him.

"The rocket ran into one of the Van Allen belts, that's what they're talking about."

Lenel grimaced. "Hogwash! The belts wouldn't cause a rocket to explode."

"Actually, since this rocket carried a signal bomb in its nose cone, the sudden shift in magnetism could have activated the detonator cap."

Lenel disagreed and began explaining why when Freiling interrupted with views of his own. Soon all the old men were talking at once, shouting to be heard over the others. Just as the argument began degenerating into finger-pointing and name-calling, Okun held his hand high in the air and screamed over the top of the noise.

"Excuse me! I have a question!" The room went suddenly quiet. "What is a Van Allen belt?"

Cibatutto recited from memory. "The Van Allen belts are two rings of high-energy-charged particles surrounding Earth, probably originating in the Sun and trapped by Earth's magnetic field. The lower, more energetic belt, is at an altitude of 185 miles from Earth's surface while the outer belt is at ten thousand miles. They were discovered by physicist James Van

Allen. Their shape and intensity vary significantly with fluctuations in the solar wind."

The older scientists stroked their beards in contemplation. Okun, with no beard to stroke, came up with an idea. "These variations, do they follow any kind of a pattern?"

Again, Cibatutto had the answer. "Yes, they do. The belts experience seasonal fluctuations, but these do not correspond directly to Earth's seasons. The energy level of the inner belt remains low for several months, then erupts into short periods of intense activity."

"Hmmm, would it be possible to find out what season the belts were in on July 4, 1947, between the hours of 10 P.M. and midnight in New Mexico?"

"I don't see why not." Cibatutto brought a thick reference book into the kitchen and began working through a series of mathematical equations. Okun was too eager to let the man work in peace.

"How often does this inner belt thingie erupt?" Brackish asked.

"About five consecutive days each year, sometimes twice a year. You have to run each date through the equation." When he was finished crunching the numbers, Cibatutto stared down at the results, nodding in an unconscious imitation of one of his colleagues. "On the date in question, the energy was at its peak."

Okun grinned and turned to the others. "Anybody up for a wager?" The scientists, accustomed to taking money from men who asked them such questions, were all ears. "You guys choose whichever alien encounter you think is the most real, the one you think really happened, and I'll bet you a month of washing the dishes that it happened during one of these flare-ups."

"Eau Claire, Wisconsin," Lenel said without hesitation.

The other men agreed. Next to Roswell, this was the case with the most convincing physical evidence.

In the Eau Claire case, a policeman claimed to have "surprised" an alien saucer hovering over a farmhouse. When the craft moved away, he pursued at high speed until it fired a blue ray, which struck his vehicle and knocked him unconscious. An examination of the car revealed it had undergone a massive failure of the electrical system. Everything from the ignition to the taillights was ruined. The spark plugs and points were melted. The officer involved lived through the experience, but died six months later of nervous depression. His vehicle was taken to the UFO evidence compound at the Air Force Academy.

Cibatutto worked the date of the Eau Claire event through the equation, then made an announcement. "The good news is we seem to have found a connection between the alien visitations and the activity of the Van Allen belts. The bad news is each of us has to do the dishes 1.55 extra times this month. I propose we go in reverse-alphabetical order." The old men cheered and slapped Okun on the back.

"Progress of this magnitude deserves more than dirty dishes," Dworkin declared. "It calls for champagne!"

If the group's new theory was correct, it would be the single most important discovery about the aliens since their ship had crash-landed twenty-six years before, more important than Okun's unproved discovery that the ships must fly in groups. If the visitors only penetrated earth's atmosphere during these short bursts of radioactivity, it would mean two things. First, researchers could weed out the many bogus sightings and reports of contact in order to concentrate their attention on the real McCoys. Second, it would give them the power to predict when the creatures would come again.

While the older men set to work finding all the files that fell into one of these windows, Okun checked the dates of the case studies he'd already looked at. To his surprise, only one of them turned out to be true—the Bridget Jones incident. The lying girl had been telling the truth after all.

It turned out to be a long day of pulling reports, but their enthusiasm was high. They brought a radio into the stacks and sang the songs they knew the words to. Even Lenel was cheery. As they searched, Okun had the bright idea of calling Radecker and telling him what they'd learned. Dworkin called him over and explained why that might not be such a good idea. "Yesterday in Los Angeles, as we were parked in front of your house, I watched your expression change when we learned your mother wasn't at home. It occurred to me then how much I'd like for you to be able to leave here when your contract is finished. I think that's what you want for yourself. So call Mr. Radecker if you like, but remember this: *the more you know, the deeper you're buried.*"

9

Mrs. Gluck and Her Daughter

Okun didn't understand the precise relationship between the Van Allen belts and the arrival of the space-ships. And he didn't much care. What was important to him was that the dates matched. Now he had a way of sifting through the rubbish and finding the gold. But he was dismayed by two discoveries. First, there were hardly any real reports. Lenel hadn't been exaggerating when he said 99.9 percent of everything in the stacks was a bunch of hooey or bullpucky or whatever he'd called it. After several days of combing through the files, they had found about four hundred case studies occurring during the specified five-day periods. Then came the long process of poring over them and throwing out the fakes that happened to have been reported during those times. The scientists ruled out all but sixty-two of the reported sightings and encounters. Only twenty of these had occurred later than 1960. And four of those were mere sightings. That left only sixteen good reports.

One of them was the Eau Claire, Wisconsin, incident.

One was the Bridget Jones case, where the central witness was dead.

Then there were thirteen people who claimed they had been abducted. And that's where things got interesting. All told very similar stories. They had been driving along lonely roads or at home engaged in some quiet activity when they suddenly stopped whatever they were doing. The drivers pulled to the side of the road. The people taken from their homes sat down or stood still. All the abductees described being surrounded by short, quick-moving creatures with enlarged heads. Many claimed they had been flown to a spaceship, where various experiments were performed on their persons. Six of them described a leader who was much taller that the others. Okun knew from other reading he had done that mentions of a much taller leader were common.

But there was one report that stood out from the others. It was about a woman who claimed she had been interrogated about a Y-shape. Her file said she was a person in the public eye, and care was taken to expunge any clue to her identity. But Okun knew her name was Trina Gluck and she lived in Fresno. In fact, he knew her street and house number. Scrawled onto the front page of the document in a handwriting style he was learning to recognize was the woman's name and address.

Two weeks later, he rode into Las Vegas with the boys. As always, the van dropped them off in front of their bank, Parducci Savings. Nothing on the outside of the building let on that it was a bank. There was no logo, no place to park, no slot for night deposits. Inside, the lobby looked like someone's living room, with lots of family photos on the walls and too much furniture. There was a counter with two teller's windows and behind that a couple of doors leading to private offices. These doors were never open. Salvatore Parducci, a heavyset man with an appetite for fine suits and gold bracelets, was the manager. He spoke in a luxuriously soft voice punctuated by sudden bursts of loud, braying laughter.

Okun knew there was something unusual about the bank on his first visit. Moments after opening his new account, Salvatore came around the counter with his arms spread wide and embraced him. While he was being squeezed against the powerful man's girth, Salvatore looked down, and purred, "Welcome. My family thanks you for trusting us with your money." On another occasion, Okun watched a helicopter land beside the building. An old lady stepped out of it carrying a casserole dish and came inside. It turned out to be Signora Parducci, delivering lunch to her son. She flirted shamelessly with Cibatutto in Italian before disappearing into one of the back offices. Very shady.

This morning's transaction had been uneventful except for Okun withdrawing an unusually large amount of cash, three hundred dollars. "Feeling lucky," he explained with a grin.

It was a sunny morning, and the old fellows were in high spirits. They were marching down the boulevard toward a café that offered one-cent breakfasts. After that, it was onward to the casinos for a day of cards. Okun seemed preoccupied. He kept to the back of the pack, fingering the wad of cash in his pocket. "Hey, you guys," he called. The old men stopped walking and turned around. "Nothing personal, but I think I'll try my luck at one of the smaller casinos today. By myself." His friends were visibly disappointed.

"Hey, what happened to all for one and one for all?" Freiling asked. "We're supposed to play as a team." When that approach didn't work, he tried another. "We'll let you win a few."

"It's not the money. I just feel like being alone today."

"Completely understandable," Lenel declared. "I'm tired of looking at these ugly old coots myself. It wouldn't hurt to have a break."

"Dr. Freiling," Cibatutto cried. "This man called you an ugly coot!"

Freiling put up his dukes. "Who said so? I'll knock his block off."

As the two men began sparring, Dworkin came a step closer to his young friend, and silently pronounced the words, "Be careful." Okun wondered if he knew.

An hour later, he had rented a car and was heading west.

Brinelle Gluck was the girl he'd always wanted to meet—nerdy, artsy, and, in her own way, beautiful. It was love at first sight. She was a couple of years older and a couple of inches taller than him and as slender as a microscope. From her moccasins to her perfect miniature breasts to her long straight hair, she was, for him, a vision of loveliness. He immediately regretted having dressed like a total square.

"Do I know you?" she asked when she opened the door.

Hating to begin anything with the word "no," he answered, "Maybe in a past life. Were you ever a monkey in Tibet?"

Instead of slamming the door in his face, she actually thought about it for a second before she answered. "Yes, now that you mention it, I was."

They both laughed at her reply and spent the next thirty minutes rambling through one topic after another. After reincarnation, they talked about Brinelle's poetry and modern dance, the Beatles, Bangladesh, biointensive gardening, the world's scariest roller coasters, and the Carlos Castaneda books. Okun felt his heart racing with excitement when she reached out and briefly touched his chest. She fondled his ankh.

"I don't usually like jewelry, but that is the most outtasight piece. Where'd you get it?"

The question caught him off guard. "Um, I can't remember. I've had it for years."

When she asked him his name, he blurted, "Bob. Bob Robertson."

"I'm Brinelle Gluck. I wish I had a nice normal name like yours. You have no idea what it's like to get teased about your name all the time. So, Mr. Bob Robertson, what do you do? Got a job?"

"Yeah, I guess you could call it a job."

"What is it you do?" Okun was starting to get uncomfortable with this part of the conversation.

"I'm a scientist."

"Really? What branch of science?"

"Boring stuff, planes, rockets, just a lot of technical stuff."

"I see. Where do you do all this boring stuff?

"Labs, mainly."

"No duh. I mean what's the name of the lab. My dad knows hundreds of people who work at Livermore and Stanford and UCLA."

He really liked this girl, and he wanted desperately to tell her the truth or at least to explain that he wasn't allowed to say. But he'd been coached a thousand times never ever to give that response. It aroused suspicion and curiosity, two things to which Area 51 was allergic. He had been told to turn and walk away or, if that wasn't possible, to lie.

"I work at JPL in the microcircuitry division. We do the circuit boards and harness wiring for the space program, mostly satellites."

Then she did something that broke his heart. She nodded.

It was a big dopey nod with an expression on her face that showed how impressed she was. She had just gotten around to asking him why he'd knocked on the door when the phone rang.

"I gotta get that. Come in and sit down." Brinelle disappeared into another room.

The house was impressive. It was a small palace built in the Spanish style, with lots of exposed wood and high, white-washed ceilings. He wandered into the sunken living room and examined a painting. It looked vaguely familiar, and he wondered if it might be the work of a famous artist. It was that kind of house.

He sat down on the sofa and let his life flash before his eyes. *This chick is mondo diggable,* he told himself. *I haven't known her an hour, and I've already lied to her a couple of times. If I keep working at Area 51, I'll never be friends with her or anyone else. There are too many secrets to keep.* Suddenly, he pictured himself at forty, still with long hair, still puttering around with the spaceship, still single. When Dworkin and the others were gone would he continue to work down there alone?

Contemplating these matters, he reached into a bowl of nuts on the coffee table and was trying to open one with his teeth when another woman walked into the room. "And who might you be?" she asked.

"Um, hello. Is your name Gluck? Trina Gluck?"

"It might be. Who are you?"

"Hello, I'm Bob. Bob Robertson. I work at JPL in the microcircuitry division. We do a lot of the electronic work for the space program. I was just having a very pleasant conversation with your daughter."

The woman, elegant, in her late fifties, was obviously Brinelle's mom. From the way she was dressed, it looked like she'd just come back from a social function.

"Are you a friend of my daughter's?"

"Sort of. I mean, I hope so. But actually, I'm here to see you. I recently read the report on your abduction and wanted to ask you some questions about it."

Instantly, Okun knew he'd said the wrong thing. The woman's expression turned ugly. "Get out of this house before I call the police."

Okun tried to make her understand how important it was, but she wouldn't listen. Brinelle came back in and tried to take his side, but her mom was irate, screaming at the top of her lungs, tears on her face. When he stopped in the doorway, she began pushing the door closed. "Dr. Wells sent me," he blurted out, just as the door slammed in his face.

He stood on the doorstep, stunned. How could he have been so stupid? Up to that moment, he'd treated it all as a game, the Great American Flying Saucer Hunt. But obviously, it was a deep personal wound for this woman. The instant he'd mentioned the word abduction, a wave of pain had broken across her face. For Trina Gluck, it wasn't a game. Okun started off down the brick driveway when the door opened again.

Mrs. Gluck stepped onto the porch and waved him back inside. "If Dr. Wells sent you, you can come in."

The kidnapping, as she called it, had taken place about ten years earlier, shortly after her husband, a congressman, had declared his candidacy for one of California's Senate seats. It was Memorial Day weekend, and Brinelle was away at her first slumber party. Trina's husband was in bed reading. She was in the bathroom brushing her teeth when her arm suddenly relaxed to her side. A moment later, the toothbrush clattered into the sink. Although she'd never so much as imagined an encounter with aliens before, she somehow knew immediately what was happening. She was terrified and felt the impulse to scream, but couldn't. She still had control over her eyes and tried to turn toward the door, but her neck would not cooperate. She felt the first one come into the room a moment before she saw its reflection in the mirror. She described it as being about three or four feet tall with a large head and shiny silver eyes, but it moved about the room so quickly she couldn't get a good look at it. After the first one examined her hair and nightgown, others came through the doorway.

One of them stood directly behind her, hidden from view, and identified itself to her as "the friend." This creature spoke to her using her own voice for what seemed like a long time. The distinction between her own thoughts and those of the friend began to blur. She felt small hands touching her body in several places and heard them rummaging through the drawers and cabinets. She felt her shock settling into anger and struggled to regain control of herself. When the friend asked how they could help her relax and cooperate, she asked for her husband. Go get my husband out of bed. But a moment later she heard her own voice reply, "Your husband is asleep now."

She was taken outdoors and laid on her back in some of the bushes by the side of the house. The friend made her understand she had a skin disease, something contagious on her stomach and pelvis. Small hands lifted her nightgown while other hands lifted her head so she could watch the operation that would cure her. Silently begging them to stop, she watched a needlelike instrument slice into her skin. The blade opened a bloodless incision down the left side of her belly, from the rib cage down to the hip. A second instrument she couldn't see was inserted into the opening. As it slid between her skin and stomach, the friend congratulated her on being clean again. Still listening to her own voice being used by another being, she was given a brief lecture of some sort. It might have been on hygiene, but she couldn't be sure.

When the operation was finished she was put into a sitting position, then lifted up into the sky. It was the sensation of sitting in a strong net and being lifted by a very fast crane. She watched as the lights of the city receded between her knees.

Then she was in a gray room. She heard the soft rustling of their movements, like pieces of silk being rubbed together. She rolled her head to the side, and noticed she was lying on a platform or table a few feet above the floor. The room appeared to be circular, almost spherical in shape. A bank of windows was set low against the wall, almost part of the floor. Nearby she noticed a pile of clothing, old dirty clothes, and she had the sense that someone had been sleeping there. The friend came and repositioned her head so that all she could see was the blank gray ceiling. She was told that the examination would continue.

Then a new creature stepped into her peripheral vision and approached the table. It was much taller than the others, but she felt that it was different in other ways as well. It seemed to be a leader of some sort. It leaned in and brought its face closer until she could see her distorted reflection in the bulging eyes. They reminded her of insect eyes although the face around them was nearly human in shape. She closed her own eyes, hoping that if she ignored this tall creature, it would back away. But it continued hovering over the table, studying her.

Without using an audible voice, the leader began pronouncing a series of words or ideas, as if it were reading down a list. She knew she was being asked about each item, but did not understand her role in the exchange. The only one of these "words" she could recall later was the letter Y, and only because it had been asked of her repeatedly. Several times, the tall creature probed her thoughts for the meaning of this symbol. She tried to cooperate, thinking they might spare her life if she could give them the information they wanted. It was clear to her it didn't mean the letter Y in the alphabet. It occurred to her that it might be a place, a landmark in a city perhaps. She thought of the Space Needle in Seattle and the arch in St. Louis, but the creature seemed dissatisfied with these answers.

It stood up, and, as it moved away from her, she must have lost consciousness.

"My husband woke me up at two in the morning saying he'd had a dream someone was trying to break into the house. He went downstairs to look around and noticed the security alarm had been disarmed. It never worked properly after that, and we ended up having to have it replaced. I asked him for a glass of water because my throat felt dried out. When I sat up to take it, he noticed there were leaves and dirt all over my back and in my hair. We decided that I must have been sleepwalking and that I was the one who had turned off the alarm. We went down and checked the side of the house, because the leaves in bed matched the japonicas growing out there, but nothing looked unusual, no signs of struggle or anything like that. I told him about having this sensation that I'd gone somewhere, but at that point it was still buried at the back of my mind.

"We talked about it the next morning over breakfast, and I mentioned to him again about this sense of mine that I'd been carried off somewhere. He wanted to call the police, but I wouldn't let him. When he left for the office, I went up to the bathroom and took a shower. Then it all came back to me in a crash when I opened the medicine chest and saw my toothbrush hanging in the rack next to his. I never put it there. I was always very meticulous about standing it in the little ceramic cup. That little detail caused an avalanche. I remembered the whole thing at once. I didn't stand there remembering it piece by piece. It all came back to me in a single moment. I looked on my stomach and found a thin red mark, like a scratch, where I remembered them cutting me open. Later our doctor told me it was a scar. He said it was so thin that I must have had it since I was a child. But I know I didn't.

"We called the police, and that was a mistake. I felt utterly violated, like I'd been raped, and when I told everything to the police it was clear they didn't believe me! Then the FBI showed up and the CIA and the Army. I was going through a severe nervous breakdown, and they behaved as if I were making the whole thing up to get some attention. That's probably been the hardest part of this whole thing, being isolated and made to feel like I did something wrong. Dr. Wells was the first person who tried to understand what I was going through. He put me in touch with Dave Natchez and the survivors group, so I had some support, someone who believed me. Well, my husband believed me; without him I probably wouldn't have survived. Does that answer your questions?"

Okun felt a little overwhelmed by everything she'd told him. "Yeah, I think so."

"So how is Dr. Wells?" she asked, trying to lighten the mood. "Still crazy, I hope."

"Unfortunately, Dr. Wells passed away."

"How awful. I'm sorry to hear that. Were you close?" Not knowing how to answer the question, Okun merely shrugged.

She went on. "I wish I'd written back sooner. I got a letter from him about six months ago, and I just haven't made time to answer it. Oh, I feel terrible."

"Six months ago?"

"Yes, I know. I have no excuse. I could have found the time."

"Could I see the letter?"

"Certainly." It bore a postmark six months earlier. The envelope was printed stationery from somewhere called Sunnyglen Villa in San Mateo, a town at the base of the San Francisco peninsula. The letter was only a couple of sentences long and revealed nothing.

"Do you have a phone I can borrow?"

He called Sunnyglen Villa and asked to speak with Dr. Immanuel Wells. The soft-spoken woman on the other end said Mr. Wells was ill and couldn't take any phone calls. She offered to take a message, asking if he was "with an agency." Okun said he was an old family friend and said he'd call back later. He stared down at the envelope, wondering what sort of mental institution would give itself a name like Sunnyglen.

It was the middle of the afternoon. If he was going to get back to Las Vegas before the van picked them up, he'd have to leave soon. After he thanked Mrs. Gluck for sharing her story, Brinelle walked him out to his car.

"Hey, what's your hurry? Why don't you stay for dinner?"

"Gotta get back to work."

"You're gonna drive to San Mateo right now, aren't you?"

Okun laughed. "I wish. No, seriously, I have to get back to Pasadena."

"I see. Paranormal investigator all day, jet propulsion

engineer all night. Don't you hate it when people lie to you, Bob?"

"Yeah, as a matter of fact I do."

"Hey, I've got an idea," she said brightly. "Let's go visit Dr. Wells together. We can crash at my friend's place in Palo Alto."

Okun couldn't tell if she was being serious or not.

10

Disappearing Act

Yes, Okun hated it when people lied to him. He talked about the lies Radecker had told him as he drove toward San Francisco. And the more he talked, the angrier he got. "He told me my job was to make the spaceship fly. Fine. But when I tell him I need a second ship to make it happen, he tries to hide the information from me! What is that about? When I tell him I want to talk to Wells, he tells me the guy is dead! Screw you, Radecker!"

Later, he would claim that this tremendous sense of anger was what motivated him to drive north that afternoon instead of east like he was supposed to. But even in the middle of his yelling fit, Okun realized there was more to it than rage. He was curious. He wanted to meet this Wells character, see what he was all about. And there was something else, a need to assert himself—to take control of his research and stop putting himself at the mercy of Radecker.

Brinelle had talked Brackish into going to San Mateo, but not into taking her along. As groovy as the idea sounded, it wasn't worth the risk. He didn't want to read a newspaper article about her unfortunate collision with a postal truck. So he drove up the coast by himself, bought a map, and followed the address to an industrial area near the freeway.

Sunnyglen Villa turned out to be a slightly run-down Victorian mansion sandwiched between a bus yard on one side and a warehouse on the other. The property was surrounded by a tall chain-link fence with razor ribbon at the top. There were bars over all the windows, even on the top floor. When a security guard stepped onto the front porch and lit a cigarette, Okun put the car in gear and slunk away. It was a strange place for a mental institution. It looked more like a prison, and Okun had a feeling they weren't too keen on visitors.

He cruised around for a while until he found a suitable motel and checked in. It had been an unusually emotional day for him, and that night he did something he only did when he was feeling blue. He wrote lugubrious poems in the journal he reserved for the keeping of scientific notes.

The next morning he walked into a barbershop and told the man, "I've got a job interview today with an insurance company. Make me look like a square."

"Crew cut?" the barber asked.

Okun nodded—a pained nod. "A crew cut sounds perfect."

When he came out, his ears felt like twin jumbo radar dishes, and he felt the breeze on the back of his neck for the first time in years. His next stop was a department store, where he spent most of the money he had left on a business suit and a briefcase. He changed in the store's parking lot, getting help from a nice old lady who knew how to tie a tie. He was ready.

When he drove up, the front gate was open. He parked his car and walked up to the front door and tried the handle. It buzzed and clicked open. The inside of the place looked very different from the exterior. The entry had been converted into a waiting room like a doctor's office, with a few chairs and old magazines. A video camera in the corner slowly swept the room. There was a counter with a sliding glass partition behind which sat a willowy woman with a soft voice.

"Hi there. Can I help you?"

"I'm here to see Dr. Immanuel Wells."

"And your name, sir?"

"Radecker. Agent Lawrence Radecker, from Central Intelligence."

When the woman asked to see some identification, Okun glanced around to make sure no one was listening then whispered through the partition. "I'm on a special assignment, so I'm not carrying any ID. My instructions are to have you call headquarters, and they'll confirm. I was told you had the number."

"Oh, sure. Have it right here." She looked at him with big doe eyes. "If you'd like to have a seat, Agent Radecker, I'll call right away." She smiled and slid the glass door closed.

Okun tried to act casual. He picked up a magazine, but soon tossed it aside and began to pace. *CIA guys can pace if they want to*, he told himself, nothing suspicious about that. He glanced out the windows every few seconds to make sure no one was closing the front gate. He was already plotting a quick retreat if she asked him for the word of the day. Every morning, Radecker had a two-second conversation with someone calling from CIA headquarters. They would tell him the identification password for the next twenty-four hours, he would repeat it and hang up. The code words, of course, followed no pattern. Monday would be ZEBRA, Tuesday would be UNIQUE, and so on. He knew he'd never guess, so if she asked him, he was prepared to tell her he had it written down in the car.

"Thanks so much for waiting. If you'll follow me, I'll take you to Dr. Wells."

At the back of her tidy little office space was a thick glass door she unlocked with a key. They stepped through it into the home's dark central hallway and walked to the living room, where three men and one woman were gathered around a television watching a soap opera. All four of them were ancient, well into their eighties or nineties, and barely glanced up when the receptionist said good morning. The paint was peeling in places, and there was a slight reek of cleaning products in the air.

"Have you met Dr. Wells before?"

"Not face-to-face."

"But you know he doesn't talk anymore." She could see by his expression he didn't. "Maybe you'll have better luck with him. To tell you the truth," she said, opening a screen door, "it was a relief when he stopped. That man used to talk so darn much I had to wear earplugs."

They stepped outside onto the roomy back porch. A couple of deck chairs faced the backyard, which was a green riot of fruit trees, bushes, and weeds. A dilapidated gazebo was being strangled by heavy vines of wisteria. The lady walked up to a frail-looking man in a wheelchair and spoke as loud as her mousy voice would allow. "Dr. Wells, this is Agent Radecker. He's with the CIA, and he wants to ask you some questions." The old man didn't stir. She shrugged and smiled. "Well, good luck."

•   •   •

Okun pulled up a chair. He'd been expecting to meet a deranged and violent lunatic, but this guy, except for the wheelchair, looked like a member of the PGA's senior golf tour. He was clean-shaven, well groomed, and handsome in a balding, bulldoggish way. He wore pressed white slacks and a powder blue sweater that matched his piercing blue eyes.

"Dr. Wells? Dr. Wells? You can hear me, right? Look, if you can understand me, give me a sign. Make a movement or blink twice or something."

Without turning his head, the old man raised his right hand, then slowly lifted his middle finger.

"OK, that's a sign. Listen," he whispered, "I'm not really from the CIA. I just said that to get in here. And my name's not Radecker. I work at Area 51, and I went AWOL so I could come and talk to you. I'm probably gonna be in VDJ, very deep Jell-O, when I get back, so help me out, man."

Wells turned and regarded his visitor, waiting for him to say more.

"Hey, can you write? If I ask you a question, can you write out the answers? I brought a pen."

"What's Area 51?" the old man asked in a raspy voice. "I've never heard of that."

So he *could* talk. Okun started nodding. "Are you testing me or don't you remember? You used to work there. You know, Groom Lake, underground labs, the crashed ship?"

"Go on, I still don't know what you're saying."

Derrr. It suddenly occurred to Okun what was happening. The old man was waiting to hear some proof that he wasn't some amateur UFO investigator. "OK, I got it. Dworkin. Lenel. Vegas every Friday. There's a long table in the kitchen with two picnic benches. The tiles on the bathroom floor are mostly white, but some of them are purple, and the handles on the middle sink don't match. Hey, what's the matter?" He noticed tears welling up in the old man's eyes. "Oh no, please don't do that." It was the second day in a row he'd made somebody cry.

"I knew you'd come. I've been waiting and waiting. Why did you make me wait so long?"

"I just found out where you were yesterday."

"Didn't Dworkin send you?" He turned suddenly paranoid. "Who sent you here?"

"Nobody sent me. Relax. Yesterday I talked to Mrs. Gluck, and she showed me a letter you wrote her. Dworkin and those guys all think you're dead. That's what we were told."

"So you came to break me out? You can't do it alone; we'll need help. We'll go immediately into San Francisco. There are two television stations within a few blocks of one another. I've already written the press release, but it's in my room. Everything has been planned. I'll need one person to accompany me into the—"

"Whoa. Hold your horses there, *Kemo sabe*. You're losing me."

Wells started over and explained his plan. It was urgent, he said, that they alert the world of the impending alien invasion which, he said, could begin any minute. This was the same plan, presented to the members of Project Smudge five years earlier, which had led to his forced retirement and imprisonment. He pointed to the strings of barbed wire hidden in the foliage. He began explaining, in too much detail, the sequence of events leading to his ouster from Smudge, and expressed his deep loathing for the men who had opposed him.

Without stopping, he segued back to his moment-by-moment plan for breaking the story to the news media. Every movement had been scripted in his mind, every enemy reaction anticipated. It was a chess game pitting himself—and a few assistants—against the worldwide conspiracy to keep the matter quiet. As he spoke, Okun realized that Wells was, indeed, crazy. He wasn't the incoherent lunatic he had expected to meet, but he was obsessive-compulsive to the nth degree.

"It may already be too late, but we've got to try. Every man, woman, and child must devote himself to the salvation of the planet. Once they hear, once they understand that we face annihilation, they will make the necessary sacrifices. Everyone working together. It will require the transformation of the world into a single, tightly organized war machine. Politics, economy, society, all must change if we hope to survive." He said everyone who knew and didn't tell was a war criminal worse than Hitler, the worst filth on the planet, and in the future he would call for their public executions. Okun himself was one of the conspirators, but wisely didn't point that out to the old doctor.

Obviously, once you were on this man's enemy list, there was no getting off it. So Okun, who'd spent the last couple of days acting, assumed yet another role. "I'm going to help you. I'll come back with reinforcements later, but right now let me ask you a couple of questions. The first thing is the addendum to your report. I read the part you wrote after the Roswell thing, but the part you attached later was missing. What was in it, your ideas about an invasion?"

"Don't belittle me, young man. These are not merely ideas. At the time of the encounter I believed I had been given a glimpse of the EBE's home planet. Later I came to believe I had been shown the planet which had once belonged to the host animals, the ones they had gutted and used like a suit of clothing. Have you seen the photographs of the larger bodies?"

"Yeah, they're horrible-looking."

"Before the planet I saw was ruined, it had been a jungle, a lavish hothouse of dense plant life. Endless, stretching to infinity. Even below the surface, it teemed with vegetation. Think of the differences in anatomy between the two creatures. Which one would be better adapted to this planet? The tentacles would allow the larger being to climb and reach and grasp. The other one was all wrong. Its body was too delicate for an environment like that. I'm sure the little fiend didn't show me his planet. I think he was explaining why he had come to ours. It's because they'd slowly ruined that place he showed me, consumed everything on the surface until they were reduced to tearing shreds of moss off the walls of caves. I think they're coming here to eat."

"Groady."

"Another thing. If this creature really was a scientist, then what was it doing hauling food around? That doesn't make sense to me. Because I had shared a personal memory with it, I assumed it had done the same. It certainly *felt* like a personal memory, so immediate, so real. But how could those two animals be the same? Then it occurred to me: they share thoughts, they share a mind, they must share a memory."

"Exactly. That's the same principle they used in developing their ships. They share an energy source just like they share mental activity."

"They're a hive, my friend, and that makes them dangerous. Individually, they may not be as intelligent as you or I. But collectively, they may be more powerful than we can imagine. Did Sam ever tell you about my experiments with the bees?"

Okun shook his head.

"I kept a hive for about six months out in the old shacks next to the main hangar. As an experiment, I began hiding their food source. But every day they'd find it within minutes.

I expanded the radius to about two miles around the hive, moving the food to random locations at random times of the day. Then the scariest damn thing started happening. After about three months of this, I'd go to the place I had decided to put the food and they'd be waiting for me! After that I tried as many tricks as I could think of to fool them. And they'd work for a while, but they never worked twice. This went on until it occurred to me that they had learned to anticipate me. They'd learned my moves well enough to predict my behavior. In the end, I set the hive on fire. Now if bees can do that, imagine what these other monsters are capable of.

"And we're not even making it difficult for them. We bombard space with radio waves advertising our position. That must stop at once. They're out there right now watching us, studying us, waiting for the moment to strike."

"You're absolutely right. So, you think there's more than one ship?"

"Are you stupid? Don't you understand what I'm telling you? There are *hundreds* of ships like the one we recovered, and they are nearby. They come every few months and snoop around our military installations or experiment on people and animals. Don't you know about all those bloodless cattle mutilations? Call the Pentagon and tell them to send you the files. Soon the time of study will be over, and they will attack. We don't know how powerful their weaponry is, but our Air Force won't stand a chance against the speed and maneuverability of their ships. In a few months all of our planes and missiles will be spent. Then they'll start picking off our ground forces. There won't be time to build the weapons we're going to need. We must sacrifice now to build a space defense network of our own. Satellite lasers, deep-space torpedoes, orbiting minefields of nuclear warheads. If we have time, we can put factories in space capable of building a fleet of warships, then launch an attack of our own. It may already be too late, but we've got to try. You have to get some good men and storm this place."

In a strange way, the more he talked, the more sense he seemed to make. Okun was tempted to ask about these other visits, but steered back to his original topic. "I'll look for the guys later. But right now I want to get my hands on a second alien ship." He explained the experiment which proved the captured saucer could only fly with a companion. "Do you know if the government has any more of them from another crash?"

"What about Chihuahua, Mexico?"

"What's that?"

"Have you seen the Majestic 12 documents?"

"The thing they wrote up for Eisenhower? Yeah, I saw them."

"It's in there." Okun had read the top-secret documents but had concluded that they were fakes, just more disinformation generated by the forces of darkness. It had a description of the "seized flying disk" that was full of inaccuracies. There had been one paragraph in the document that had been blacked out.

"So what's this Chihuahua thing about?"

"Simultaneous with the crash at Roswell, another streak of light had been observed moving due south. The Army collected scores of 'hard' sightings from people on the ground all the way from Roswell to Guerrero, a town in the mountains of Chihuahua State. "A few days after the crash, we sent troops across the border. Just barged right in and surrounded the area where the local people said the thing went down. They searched for a long time, but didn't find anything."

"But you think there's one down there?"

"I don't know. I always meant to go down there and look around for myself, but I never did."

"And where was this exactly?"

"Right outside of Guerrero." Once again, Wells began to explain why he had to get to the television station, but Okun interrupted him immediately.

"One last question. The Y. I saw it on one of the monitors inside the ship when we pumped some power into the system. I thought it was some kind of an SOS. Dworkin told me you had that same feeling."

This time Wells only shook his head. "I haven't figured it out. You say you spoke with Trina Gluck."

"Yes."

"Did you believe her?"

"I don't think she's lying. Yeah, I guess I believed her."

"If she's right, the aliens don't know any more than we do what the Y is. For years I believed it was the alien equivalent of our SOS, but if so, why don't they recognize it?"

"Agent Radecker," the nurse called from the doorway. "You have a telephone call, sir."

"Our reinforcements?" the old man asked eagerly.

"Either that or VDJ." Okun extended his hand. "Thanks a lot for your help."

Wells looked at the hand, horrified. "You're leaving? You're going to leave me here? NO! You tricked me! You're with them, aren't you? You never had any intention of helping. Get away from me, you filthy murderer."

All the way through the house and back to the office, Okun could hear the old man howling curses at him. And it didn't look like life was going to get any better. He was fairly certain that once he picked up the phone he would be nailed by some internal security guy in DC.

He took a deep breath and picked up the receiver. "Radecker here."

"I thought your name was Bob Robertson."

"Brinelle?"

"Yeah. Listen, Secret Agent Whatever-Your-Name-Is, you are majorly busted. Two guys were just here from the FBI asking about you and, sorry, but we had to tell them where you were going. So you might want to get out of there."

"Thanks, Chief, I'll get on that right away."

"Are there people standing there listening to you?"

"Affirmative."

"And you want to sound like you're on official business?"

"Exactly."

"Cool. You better hit the road, but use that phone number I gave you, OK?"

"Will do. Over and out."

Okun started out the door, but thought better of it. Why should he run? What did it matter *how* he got back to Nevada? It might be a more pleasant trip if he had some company. So he sat down in the waiting room and looked through some magazines until he heard a car skid to a stop in the parking lot.

11

A Death in the Family

Brackish Okun spent the night behind bars. As he'd guessed, the FBI guys who took him into custody drove him all the way to Nevada, to the main entrance to the Nellis Weapons Testing Range. They were very polite with him the entire time, even friendly. He was never handcuffed or treated as a prisoner in any way—except for them following him into the rest room when they stopped for lunch. But it was a different story when they handed him over to the Military Police waiting for him at the front gates. He was searched, handcuffed, and tossed in the back of a Jeep. The MPs drove him to the Military Intelligence building and locked him in a windowless cell. He was woken up in the middle of the night and taken to an interrogation room, where he was questioned by a pair of officers. They demanded to know everywhere he'd gone and everyone he'd spoken with during his twenty-seven-hour absence. They warned him, however, not to tell the *whole* story. If he had divulged any compartmentalized information, anything about the work being done at Groom Lake, they wanted to know to whom he had done so, but reminded him they were not cleared to hear such information and telling them would constitute a violation of the law.

He told them the whole truth, but they acted as if they didn't believe a word of it. They grilled him for two hours, subtly leaning on him to change his story. When the session was over, he was taken back to the cell. At 7 A.M., he was awoken once again, this time by Radecker, who stood on the other side of the bars looking like a high-pressure radiator hose about to split open and spray the room with dirty boiling water. He screamed at Okun for a long time, telling him what a stupid and dangerous thing it had been to disappear like that. When the enraged CIA man stopped for breath, Okun tried to lighten the mood.

"Aren't you even gonna compliment my haircut?"

Radecker skewered him with a hard stare. "I trusted you," he hissed, "and you double-crossed me. You stabbed me in the back. Now you're going to pay the price. There's going to be a court-martial. A legal team is preparing charges against you right now. You're looking at some serious prison time."

"For what?"

"Let me see. Being absent without leave, impersonating a federal officer, trespassing, violating the Federal Espionage Act. All together you shouldn't get more than ninety-nine years. You'll be eligible for parole in about twenty."

"I didn't reveal anything," Okun assured him. "I swear. The only person I talked to was Wells."

Radecker flashed him a wicked smile. "Wells no longer has a security clearance. He doesn't have any official ties to this program. You blew it."

"You're kidding me, right? I didn't tell him anything he didn't already know."

"The guys outside don't know that. I guess I could talk to them for you, explain the situation, try to get the charges dismissed. But I'm not going to do that, and I'll tell you why. Because you intentionally embarrassed me. I get sent out here to baby-sit your hippie ass, and you pull this stunt. Where do you think that leaves me? I'm finished at the CIA, I'm a joke. Even the friggin' FBI is laughing at me."

But Okun was never charged with any crime. Apparently, he had unseen friends in higher places. A phone call from the Deputy Director's Office of the CIA instructed the base's legal affairs office to drop the case and overlook the entire incident. Radecker was told to restrict the young scientist to the labs and immediate environs, but to take no further disciplinary action. He was furious, but powerless to strike back.

When Okun returned to the underground labs, the mood was indeed somber. He wasn't the only one in the boss's doghouse. When Brackish had failed to rendezvous with them for the ride back from Vegas, the old men had tried one trick after another to stall the van's departure. First Freiling wandered off, pretending to have a senile episode, then Lenel complained of chest pains and was taken to a hospital. At dawn, when Okun still hadn't returned, they gave up and came home. Radecker was convinced they were in on the plot. The Vegas trips, he announced, were history. The old men would be allowed to drive into town only long enough to transact their banking business and fill their prescriptions at the pharmacy before returning to base. For Dworkin and company, being robbed of their only form of recreation was a crushing blow, and they couldn't help blaming Okun.

Spirits were low, and there was a poisonous atmosphere in the labs. Cracks began to appear in the block of solidarity shared by the older men. They began to quarrel with one another, and they made no secret of the fact that they were angry with Okun. Lenel confronted him one morning, asking if his "lark" had been worth it.

"What was so important that you had to go talk to him?" When Okun tried blaming the whole thing on Radecker and his lies, Lenel asked him again. "We told you Wells was crazy. Now I'm asking you if you learned anything by going to see him?"

Rather than answer, the young man with the crew cut retreated to his room. What *had* he gained by taking his trip up the coast? The onetime director of Area 51 had told him several interesting things, but nothing he could really use. The matter of the telepathic Y-message remained a mystery, and he had less freedom than ever to research the possibility of a second ship. Perhaps the only thing he'd really taken away from the meeting was the haunting vision of the earth being invaded by a conquering species from a distant galaxy. As preposterous as some of it had sounded at the time, Wells's words were taking root in Okun's imagination and growing stronger by the day. He tried to talk to the other men about them, but it was almost as if they were afraid of these ideas. Why else would they dismiss them so quickly when there was ample evidence to support them?

Radecker wasn't finished. He instituted an insidious new paperwork regime. Crate after crate of new equipment had begun to arrive for work on the retrofitting project. Under the new system, every piece of every shipment had to be cataloged in triplicate before it could be used. This meant separate forms to fill out for each bolt, each O-ring, each spool of wire. Then there was another piece of administrative sadism—the daily work proposal. The first hour of every morning was spent filling in these tedious forms.

Things improved slightly over the next two weeks. Cibatutto rigged up a discarded telex machine to help them get around some of the new paperwork, and Dworkin introduced a new card game—bridge—which the old men quickly mastered. One Friday night, Radecker came into the kitchen and found them playing a rowdy game of cards while Okun watched. Just when the wounds Okun had caused began to heal, Radecker tore them open again. He realized Okun had gotten away with humiliating him without suffering a scratch. Something must have snapped, because the next day he dug his claws into Okun the only way he knew how. If he couldn't punish the boy genius directly, he would hit below the belt. He had Freiling sent to a nearby Air Force base for psychological testing to determine if he was mentally fit to continue working at the highly classified labs. Freiling returned shaken and confused. The shrinks had ganged up on him, he said, deliberately done things to confuse him. The old man was terrified at the prospect of being sent to a retirement home—prison like the one Okun had described in San Mateo.

The whole group of them marched off immediately to Radecker's office, but he wouldn't talk to them. "I thought we had a deal, Mr. Radecker," Dworkin called as politely as he could through the closed door.

"Don't talk to me about it; go ask Okun. And think about this the next time one of you decides to cross me." They spent the rest of that Saturday taking care of Freiling, assuring him they wouldn't let him be sent away. When he finally relaxed and fell asleep, it was late at night.

Okun came into the kitchen and found Dworkin sitting there in the dark.

"What's goin' on, can't sleep?"

"A case of indigestion," Dworkin said. When Okun switched on a light, he saw a glass of water and a bottle of pills on the table. "It's probably just heartburn caused by a stressful day."

"You sure you're all right? Should we call somebody?"

The old man laughed. It wasn't that serious. He invited Okun to sit down, and asked him about his visit with Wells. He wanted to know all about the place he was being held and what he had said. After listening for a while, he asked Okun for his opinion. "Do you think he's right? Are we criminals for not telling the world?"

"Maybe. Especially when you look around here and consider the kind of manpower the government is devoting to this research. There ought to be hundreds of people down here, and what have we got? Four men over seventy years old and one doofus who doesn't even have a Ph.D. They aren't taking this project seriously at all. I think Wells is right about one thing. We need to get lots of people working on this. If word got out, people would have to take it seriously and band together to get ready."

"Possibly," Dworkin mused, "but I'm not convinced people would band together. I think it more likely that society would disintegrate. The way you reacted to learning about the ship and seeing the alien bodies was far from typical. When people really begin to believe we are facing annihilation, as Wells does, they tend to withdraw into themselves. I can imagine groups of frightened people abandoning their normal lives and retreating deeper into private misery, or forming private armies and taking to the hills. But that's all specula-tion," he said, finishing off his glass of water, "and it begs the question, because people are not going to be told. Even if one of us succeeded in putting ourselves on the evening news and telling the whole thing, no one would believe us. You know what happened at Roswell. They're quite skilled at making intelligent persons seem crazy."

"So what's the answer? Just continue going through the motions down here?"

Dworkin stared into his empty glass for a few moments. "I've spent most of my adult life in these rooms, and I'm not sure I have anything to show for it. I was married, you know."

"No, I didn't know that. Any kids?"

"No, thank heavens. But if there had been, I still would have left them. Dr. Wells and I had our differences over the years, but we always agreed the work being done here was important enough to justify our personal sacrifices. The work has been everything, and now I'm afraid it's over."

Okun knew what he must be talking about. "Because you're getting too old?"

"Precisely. It's been a few years since we've lost anyone, and I've allowed myself to forget what it feels like. If he sends Dr. Freiling away, we'll be reduced to four. Soon we'll all be gone, and I worry about what will happen then. I don't know if you are prepared to carry on here by yourself."

They let that idea hover in the air for a while. Brackish considered the possibility of following in Dworkin's footsteps, trading in all his possible futures for the lonely life of a lab rat. He thought briefly of Brinelle, her gangly limbs and wide smile. He knew he'd probably never see her again, but for the moment he let her represent everyone he might meet. Did keeping the labs open mean he would never again have a crush on a girl? Or decide at the last minute to go catch a movie with some friends?

"If these creatures ever did turn hostile," Dworkin pointed out, "you may be the only person in the world who could have us prepared. So far your sponsors in Washington, whoever they are, have denied you nothing. It might be time to petition them for some new personnel. I doubt whether we old fellows are going to be around here much longer."

Okun waved him off. "It's nothing we have to decide tonight. I've still got three years on my contract, and you four guys are going to outlive me by a decade. Now, come on, you should try to get some sleep."

"You're right." He sighed. "I'm feeling awfully tired."

In the morning, Dworkin didn't join them at breakfast. When they went in to check on him, they discovered he'd died in his sleep. One day after learning that Freiling's neck was on the chopping block, they had lost their leader. While Cibatutto got on the phone and began making burial arrangements, the others retreated to their rooms and their personal despair.

"Six down and three to go," Lenel whispered as the minister delivered a brief eulogy over the body. The ceremony was the same one given to the men who had died before Okun arrived. It was all part of a package plan offered to them through their bank. Parducci Mortuary offered embalming, makeup, coffin, a catered open-casket viewing period, transportation to the cemetery, flowers, and interment services all for one low price. The only thing not included was a police escort to the cemetery. The Parducci family was not friendly with the police. When the minister was finished, he announced there would be a few minutes for those assembled to wish Dr. Dworkin their final farewells. There were more people in attendance than Okun had expected. Two of Dworkin's sisters were there and brought their families with them. There were four or five scientists who had worked with him earlier in his career,

Ellsworth, accompanied by two other officers, and Dr. Insolo of the Science and Technology Directorate. Everyone formed a line and filed past the open casket, pausing to say a few words or lay a flower on Dworkin's chest. When Okun approached the pine box, he hardly recognized the figure inside. The cheeks were too rosy and the hair was fluffed up in a way Dworkin had never worn it. When someone behind him uttered the word "lifelike," Brackish felt his heart drop halfway to his knees and quickly headed outside to get some air.

He dumped himself onto a bench next to the chauffeur of the hearse, who was reading a newspaper. "How's it going in there?"

"Tough. Very tough." Okun's voice broke.

"Were you related?"

"Kinda."

The man nodded as if he knew what that meant. The two of them sat there for a few minutes watching the traffic on the street until the driver returned to his reading. Okun was thinking about what Dworkin had said about not knowing if he was prepared to continue the work. He felt a sudden urge to run away, to disappear into the city and hide, to start a normal life like the one the man next to him had. He turned to ask a question, but something caught his eye before he could. A headline on the newspaper read "Chihuahua Quake Darkens Parts of Texas" and then in smaller print, "Electromagnetic Mystery Hampers Construction Efforts." He leaned in closer and started reading the story off the back of the man's paper. The farther down the page he read, the more he nodded. At the end of the column, it said "continued on A6."

Under the watchful gaze of a security agent posted in the parking lot, Brackish went to the van and retrieved his journal notebook. He quickly looked over the notes he'd made after his conversation with Wells. "This is it, this is the real enchilada," he said to himself. He strode back to the ceremony. As he passed the chauffeur he snagged the paper out of the surprised man's hands and carried it inside.

The three older scientists were gathered around the open casket, solemnly conversing with their deceased friend. Okun joined them, thwacking down the newspaper on the coffin so he could straighten it out. "You guys," he said in an excited whisper, "I found it. It's in Mexico."

Bad manners were one thing, but this was flagrant boorishness.

"Brackish, this is neither the time nor the place," Freiling pointed out.

"He's right," Cibatutto growled. "For Sam's sake."

Okun looked them in the eyes. "Sam told me that he always sacrificed his personal happiness for the sake of the work, and I'm sure he'd want me to read you what's in this article right this second."

Somewhat reluctantly, they made room for him and he stepped up to his place at the head of the coffin, where he kept the paper low and read in a whisper.

"'A massive earthquake measuring 8.2 on the Richter scale rumbled through the desert state of Chihuahua earlier this week, destroying villages, damaging highways, and toppling dozens of high-voltage power poles that bring electricity to the state as well as the Texas towns of Sierra Blanca and Van Horn.'"

"Get to the point."

He skipped down the column.

". . . 'but attempts to run power through the Nuevo Casas Grandes area have been delayed by severe damage to local roads and the inability to use radio or phones in the area. Indeed, nearly all electrical devices brought to the region known to locals as La Zona del Silencio, or the Silent Zone, experience some sort of disruption.

" ' "It's been this way for a long time," said Octavio Juan Marquez, a spokesman for the power company. "Our radios don't work in some of the hills out there. We get a lot of static in some areas, and in others they die out completely. The local people say it's caused by the *chupacabras*, furry animals that hunt little children at night," he said with a laugh.

" 'But for residents of the mud-and-thatch villages that surround the area, it is no laughing matter. Speaking through an interpreter, an Indian woman who lives in the area said, "What makes it so scary out there is how quiet it is. No plants grow out there anymore, and animals don't go there, not even insects. That's why people say the *chupacabra* live out there."

" 'The untraceable atmospheric disturbances have baffled experts since they began in July of 1947. U.S. troops stationed farther south in the town of Guerrero conducted an extensive geological survey of the area during the early 1950s, attributing the phenomenon to the huge amounts of iron ore found in the ground.' "

As Okun turned to page A6, he glanced up long enough to see that the scientists realized he was onto something. Any lingering doubts any of them might have had were erased forever when Okun turned the page. There was a small photo of construction crews working on the downed power lines. A long line of giant power poles stretched away into the distance, each one of them shaped like a giant Y.

As far as Okun was concerned, there was no need to read any further. He looked around at his fellow scientists with a look that said, *You know what we have to do now.*

The four men stepped outside and Okun ran through his theory on how the whole thing worked. "OK. We were right. There was another ship flying with the one at Roswell. They were scouting around or whatever when the missile was fired from Polynesia. The blur that moved across the radar screens before the rocket exploded must have been yet another ship. Maybe that ship was hit, or sent out a retreat signal or perhaps—I haven't figured that part out yet. But we do know the Roswell ship took off north and another ship flew south. The Army thought it crashed near Guerrero, and they invaded Mexico looking for it, but they were too far south. The Y must have been a signal from the downed ship."

"Then why didn't that third ship on the radar screen come and pick them up?" Freiling asked, starting to get it.

"The wires overhead?" Lenel ventured. "Maybe the field of EM waves blocked their signal."

Four heads nodded.

"But that means," Cibatutto pointed out, "during their next visit, if the aliens visit again anytime soon, they will be able to receive the signal. It's probably still being sent if we picked it up last year."

"When's the next time we'll get a window of Van Allen activity?"

Cibatutto pulled out a pen and did a few calculations on the newspaper. *"Mamma mia. Dio de cane!"*

"Translation, please."

"Three days. The inner belt's energy peaks in three days."

Okun, unconsciously fingering the ankh-shaped figurine on his necklace, looked around the group. Trying his best to sound like Dworkin, he said, "Gentlemen, we find ourselves in a rather dramatic predicament. If we return to Area 51 after the funeral, we have little or no hope of finding the second ship before our alien visitors do."

With the ceremony over and Dworkin's coffin loaded in the hearse, people began getting into cars for the trip to the cemetery. Radecker walked to the front of the line of parked cars, expecting to ride in the hearse. "Have some decency, man," Lenel snarled at him when he touched the door handle. "You helped put the man in his grave. Let him take this final ride in dignity with his friends."

The two men traded icy stares until Radecker went farther back and climbed into the van. Lenel opened the passenger side door and wondered how he was going to get inside the vehicle. Okun, Freiling, and Cibatutto were already scrunched in tight next to the driver.

"No, absolutely not," the chauffeur said. "We can't have anyone else ride in here. I'll get a ticket." But the scientists, some of the Strip's most experienced con men, could be very persuasive. The driver quickly changed his mind and signalled for Lenel to climb in. With some difficulty, he climbed onto Okun's lap, and the procession pulled out of the driveway and headed south along famous Las Vegas Boulevard. Before they'd gotten to the first stoplight, Freiling began chattering about the door.

"Did anybody check the back door? It wasn't closed all the way. When we get to the next light I'm going to get out and check it. The last thing we need is for poor old Sam Dworkin to roll out the back door and spill all over the Strip."

"Don't worry, sir, the door is closed."

"You're awfully kind to say so, and I know you mean well," Freiling doddered, "and I'm sure you're very good at your job, but at the next light, I'll just step out quickly and check."

It only took three stoplights for Freiling to annoy the man so thoroughly that he screamed, "All right already, I'll check the darn door." He got out and stormed to the rear of the hearse, opened the door, and yelled to the passengers in the front seat, "Like I said, the door was closed. Now I am going to close the door again and make sure it is securely sealed."

But before he could execute his plan, Freiling had slid himself into the driver's seat and stomped down on the accelerator pedal. The tires screamed as the vehicle peeled out into the cross traffic moving through the intersection. The sudden momentum caused the coffin to slide out the back and crash, right side up, onto the roadway. Thanks to blind luck and the quick reactions of several drivers, the hearse bolted through the intersection untouched.

While his passengers held on tight, Freiling, who hadn't driven anything in over twenty years, pushed the Cadillac engine up to seventy miles per hour while Dworkin did his part by holding Radecker and the rest of the procession at bay.

Running over traffic islands, scattering pedestrians, and ignoring his passengers' pleas for him to slow down, Freiling pointed the nose of the machine at the center of the road and roared straight through town. They were headed for the Tropicana, but their driver was so focused on weaving through traffic he didn't see it until it was nearly too late. *What, here already?* he asked himself, and pulled the wheel hard to the right, steering toward what looked like a driveway. While several nearby cars swerved, skidded, and crashed into one another, Freiling ran the hearse onto a curb, blowing out the two front tires. Undaunted, he plowed through some of the landscaping, over another curb, and up to the Tropicana's front doors. While dumbfounded valets looked on, the three elderly fugitives, assisted by their younger accomplice, jogged through the front doors.

It wasn't long before Radecker pulled up, but long enough for the old cardsharps, who knew the building well, to make themselves hard to find. Half an hour after they'd disappeared through the front doors, he had forty men scouring the building in a door-to-door search. And just in case they'd somehow managed to slip out, he called in the sheriff's office and the Highway Patrol to set up a perimeter around the entire city. They were searching every car headed out of town. Radecker asked himself where the old men would go if they had already fled the building and, to his credit, he guessed right. He jumped in the van and tore down the street. A short distance later, he parked the car on the street outside Parducci Savings and ran inside.

Salvatore Parducci was in the middle of counting a stack of bills and didn't want to lose count. He ignored Radecker's questions about seeing three old men in suits until a hand swept across the counter and scattered the money on the floor. When Sal looked up, Radecker had a pistol pointed at his face. "Yes, sir, how can we help you today?"

"Where are they, damn it? They're hiding in here, aren't they?"

"The three old men? We got a lot of retired people as customers. Can you describe them for me?" In the background there was a sudden high whine that sounded like an electric motor.

"Lenel, Cibatutto, and Freiling," Radecker said, coming around the counter to search the office. "Recognize those names?"

"Very well. My family has been doing business with them for many years." Parducci held his hands away from his body. He remained perfectly still and perfectly relaxed, even when Radecker kicked open one of the locked office doors to look inside.

"When's the last time you saw them?"

"You're not with the IRS, are you?"

"What's that?" The whine of the motor had turned to a hollow slapping sound.

"What's what?"

"That noise?"

"Oh, the noise. That thupa-thupa-thupa sound? That would be Parducci Enterprises' helicopter."

Radecker rushed to the window and tore back the curtains in time to catch a glimpse of his employees lifting off. He turned back to the heavily bejeweled banker, who explained, "We're a full-service financial institution."

By the time Radecker's second APB in as many months went out to law-enforcement officials across the western U.S., the fugitive scientists were renting a car with cash at Ontario Airport in California.

12

Chihuahua

With Okun at the helm, the crew headed south. The rental agency had put them into a brand-new Ford LTD station wagon, which bobbed and weaved down the freeway like a small yacht. Their plan was to slip across the border at Tijuana as quickly as possible. During Okun's last AWOL escapade, Radecker had mobilized a small army to find him. They could only imagine what kind of dragnet he'd set up this time.

Okun had never been to Mexico, so he didn't realize anything was strange when he pulled up to the San Diego side of the border and found himself in a long line of traffic waiting to go across.

"Something's not right here," Lenel said, leaning forward from the backseat. "There's supposed to be a line on the *other* side, not this one. Entering Mexico should be faster than this."

"Maybe things have changed since the last time you came down here." Okun shrugged.

"No. Turn around and get out of here," Lenel told him. But it was too late for that. They were in the middle of seven lanes of one-way traffic. So the older men quickly devised Plan B. One by one they slipped out of the station wagon and made their way to the footbridge. They would wait for one of the many tour groups crossing into Tijuana for a day of shopping and blend in with them. Okun thought they were being a little too careful at the time, but when he approached the gate he saw two men in suits and sunglasses walking back and forth, looking into every car. When one of them came close to him, Okun flashed him a peace sign and a smile. The man moved on without changing expression to continue his hunt. *Has Radecker figured out where we're headed?* Okun wondered. Then, he thought about the complicated path he'd taken to deduce the location of this second spacecraft. *Naw. Radecker won't figure it out.*

"Where are you headed?" the uniformed border guard asked when Okun pulled even with the booth.

"Ensenada."

"What's the purpose of your visit?"

"*Mucho* tequila."

The guy smiled, told him to drive safely, and waved him through.

He found the three old men waiting for him a hundred yards up the road. They climbed in, and off they went. Once they found their way to the road they wanted and were out of town, Okun drove twenty miles an hour faster than the rutted roads would allow.

•   •   •

That night, they pulled into the mountain town of Nuevo Casas Grandes about 10:30, expecting to find the place completely dead, out of commission until morning. All the way up the twisting road that took them into the foothills of the dry Sierra Madre mountains, they saw downed telephone poles and freshly broken cinder-block houses. But, in the "Grandes," there was little evidence of the huge earthquake that had rolled through the town a week before. The main street was lined with old wood-frame buildings. The brightest, loudest place on the block was the Taverna Terazas, which stood directly opposite the town's church. A jukebox inside filled the street with sound, adding to the noisy chug-a-lug of portable generators. A dozen men sat outside the bar, talking and laughing, chairs tipped back against the wall.

Lenel, Freiling, Cibatutto, and Okun, all of them still dressed in the suits they'd worn to Dworkin's funeral, parked the car and walked down the center of the street. Striding four abreast, they looked like a not-very-threatening group of gunslingers. The men outside the saloon were tough-looking dudes, vaqueros who looked like the real deal: dusty leather boots, dungarees, and Western shirts. They stopped laughing when the Norte Americanos walked up.

"*Hola, amigos,*" Okun called as he walked past them and through the front doors. The scientists followed him inside. The small bar was almost full. Okun came in and took a table near the jukebox, which was playing a rowdy ranchero song. Conversation lulled for a minute while the men at the bar turned around to have a look at these four dressed-up gringos, but then resumed. When a waitress walked past, Okun ordered them four beers, then leaned in over the table. "Once we find the Silent Zone, we'll drive down the line of power poles, and I'll find the point-of-view angle I got from the screen. I'll stand in the same relation to the power pole I saw in the image on the screen."

"You remember it well enough?"

"Trust me. It's Etch-A-Sketched across the inside of my brain."

"How are we going to find out where this place is?" Freiling asked.

Lenel motioned toward the bar. "Judging from the uniforms of those men at the bar, they work for the electric company. We could follow them out there in the morning."

"I have a better idea," Cibatutto announced. He paused to hand the waitress a twenty for the beers, and told her to keep the change. "We hire a guide."

"It better be somebody we don't like very much," Lenel warned darkly, "because if we actually discover an alien ship, he might not live very long."

Okun saw how it could work out. "Dr. C's right. It'll be faster if we have somebody who can take us out there. If we find a ship, we do our best to hide it from him. Two of us can stay out there while the two others ride back into town with the guy to call in our reinforcements. If he finds out about it, too bad for him. There's too much riding on this."

"Slow down, kid, you're starting to sound like Victor Frankenstein," Lenel said.

Freiling had been waiting for a lull in the conversation. He turned to Cibatutto. "I'm still wondering why you gave that waitress so dang much money?"

The answer walked up to the table. A skinny young mestizo kid, maybe seventeen, came over to their table, turned a chair around, and straddled it. "You wanna buy some pots?"

Okun did a double take. "Buy some huh?"

"Pots. Bowls. Ceramicas." He explained in plain English how Americans sometime came to Grandes wanting to buy pottery robbed from burial sites of the Mogollon Indians. He pronounced the word mo-go-YON. Others came to see the caves the Mogollon had once lived in.

"We're not here for pots. We want to go out to the Silent Zone." Okun pulled the rolled-up newspaper out of his pocket and showed it to the kid. "You know anybody who can take us to this place?"

"We will pay a hundred dollars," Cibatutto added.

"Me!" the kid yelled. "I'll take you. I'm not afraid of la Zona."

"Done. But only if we leave by dawn. *Temprano en el mañana*," Okun said, reaching across the table to seal the deal with a handshake. "What's your name?"

"Pedro." The cocky kid was grinning like he'd just swindled the gringos out of a million dollars. If he had known the risk he was taking, he would have asked for much more. Not only could he guide them to the Silent Zone, but he could lead them to the only hotel in town, and, for an extra few bucks, he would take care of getting the food and water stockpiled. He'd learned English living in Los Angeles for nine years, but his father decided it wasn't a good place for kids to be growing up and moved them back here to their hometown. Now Pedro was sitting around in bars offering strangers black-market artifacts robbed out of graves. The four men made a list of all the items they would need for the next day.

"Why do you wanna go out there?"

The four men looked at one another uncertainly.

"Can you keep a secret?" Okun asked.

"Yeah, of course."

"You really promise not to tell anyone?"

"Yeah, of course."

"We're treasure hunters," he whispered. "We work for a

mining company, and we think these hills are loaded with treasure."

The kid came out of his slouch and sat straight up. "You mean gold and silver?"

"No. I'm talking about iron ore, millions of tons of it. We read about the Silent Zone and said to ourselves, there must be iron ore up there."

That sounded boring, and the kid lost interest immediately which was just what Okun intended.

Early the next morning, they met him outside their hotel. He'd found most of the supplies they'd ordered except the flash-lights. He explained, however, that he'd gone into the church across the street and taken a bag full of candles. "I'll pay 'em back later." An hour before the first construction crews got rolling, the scientists followed their guide's directions to the edge of town, where they turned onto a dirt road. They headed out, driving the station wagon where it was never meant to go. They bounced along a badly rutted utility road, which carried them deeper into the hills. Eventually, they rounded a turn and found themselves in a huge flat valley at least ten miles wide. "This is the Valley of the Caves," Pedro told them. More than a valley, it was a huge open plain, largely barren. Towering in the distance were the Y-shaped power poles. Beyond them, sharp vertical cliffs led the way to endless hills climbing to distant peaks. Even from that distance, they could see that some of the tall poles were listing, damaged by the earthquake. As they approached the lines, they saw cranes, giant spools of wire, and other construction equipment. Some of the power lines had broken away from the poles.

They asked Pedro about the Mogollon Caves he had men-tioned the night before. He told them what he'd learned from the black-market art buyers. The Mogollon Indians had built the caves and lived in them for centuries until they suddenly disappeared about five hundred years ago. He explained how the Mogollon, like other tribes in the region, had tied cradle-boards to the heads of infants, in order to cause deformations of the skull. They weren't natural, somehow, the kid said. Their heads were weirdly shaped, they made extraordinary pottery, and they built great cities like Paquime, then vanished suddenly without a trace. Their entire civilization abruptly ceased to exist, and no one knew why.

"Maybe the *chupacabras* ate them," Okun teased.

"You laugh now," Pedro said, "but just wait till you get out there. It's not natural. Nothing lives out there, not even flies." The word *chupacabra* was usually translated as "goat sucker." The legend of these feral four-legged creatures was the State of Chihuahua's answer to the Loch Ness monster. "They live off the blood of other animals," Pedro went on. "That's why no animals will go into the Zone. Some people say they're like the pets of *los extranjeros*, the ones who came from outer space."

All heads turned toward the boy, who went on.

"A long time ago, they say a spaceship crashed down there by Guerrero, about a hundred miles south of here, and some of the Indians took care of the spacemen. They lived with the Indians for about ten years, and the *chupas* were their pets. But when the spacemen died, the *chupas* got lonely for their masters and ran away. Then they came to live in the Zone, and if any animals go in there, they kill them and suck their blood."

Okun's mind was already on other matters. "How much farther?"

"Keep going, it's still far." A few minutes later, Pedro was leaning forward, looking for something in the cliffs. "There's one." He pointed. "That's one of the caves."

When the scientists saw what the kid was pointing at, their jaws dropped. Each time Pedro had mentioned caves, they had pictured tunnels leading into the ground. But now they saw what he was talking about. High above the ground they saw a gigantic recess scooped out of the face of the cliff, two hundred feet across and fifty feet tall. Small adobe houses were built inside, some of them perched at the very edge. It was a very small town constructed inside the giant cubbyhole three stories above the ground. Without a word, they all piled out of the car for a closer look. Even though they were racing against time, this place deserved a quick tour. They had all arrived at the obvious conclusion: *This cliff dwelling is large enough to hold one of the alien ships.*

Getting up to the cave involved negotiating a series of stone stairs and rickety wooden ladders, which the older men did surprisingly well. They wandered deeper under the stone ceiling toward the nether reaches of the cave. It was deep enough to hold two vehicles like the one at Area 51. Crumbling mud-and-stone walls that showed a string of single-room apartments had been built against the interior walls. Several of the walls at the back still retained their curiously shaped, windowlike doorways. The ceilings were blackened in several places with the soot of ancient fires. Broken bottles and crushed beer cans had been scattered around by the local kids, who used the prehistoric cliff dwelling as a modern party spot.

Pedro led the men toward the edge and pointed out a narrow stone trail cut into the cliff. He called it the back door, and explained that most of the caves had such entrances. "If somebody tried to attack them, the Mogollon pulled up the ladders. If somebody tried to come in on one of these trails, you could knock them off with a big stick."

Before climbing down, the men stood at the edge of the

cliff, feeling the warm wind blowing straight up its face, and admired the spectacular view. The open sweep of the land gave way to the infinite desert stretching out to the curve of the earth. It was a beautiful morning, shirtsleeve weather and cloudless electric blue sky.

"I can't think of a better place to hide a ship," Freiling commented when the boy was out of earshot.

Back in the car, they followed the line of power poles, moving over the rough earth at speeds which threatened to snap the suspension of the heavily loaded station wagon. Pedro said they were getting close and turned on the radio, telling them, "When it goes out, you know you're in la Zona." When the radio suddenly developed static, everyone looked at one another. When it died completely, they kept their eyes straight ahead, scanning the hills for anything unusual.

"How big is this area? Where the radios won't work," Okun asked.

"Big, I don't know."

"Have you been to the other side, where the radios work again?"

"Yeah, it's over there near Galeana. I don't know how far it is."

The men in the backseat unfolded a map of the area and asked him questions, trying to determine the size of the Silent Zone. Eventually they decided the center of it was about five miles ahead. After three miles, Okun slowed down and took a long look at one of the huge steel power poles. He switched off the car and got out, still focused on the Y-shaped tower. But something else caught his attention.

"Wow. Listen to that." They were surrounded by an ocean of soundlessness. Except for the occasional puff of a breeze rustling through the weeds, there was absolute stillness. Until that moment, Okun and the others hadn't realized how much background sound they'd been listening to all day: the flapping wings of birds, things crawling through the bushes, the buzzing of small insects. Suddenly, each man could hear how loud his own breathing was.

"You see?" Pedro asked. "That's why they call it the Silent Zone."

Okun took out his notebook and examined a sketch he'd made of the Y a few days after he'd first seen it. Then he climbed on top of some nearby rocks. He moved left, then right, then forward, until what was in front of his eyes matched what he'd seen on the screen. If the pole in front of him was the one in the alien transmission, the ship must be somewhere very near where he was standing. He disappeared into some bushes growing at the base of a cliff, reemerging a few moments later and shaking his head.

"Let's try the next pole."

They drove a few hundred feet past the next pole and went through the same routine. This time, everyone helped scour the rocks and bushes along the base of the cliffs. But this proved to be impractical because it took the old men so long to get back to the car. It was already early afternoon, and, although no one said anything out loud, they all knew time was running out. Even Pedro started to pick up the pace. He and Okun working together could investigate one of the spots in five minutes. Each time they climbed back in the car, Okun stared down the long row of power lines, stretching off toward the vanishing point, and reminded himself, *We have all night and tomorrow morning—be methodical, be patient.*

They came to another set of cliffs and found two cliff dwellings in roughly the right relationship to the nearest power poles. The group spent a precious hour exploring these two caves and the area around them. As they drove toward the next pole, Lenel brought up the subject of contacting Spelman.

"It's getting late. We should call Spelman tomorrow morning whether we find it or not. If we're right about all of this, there's a good possibility there will be air traffic in this area tomorrow night. We'll explain the whole theory and maybe convince him we're not crazy."

"All the phones are dead in town. We'll have to drive clear down to the main highway again."

"And we're already down to half a tank of gas."

"Maybe we should go back into town and figure out our next move."

Okun kicked the dirt. He wasn't ready to give up, but knew the men were right.

"Hey, look up there," Freiling interrupted. "Look at that cactus and all the plants around it. Isn't that kinda fishy? All these cliffs around here are bare rock, but there's a bunch of plants all growing in one little area up there."

The crew walked to the base of the cliffs and looked up. They were standing near a twenty-foot rock wall, which led to a steep, forty-five-degree slope, which led in turn to a second set of much taller vertical walls. There was something odd about the patch of rock Freiling had pointed out. All day, they'd been noticing agave plants and cacti clinging to the rocks. After establishing toeholds on the cliffs, the plants spread their roots over the exposed surface of the rock. No roots were visible on this cliff despite the number of plants. Could there be a hidden cave up there?

Pedro climbed up the wall in front of them, then walked carefully up the slope until he came to the top. The cliffs surrounding him formed an eerie tower of ribbed rock bleached pale yellow by the elements. Great black streaks ran down them, as if someone had poured buckets of tar over the sides.

Okun went back to the car, retrieved a tire iron and a candle, then scrambled up the hill himself. When he reached the narrow shelf of flat rock at the base of the upper cliffs, he noticed a couple of strange things. The area Freiling had pointed to was smooth. It didn't match the wavy rocks of the neighboring cliffs. Also, there were long, thin cracks running through it. They looked like the ones he'd seen in plaster walls after quakes in Los Angeles.

He stepped back, spotted a squarish hole near his feet, and poked the tire iron into it. He couldn't find the back of the opening. He lay down and put his face up to the hole, but could see nothing. Running his hands over the surface of the cliff, he became convinced it was a wall built to conceal one of the caves. He picked up the tire iron and used the wedge end to begin chipping away at the face of the hillside.

The surface was hard, but it wasn't the solid boulder it appeared to be. Handfuls of sand and small stones rolled away down the slope behind him. When one of his strokes caused a dull sound, he brushed away the last pieces of debris. Something in the hole was made of a soft, patterned material. On closer inspection, it turned out to be dried grass woven to form a kind of mat. He pushed on it and felt it give. *Strange*. He slashed at the matting with his tire iron and succeeded in breaking through it. He started fumbling with one of the candles to look inside, but before he could light it, he knew he had found what he was looking for. Wafting out of the hole came a distinctive aroma, something like ammonia.

"We got it. It's here!" he yelled down the cliff. "I can smell the pod chairs from here." He lit a candle and inserted it through the hole. The cave inside was huge, narrower than the first cave but much deeper. And sitting in the middle of the space, about twenty paces from him, was a dusty alien space-craft. "Gotcha, baby," he told the ship. "I can't believe I finally found you!" He backed out of the hole and started jumping around, waving his arms in the air screaming, "It's here. It's here. I can see it. We did it!" In his excitement, he jumped too high and the gravel underfoot gave way. He crashed to his back, then started sliding down the slope. He was headed for a two-story plunge to the rocks below, but reached out at the last second and latched on to one of the bushes, his body doing a 180-degree flip. Head dangling over the edge, he smiled at the upside-down scientists. "There's a ship in there. Identical to the one we've got. I think it's time to call in the Marines."

"Young man, get away from that opening," Cibatutto cried out. Pedro had come back across the huge stone shelf to see what all the excitement was about. Noticing the hole Okun had chipped into the wall, he started poking around it, curious.

"Hey, Pedro, get away from there."

"What's in there?"

"Nothing, please don't go near it."

"Why not? I wanna see it."

Okun was too far down the slippery slope to get there in time. He knew if Pedro saw the spaceship, it would go hard on him. Desperate, Okun yelled as loud as he could. *"Chupacabra!"* The kid froze in his tracks. "We're not really looking for iron. We're looking for the goat sucker, and this is his home. Don't let him pull you inside!" Suddenly the boy couldn't be far enough away from the hole. He retreated along the narrow shelf at the base of the upper cliffs until he was around a corner.

Thirty minutes later, the five of them were standing around the car again. Pedro had found two trails running along the edge of the cliff. One of them was a switchback leading up to the top of the bluffs, while the other one came out of the hills not far from where the car was parked.

It was time to split up. Okun and Lenel would stay and investigate the ship while Cibatutto and Freiling took the kid to find the nearest phone.

"Time is of the essence," Cibatutto observed. "We've only got about twenty-four hours until our friends show up." So off they sped to find the nearest phone.

"Let's hurry up and get inside before dark."

Okun helped Lenel, unsteady, climb the narrow trail. They came out onto the great stone shelf outside of the hidden cave. Lenel sat down and watched the sun sink toward the horizon as Okun used the tire iron and his bare hands to cut a doorway into the cave.

13

The Mogollon Cave

Radecker had been so busy setting up his dragnet and feeling sorry for himself, he didn't get around to questioning the chauffeur until the next morning. The man had spent the night sleeping on a bench at the police station. He repeated everything that had been said in the car, including a verbatim account of Freiling's infernal jabbering.

"In my opinion, it's something the young guy saw in the newspaper." He described how Okun had snatched the paper out of his hands and was still holding it as they began the drive toward the cemetery. "If these guys were dangerous criminals, why wasn't I warned? And who's gonna pay for fixing up the hearse?"

When one of the cops handed Radecker a copy of Saturday's paper, it didn't take him long to figure out which story had caught Okun's eye. Now it was his turn to nod. By the time he was finished reading the story, he knew exactly where they were headed. He grinned at the chauffeur and wrote a phone number on the back of his business card. "You've been very helpful. Call this number. They'll fix your car." Then he turned to one of the cops. "I need to use a phone for a private call."

He was shown into a small office and dialed Spelman's direct line. "I think I've figured out where they're headed."

Spelman told him to hold the line, then passed the receiver to someone else. "Is this Radecker?"

"Yes, sir. Who's this?"

The man ignored him. "We found out your boys rented a car at Ontario Airport yesterday. The vehicle is a gold Ford LTD station wagon with wood-trim panels, California plates CYS 385. You got that?"

"Yes, sir."

"You say you know where they're headed?"

"I believe so, sir. But before I say anything, I'll need to know who I'm talking to and if you have proper clearance."

"This is Deputy Director Nimziki. Now where are they?"

"Mexico, sir. Somewhere in the State of Chihuahua, probably in the town of Guerrero." He went on to explain Okun's sudden interest in the newspaper and the likely connection to a paragraph in the Majestic 12 documents he had personally inked out before handing the document over to Okun. "He must have learned about it from Wells."

"You think they're down there looking for an alien vehicle?"

"Yes, sir," Radecker said almost apologetically. He'd been given very few specific instructions on how to do his job, but one thing had been made crystal clear: deny Okun access to information concerning other spacecraft. It seemed simple enough, but he had failed miserably. Okun had learned everything, despite his efforts. "With your permission, Mr.

Nimziki, I'll fly down there immediately and round them up."

There was a pause while the man on the other end thought it over. "No, that won't be necessary. You've served your purpose. Collect your things and report back to Company Headquarters for reassignment."

"Yes, sir. Thank you, sir." He hung up the phone, confused. Until that moment he had no idea who'd been pulling the strings on the project, and he was surprised it went right to the top, Nimziki's office. Everyone in the company knew the presidential appointee wasn't the real power at the CIA. Day-to-day operations and who-knew-how-many covert operations were increasingly run out of the Deputy Director's Office. It was only a matter of time until he was named to head the Agency. But what had he meant by *You've served your purpose*? That sounded ominous. At least he'd mentioned reassignment. Radecker allowed himself to be optimistic in spite of the mess he'd allowed to happen. Perhaps he was going to be promoted after all. At least he knew that wherever they sent him, it couldn't be any worse than being trapped in Area 51.

The front wall of the cave was an ingenious construction of meticulously stacked stone, woven grass, and mud. After baking in the desert sun for twenty-five years, it was almost as hard as solid stone. When Okun hesitantly stepped through the opening, he noticed another curious piece of construction material: a large section of shell armor. He recognized it as the circular door of the alien ship. The last light of day was coming through the squarish hole Okun had found earlier. When he lit one of the candles and approached the hole, he made a rather gruesome discovery. Something was lying in front of it. The thing looked like a degraded plastic bag with hands and feet. He moved closer and discovered it was the decomposed body of an alien. The hands and feet, made of a thicker, tougher material than the rest of the body, were decaying more slowly. Lenel came up behind him, holding a candle of his own.

"He must have been looking out his little window waiting to be rescued when he died. The electromagnetic field generated by the power lines must have created a ceiling which allowed the signal to travel laterally, but not upward. That must be why the aliens never located the distress signal."

Okun lowered himself toward the body until his face was only inches above the decomposed corpse and looked through the opening. "Guess what the last thing he was looking at when he died?"

"A large Y standing in a desolate landscape?"

"Bingo."

"It looks like this one has been dead for years. But we picked up his visual signal less than two years ago. Does it mean there's a telepathic interface between the creatures and their ship?"

"Makes sense. And this little guy must have programmed the ship's sending unit to repeat the message endlessly." He looked over his shoulder at Lenel. "Now I know why the image felt so lonely. This would be a crummy way to die, marooned in a cave on some foreign planet."

Lenel grunted. He wasn't about to start feeling sorry for the extraterrestrials. He walked deeper into the darkness to take a look at the ship. They lit a dozen candles, which cast an eerie, dancing glow around the ceiling. Like the first cave they'd explored, this one had mud-brick apartments standing side by side around the perimeter of the space. Staying close to one another, the two men began walking around the ship.

"This one didn't crash," Lenel observed. "There's no sign

of damage anywhere. The shell armor seems to be in perfect condition. I don't even see scrape marks."

Okun squatted down. "One problem. Where are the thrusters? This baby's lying flat on its belly. Shouldn't it be raised up off the floor?"

Lenel shrugged and moved on. They walked all the way around the exterior of the ship, pausing to make an investigation of the small rooms farthest from the mouth of the cave. They found several Mogollon artifacts, including what seemed to be a grinding stone, but no evidence at all that the alien had used the rooms. As they returned to the ship and came around toward its nose, Okun's attention was drawn to something happening behind the windows. He was about to say something when he took another step and fell into a hole. The sudden scream and downward flicker of candlelight scared Lenel half to death. "Okun? What happened?"

"I'm OK," he said, "but be careful. There's a hole over here." When he struck a match and relit his candle, Lenel came to the edge of the three-foot-deep pit. He reached a hand down to help Okun climb out, but Okun didn't take it. He was sniffing. "The ammonia smell is stronger down here." He turned around and noticed he was in a trench that led in the direction of the ship's door. "It looks like this tunnel leads inside the ship. Should we go in?"

"What if I said no, that we should wait for the help to get here?"

Okun admitted, "I'd probably go in anyway."

"So why are you even asking?" the habitual sourpuss snapped. "Help me down into this hole."

They crawled the thirty feet to the center of the ship on their hands and knees, the ammonia smell growing stronger. When they were under the open hatch, Okun saw the light of his candle flickering across the dark interior of the ship.

Something suddenly struck him as terribly wrong. As Lenel caught up with him, muttering something under his breath, Okun reached out and arrested the old man's progress with a hand clamped onto his shoulder. He was looking up into the ship in a way that made Lenel very uneasy.

"Now what?" he whispered.

"Listen. You hear that?" Okun was moving his index finger around in a very slow loop to show how the sound was repeating itself. After watching him do this for a minute and not hearing anything, Lenel spoke a few decibels louder than he needed to.

"My ears are shot. I can't hear anything."

Cautiously, Okun stood up, not sure he was going to like what he saw inside. Was it possible there were survivors after all these years? He thought of Trina Gluck's story, and how she'd been nose to nose with the Tall One. Although there was no one moving inside the ship, he was amazed when he located the source of the repetitive noise: the instrument panel at the front of the ship was surging to glowing life every few seconds. He climbed inside and walked to the front of the ship. He knelt and timed the surges against his wristwatch. To find part of the ship working didn't amaze him. He'd expected to discover the signaling system still carrying the message with the Y. But what he saw happening around him made no sense. *All* the systems were pulsing to a very slow heartbeat. "This is impossible," he yelled. "This thing is using way way way too much energy. Why does it have so much juice left?" He turned and went to confront Lenel with these questions but suddenly leaped backwards, sprawling against the dashboard, his heart suddenly pounding like a fire bell.

"What's the matter with you now?" Lenel demanded, crawling into the cabin.

A speechless Brackish could only point to something on

the floor. Lenel walked over and found three more decomposed bodies in the corner. They had been left in sitting positions, but, over the years, the heads and chests had collapsed in on themselves, sinking to the floor. Three sets of legs pointed toward the front of the ship. Okun had been so intent on checking the instrument panel, he'd literally walked right over them without noticing. The papery remains of a leg had been packed down under his shoe.

"Don't worry. They're just as dead as the one outside, and you didn't seem scared of him."

Okun looked at the cadavers like he'd just swallowed a mouthful of chunky milk. "But the way they're sitting there. Creep-o-rama extraordinaire."

"What's this power issue you were hollering about?"

Brackish got back to business. "Look at these instruments!" The two of them watched the instruments run through their four-second cycles. The yellow shell glowed dimly, the bony arms of the steering mechanism twitched, the set of tubes under the pod chairs expanded. "Where is all this energy coming from?"

"Beats me." The old man shrugged. He started to say something else, then stopped.

"What? What were you going to say?"

"Based on what we know about these ships, what's the most logical energizing source?"

Okun's mind toiled in darkness for a few moments until a lightbulb popped on. "You're suggesting these power surges are coming from another ship? Which must mean there's another alien vehicle within transmission range. Which means . . ."

"Exactly. They could be on their way down here right now."

This theory did not brighten the mood of any of the lifeforms inside the cabin, living or dead.

"Wait a sec," Okun complained. "We worked out the Van Allen connection a couple of times. We're supposed to have until tomorrow!"

"Don't get your knickers all twisted up, son. It's only an idea. Who knows where this power is coming from. Maybe this ship is using the earth's natural electromagnetism as a battery, or maybe this is what happens every time the belts show increased radioactivity."

But half an hour later, the instruments were pulsing in three-second cycles. Both Okun and Lenel were convinced an alien ship, perhaps even a small armada of them, was approaching Chihuahua.

"I figure we've got an hour, maybe two if we're lucky," Lenel said. "This ship is in perfect shape. We've got to learn as much as we can before they get here. I'll go below and try to get a look at the aqua-box. You stay here and learn what you can about the control mechanisms." Okun, mind racing in a thousand directions at once, vaguely agreed. "And because this is an emergency, I'm going to lend you my secret weapon." Lenel reached into his breast pocket and pulled out a three-inch-long screwdriver. "Pull that panel apart and make us some schematics drawings we can use on the ship back home."

As Lenel trudged off, Okun absentmindedly set to work prying the control system components out of their fittings. When he began to sketch, his mind began to wander. He'd poured his heart into finding this ship, and now it looked like he was going to lose it again. He wondered how tough the aliens really were. Could he and Lenel, like the ancient Mogollon Indians, defend their cave? He imagined pelting the unwelcome visitors with rocks as they tried to climb the hillside. If that failed, there was always the tire iron.

When they saw Mad Dog Okun at the top of the slope wearing a menacing sneer, would they turn and run? Would they fight? Or would he feel his body go numb and the weapon drop from his hands like Trina Gluck's toothbrush had dropped into the sink?

Then there was another possibility. When the approaching aliens were close enough, the craft he was sitting in would most likely be able to fly. He pictured himself glued into the pilot's pod chair. When the first eebie showed itself in the freshly cut doorway, he would slam the ship in gear, blast through the wall, and fly north to Groom Lake before the aliens knew what hit them. Two drawbacks of this plan were that Okun had never flown any type of aircraft in his life, and he didn't have the foggiest notion of how the ship's controls worked. He went back to the tire-iron scenario.

He had finished sketching the major components of the control systems into his notebook when he heard Lenel cursing and grumbling below the hatchway. He checked the cycles again. The power throbs were coming every second and a half now and appeared to be growing stronger. Very soon, the ship would be receiving a continuous flow of energy. Staying as far as possible from the straight-legged remains of the three bodies, he went to see what all the noise was about.

"I can't dig this out. I'm too damn old." Okun stepped down into the tunnel and checked Lenel's progress. He'd managed to dig about a foot and a half back toward the aqua-box. That left three and a half feet to go. Okun took the tire iron and began working furiously, driving it into the earth walls and breaking off handfuls of dirt with each thrust. He should have been doing this job all along. None of the schematics he'd made would be worth anything if they couldn't figure out the power-generating system. But the floor of the cave was packed hard, and it quickly became clear he wouldn't reach the door to the aqua-box in time.

He and Lenel both froze when they heard an unfamiliar sound. It was coming from inside the ship. When they looked inside, they saw that the lights on the instrument panel were no longer strobing. The ship was up and running.

"It's time to get out of here."

"Not yet," Okun said. "We've got to get a look at the power system." He proposed the idea of defending the cave to Lenel, who looked at him like he was crazy, then got down on all fours and started crawling out from under the ship.

"You stay here if you want to. That's not the way I want to die."

Out of frustration, Okun stabbed the earth several more times with his tire iron. But then, realizing it was too late, he collapsed against one of the walls, sweating profusely. As he was considering his next move the whole ship seemed to let out a shuddering moan. There was a loud cracking noise as it began to lift off the ground. It rose slowly, an inch at a time.

Lenel, candle near his face, seemed to rise with it. Standing on his knees, he straightened up as far as the rising ship would allow. He had a wide-open expression of wonder on his face, like a kid watching a magic show. He let out a giddy laugh, looking back toward Okun. "Will ya look at that! It's the most beautiful thing I've ever seen." The ship continued lifting until it cracked hard against the stone ceiling, sending a few chips of rock skittering down its sloped sides.

"The thruster rockets seem to be in good shape. Looks like they dug holes for them to sit in."

The black alien ship, a perfect twin of the one at Area 51, floated three feet above the ground, as mute and mysterious as a sphinx. Okun, oedipal, wanted to solve one more of its riddles before he left the cave. Ignoring Lenel's protests, he wriggled himself into the freshly created gap between the hull of the ship and the floor of the cave. He began pulling at the cover door of the aqua-box.

"Uh-oh," Lenel said. "What's that?"

"What's what?" Okun grunted between tugs.

Lenel shuffled toward the door to the cave, leaned outside, and searched the sky. Many miles from the nearest city lights, the stars shone down unobstructed and seemed to form a plush and twinkling blanket in the sky. While he was watching, one of these stars seemed to split in two. Part of it remained high in the atmosphere while another one moved closer.

"We've got company! They're here." Lenel turned around and shouted. "It's time to go."

"Almost. I've almost got it." With a final yank, Okun liberated the door from its slot. It came free of the ship and landed heavily on top of him. When Lenel heard the ooof! sound, he repeated his warning that it was time to leave.

"Start without me," Okun called from beneath the door. "I'll catch up."

Lenel poked his head out the door indecisively and looked at the stone shelf leading to the trail. "All right. I'll take the same path we came up on. Meet me at the bottom of the hill. How much longer are you going to be?"

If Okun couldn't find a way to get his head and chest out from under the heavy section of shell armor, he was going to be there permanently. "A minute or two," his muffled voice answered.

"OK, two minutes. No longer!" Lenel warned. He could see the swirl of green light coming from beneath the ship and knew Okun had gotten the door off. He stepped through the opening and began edging along the top of the slope.

Okun concentrated on making himself very skinny and

eventually succeeded in worming out from under the door. Then he looked up and beheld the spectacular play of light caused by the aqua-box, its energy racing around the inside of the chamber like a transparent cyclone of crystal green water. An exact clone of the one at Area 51, it exhibited the same paper-thin walls of rock, the same hairwidth filaments arranged in a complex geometrical pattern. But there was one important exception: floating in the center of the hexagonal chamber, suspended in midair, was a small piece of metal shaped like an ankh. Like a gyroscope, it was spinning and rolling while remaining in one spot. It seemed to be gathering the energy off the sides of the hexagon and sending it out in a controlled manner. Each of the ankh's four arms sent out a razor-thin beam. He remembered the chaotic way the other ship's box had purged the system of energy and how the ships would have had to fly improbably close to one another. This was the answer, and it had been hanging around his neck the whole time. Incredible!

When something moved across the doorway, Okun reached out and grabbed the tire iron. But it was only Lenel, who immediately concealed himself behind the rock wall. "Too late. They're here." He pointed up through the ceiling. "They've found us, and it's too dark out there for me to see where I'm going."

Okun gathered up his possessions. He'd seen how the aqua-box worked. He was ready to help Lenel make his escape. But as he made to leave, he decided he needed to try one last experiment. He slipped his necklace off and tried to undo the knot, but couldn't. "Might work anyhow," he muttered. He wanted to switch the two ankhs, to make absolutely sure they were interchangeable. He reached up and pulled the spinning piece out, preparing to switch them. Immediately the ship lost power and began settling toward the floor. Okun hadn't counted on that. He shoved the new piece into the chamber and closed his eyes tight, expecting to feel the weight of the ship crush down on his chest. Luckily, it accepted the second ankh, leather string and all.

If I take both ankhs, they won't be able to fly this ship out of here! He decided to go for broke.

"What in Hades are you doing over there? They'll be coming through the door any second. Let's get—" Lenel, glancing outside, saw something that stopped him in mid-sentence. Hovering directly overhead was the nose of an alien saucer. It crawled forward until it was away from the cliffs, then turned itself around and crept closer. Peeking around the corner of the doorway, Lenel had a clear view through the windows into the interior of the craft. A hand-ful of the large-headed creatures were gathered at the windows, inspecting the cliff.

"How we doin' over there?" Okun called over his shoulder. He was too focused on his task to notice that Lenel's answer was an unintelligible stammer. He was trying to get his ankh out of the aqua-box without having the ship squash him. He had crawled back into the trench and was reaching with the tire iron, trying to snag the loop of leather string. But this was as difficult as a carnival game owing to the fact that the spin-ning ankh was moving the string in all directions.

The hovering saucer pressed in closer. Lenel picked up a large rock and stood with his back pressed to the wall, his eyes glued to the doorway. He planned to clobber anything that stepped inside. He felt the nose of the spacecraft bump against the wall and wondered if they were going to use the ship as a battering ram to open the cave. He found his voice long enough to whisper hoarsely across the darkness of the cave: "They're right outside."

One last try, Okun told himself. *I know I can get it*. But before he could take a final stab at the dancing leather string, a powerful blast of white light entered the cave from outside. It was sweeping across the floor and heading his way. Faster than he knew he could move, he rolled into the trench, hiding himself a split second before he was seen. The search beam scanned the cave's interior for several seconds before abruptly shutting off.

"Now do you believe me?" Lenel's voice was trembling. "Please, Brackish, let's go."

Cowering in the trench, Okun asked if the ship had moved away. Suddenly his idea about challenging the aliens had vanished. When Lenel reported that it had flown a little way off, Okun leaped out of the trench and ran for the door. Without a word, he helped his old friend step through the hole and out onto the ledge. The spacecraft was hovering near the bottom of the cliffs, not far from where the station wagon had been parked a few hours before. Okun was more terrified than he'd ever been. He felt the strong urge to sprint away down the cliff and be well hidden by the time the aliens came out of their ship. But he couldn't abandon Lenel, especially after making him wait so long to escape. He tried to pull the man along gently, but was afraid of knocking him off-balance. When they came to a flat section of the stone ledge, he left Lenel for just a moment to run ahead and check the switchback trail Pedro had shown him that afternoon. It looked too treacherous for the old man. As Lenel took the last few steps toward Okun, he lost his way and walked off the narrow trail. He landed on the gravel slope and crashed hard against the rocks. By the time Okun got to him, he had slid ten feet down the hill and was clutching a handful of shrubs. Desperately searching for a way to reach his friend, he heard the old man whimpering in pain. Even the quietest sound was a roar of noise in the Silent Zone.

"Lenel," he rasped, "reach up here and grab my hand. I'll pull you up."

The old man shook his head. "I think I broke something. You get out of here. Get back to Area 51."

"Not without you I'm not." Okun wedged the toe of his shoe into a fissure in the rock and started lowering himself head-first down the slope. Before he could grasp the old man's wrist, the root of the bush Lenel was holding gave way, and Lenel began sliding down the rocky slope. Horrified, Okun made a last desperate lunge, but couldn't reach him. The old man slid away until he plunged over the side of the lower cliffs and landed a second later with a sickening thud.

"Lenel, are you all right?" he whispered, knowing his voice would carry to the bottom of the cliffs.

No answer. He was about to start down the hillside to find his friend when he heard a metallic click echo through the valley. Then he watched a circular pool of light form on the ground below the ship. The hatch door had been opened. Adrenaline pumping, he ran a few more strides along the trail before diving into a shallow foxhole near the base of the trail leading to the top of the cliffs. Climbing the trail now would definitely expose him.

He looked down on the ship until he saw the little beings step onto the ground and begin wandering around the area. They moved toward the base of the hill, to the place where Lenel's body must have fallen. Although he couldn't see Lenel, he could see the creatures standing around him. He wanted to shout at them to get away from his friend, but was too terrified even to move. Suddenly, they abandoned Lenel and began climbing the hillside. Okun knew that probably meant the old man was dead.

Peeking and ducking, he watched the aliens trying to climb the first steep wall toward the cave. From everything he'd learned about them, he expected them to be much more nimble. But they were having just as much trouble as he had had with the rocky terrain.

It occurred to him he could probably make a run for it. In fact, he probably *should* because his foxhole was only seventy-five feet from the opening. When they realized someone had been messing around with their ship, wouldn't they come out and search the area? *Maybe they'll think Lenel was in there by himself.* No, he had to get out of there immediately. He reached down to grab his notebook and his ankh and realized he'd left them inside! He slapped himself in the forehead. The searchlight scanning the cave had scared him so badly, he'd forgotten to pick up his things. He'd come all this way only to blow it at the very end. He briefly considered making a mad dash back to the door, ducking inside to grab his possessions and racing out again. But, like the other heroic plans he'd made that evening, he thought about it too long. Soon six of the awkward little creatures were approaching the mouth of the cave. At the bottom of the slope, he spotted a taller creature, climbing the hillside even more awkwardly than the others. *That must be The Tall One.*

The smaller aliens had already been inside for a couple of minutes when the Tall One reached the top of the slope. They came outside and flitted around the taller creature, seemingly agitated. As Okun watched this scene unfold, the Tall One turned its head in a very deliberate way and seemed to look directly at Okun across the darkness. Okun ducked out of sight, fighting to control his fear. It was dark; maybe he hadn't been seen. His heart racing like it was going to explode, he quietly turned on his back and tried to clear his mind. He knew he had to stay hidden, but he also knew he had to run. He heard the sound of their feet moving across the gravel again. Were they moving in to surround

him? He flipped back over and glanced up at the switchback
trail. It was time to find out who could run faster, a terrified
earthling or these creatures from who-knew-where. But
when he peeked once more over the edge of his hiding place,
the creatures were in retreat. The six smaller ones were
marching away down the hillside and the Tall One was disappearing alone into the cave.

They climbed down the lower cliff and didn't walk over to
Lenel's body. They went straight to their ship and climbed in.
Okun counted them again to make sure none of them were
sneaking around to ambush him. A moment after the circular
door snapped closed, there was a whirring hum and the sixty-
foot craft zipped straight up into the air, disappearing into
the canopy of stars at a fantastic rate of speed. When the ship
was gone, the zone of silence swallowed him once more. He
heard the Tall One moving around inside the cave. Somehow,
being left alone near this most terrifying of the aliens was
worse than being near all six of the others. *Is the Tall One
reading my mind right now? Does he know I'm out here?*

No longer indecisive, Okun began his escape. He pushed
himself quietly away from the gravel of his hiding place and
stepped back onto the trail. He began climbing the narrow
trail to the top of the cliffs, which was littered with pebbles
and sand. Each footstep became a matter of life and death. To
help him find the Zen of the moment, he imagined himself as
Grasshopper, the young Shao-Lin priest from the *Kung Fu*
television series. Hands gliding through the air, knees bent,
Okun climbed the treacherous slope as delicately as if it
were a rice-paper carpet he could not afford to tear. When he
reached the top of the bluff, he found himself on a large
mesa. After a final glance over the side to make sure he
wasn't being followed, he tore away at a dead run. He ran as
fast as he could in a straight line across the open plain,

looking over his shoulder every few seconds. When he got to the far side of the plateau, he wasted no time. He ran down this new set of slopes which were every bit as treacherous as the ones outside the cave, something he could never have done if his system weren't overloaded with adrenaline. It didn't matter to him that he was running ever deeper into a water-less no-man's-land where he might die of thirst or starvation. His immediate problem was getting as far away from the cave as humanly possible. He wanted to be miles away when the Tall One came out of the cave to look for him. After twenty minutes of sprinting, a stabbing pain in his side forced him to stop. He limped to a place between two boulders and col-lapsed in the sand, gasping for air and dripping with sweat. He was sure they wouldn't find him here, even if they came looking.

When he'd been lying there long enough for his breathing to return to normal, he heard a droning sound in the distance. He listened to the sound for a long while until he recognized what it was—an airplane engine. It was coming from the direction of the power lines. Cibatutto and Freiling must have reached a phone and called in the Marines. He wanted to run back the way he'd come and help them locate the cave, but he was beyond exhaustion. All he could do was hope the military found the spot before the Tall One escaped with the ship. Struggling to keep his eyes open, he listened to the plane's engine purring in the distance.

14

The Okun Era Begins

Even before he opened his eyes, he felt the presence standing over him. He was lying on his stomach and felt every nerve ending in his body tingle to full alertness. His deepest instincts told him not to move, not to change his breathing. He was certain he was being watched.

A voice asked, "Mr. Okun?"

Brackish deftly flipped himself onto his side and cocked his leg back, ready to mule-kick his attacker, when he noticed he was in a hospital. The doctor at his bedside, who had almost taken a face full of foot, was a young man with a goatee, a buzz cut, and a very intense look on his face. He hadn't flinched.

"Feeling better this morning?"

"Dude, I was just about to kick your teeth out. You're supposed to get out of the way when that happens."

"Much better than yesterday, I see."

Okun looked him over. "What do you mean? How long have I been here? Where am I? What's wrong with me?"

The man arched an eyebrow. "Much much better." He introduced himself as Dr. Issacs and explained they were at Fort Irwin, California. Okun had been there for a week, and although there was nothing physically wrong with him, he was suffering from an extremely unusual form of memory loss. Although Okun could remember everything that had gone on in Mexico, he could recall none of his stay in the hospital. Each morning for the past week, he had woken up anxious to tell about the alien ship he'd found. Although he was only half conscious, he managed to relate the story accurately and in some detail. When Issacs and the other doctors explained to him that he'd already told them about the trip south of the border, he became quarrelsome, refusing to believe them. Each morning he asked if the ship had been recovered, if Lenel was dead, and whether his ankh necklace had been found. He remembered the answers he received until he slept again—whereupon he forgot everything. Even when he drifted off for a ten-minute nap, he woke up surprised not to find himself in the desert. Dizzy and confused, he began asking the doctors where he was, how long he'd been there, whether the ship had been recovered, and if Lenel was still alive. Issacs, who was not a psychiatrist, said it was a case of amnesia unlike any he could find described in the medical literature and had no idea of how to go about treating the condition. Gazing steadily, almost menacingly, down at his patient, he expressed a guarded optimism. "You've seemed groggy all week, but today you appear to be quite alert. I take it as a good sign."

Okun looked confused and opened his mouth to speak.

"Before it occurs to you to ask," Issacs cut him off, "let me assure you that Dr. Lenel is alive and well. He broke two ribs and fractured some bones in his left hip, but his doctors expect him to recover nicely. Your story matches his in every detail up to the point where he fell down the hill, and we have no reason to suspect your account of the facts after that point."

"So, what you're telling me is"—Okun wanted to get this straight—"I keep not remembering yesterday."

"Precisely. Or you might say you keep on un-remembering it in your sleep, and I don't mind telling you that the whole thing has begun to get on my nerves. We've had the same conversation every day this week." He explained that the two of them had spent hour after hour arguing because Okun refused to believe Issacs when he said Okun had told him the same exact story the previous day. "Frankly," the stolid young doctor said, "it's become incredibly tedious."

Okun was beginning to wish he'd kicked this guy when he had the chance. He tried to remember yesterday. The last thing he could recall was finding the spot between the boulders and listening to the plane's engine. He started to ask Issacs something, but the doctor held up his hands.

"Before you begin asking your usual questions"—he rolled his eyes wearily—"perhaps you'd allow me to answer them for you. First: the search planes located the cave shortly after dawn on Monday morning. The exterior wall had been destroyed, very possibly broken from the inside out, but there was no other evidence of the ship you and Dr. Lenel have described. Second: *no*, your necklace was not in the cave. Third: *no*, the other ankh was not in the cave either. Fourth: *yes*, the recovery team headed by Mr. Jenkins searched in the loose earth where you had been digging. Fifth: you were found by two members of the search party, a pair of agents from the CIA's Domestic Collections Division. Am I going too fast for you?"

"No one even saw the ship leaving the cave?"

"Radar abnormalities were observed in the region, but no definitive sighting was made."

"So, basically, we came away empty-handed?"

"Yes, it seems so."

Okun buried his face under his pillow and briefly considered smothering himself. Issacs, who briefly considered helping him, went on. "I'm very encouraged by the fact that you appear to believe what I'm telling you this morning. It may mean you're cured. Today is different for another reason as well. Colonel Spelman is visiting from Washington and is waiting to see you. I'll show him in."

A groan came through the pillow when Okun heard he would have to face Spelman. He was positive he was about to be bawled out by an irate soldier for all the rules he'd broken and all the damage he'd caused. But when the barrel-chested officer came into the room, he was all handshakes and smiles. He didn't seem angry at all.

"Nonsense," Spelman said, when Okun began apologizing for the way he'd chased after the second ship. "You did your best. If we had trusted you a little more, and sent you down there with some military backup, we would have captured the thing and maybe even taken some prisoners. But we were a little nervous after your visit with Dr. Wells. You couldn't have played it any better than you did."

"I need to get back there, Colonel. I need to search the cave for something. See, I had this necklace with a little piece from the ship shaped like an ankh—that's the ancient Egyptian symbol for life. Anyhow, I—"

Spelman turned away, and said, "Dr. Issacs, would you mind stepping outside for a moment and keeping the hallway clear. Mr. Okun and I have some issues to discuss." When the doctor had gone, the colonel reached into his breast pocket and pulled out Okun's leather necklace with the ankh still attached. "When the DCD found you sleeping between those rocks, this was lying at your feet. They brought it directly to me."

"Impossible!" Okun gasped. "I left the necklace inside the cave. I'm positive about that."

"That's what I heard."

"Then how did they find it next to me?"

"I was going to ask you the same question."

Okun shuddered at the idea of the Tall One stealing up and examining him while he slept. *Was that all he had done?* The two men talked for a long time before agreeing the facts seemed to indicate that the Tall One had wanted Okun to have the ankhlike instrument. *Why* he would want this was another question altogether. Spelman had a theory about it. He began by asking if Okun was familiar with the Bridget Jones incident. Okun said he was. "Then you know these creatures possess implant devices our technology is unable to detect. As soon as you were brought here, we ran a number of X-rays and other tests, and while we were unable to find anything unusual, we can't rule out the possibility that you've been tagged somehow."

"Come again?"

"When the Jones girl found the object, she described a depression in the grass shaped like a man. I've always felt the eebies must have been on the verge of implanting the BB-sized device into the police officer when they were interrupted, probably by the girl's arrival on the scene. We have every reason to believe your encounter with these creatures was more than one of physical proximity. Ask yourself why you were still asleep so late in the afternoon when they found you? Where did this strange thing about forgetting the previous day come from? And I don't need to tell you how often abductees tell us about experiencing false memories or how they lost track of themselves for a day. Maybe your encounter was more involved that you can recall."

Okun considered this possibility. "Have I developed any strange powers like she did?"

Spelman shook his head. "Except for being groggy and argumentative all week, Issacs tells me you're normal. Keep in mind this implanted device business is only a theory, a worst-case scenario. But it's at least possible they gave you back the necklace hoping you'd carry it to another one of their ships. If they've marked you in some way that allows them to track your whereabouts, you could lead them to Area 51. It might all be a ruse to hunt down their missing ship."

"I see. So I'm probably banished for life from going back there."

"Actually"—Spelman smiled—"that's another thing I wanted to talk with you about. We are prepared to offer you the position of Director of Research at the facility. It would always be a risk moving you in and out. But if we took certain precautions, we feel confident you and the ship would be safe."

"What kind of precautions?"

"You told Dr. Issacs the downed vehicle was emitting a beacon signal."

"Right. The image of the Y. You already know about that, too?"

"Yes, you told us on Tuesday. You said the electromagnetic field generated by the power poles must have created a roof which prevented the space-based aliens from receiving the distress signal."

"So you're saying we could rig up some mobile unit to generate EMF waves, and I'd travel to the labs under it? *Très* cool. But wouldn't it just be easier to hire somebody else?"

The two men looked at one another for a long beat. "At this point," the colonel said, "we don't feel anyone could replace you. You know so much. It would take many months, perhaps years, for someone to learn what you already know."

Okun heard Dworkin's voice ringing in his ears, *The more you know, the deeper you're buried.*

Spelman stood up, preparing to leave. "You're the only one we're considering at the moment. It's the job we had in mind for you when you were recruited. Take some time to think it over. We know from Agent Radecker there are many changes you'd like to make at the labs. As Director of Research, you would have the power to make them. But once you're in the door, you'll have to stay down there. You won't be able to sit outside and do your watercolor painting anymore, and there won't be any weekend trips to Las Vegas." Before he turned to go, he added, "As much as I'd like to see you accept this assignment, I have to admit I don't know how I'd choose. Here, hold on to this while you make up your mind." He handed over the ankh and leather necklace.

Before Spelman was quite out the door, Okun asked one last question. "I take it Radecker's no longer the director. He's not here at the hospital, is he?" Okun didn't need any more grief this morning.

Spelman suppressed a smile. "Agent Radecker has been promoted. He's now the Chief of Intelligence at the CIA office in Barrow, Alaska. Just above the Arctic Circle."

The next day, Okun remembered yesterday.

Soon afterward, he was discharged from the hospital. But not before he'd developed a grudging admiration and bickering friendship with the multitalented Dr. Issacs. No older than Okun, he was a pathology intern at Bethesda Naval

Hospital in D.C. He held a B.S. from Cornell in astrophysics and claimed to be an expert in ancient mythology. Since his first days at Area 51, Okun had seen the need for medical expertise in the labs. Further autopsies needed to be performed on the recovered aliens, tissue samples needed to be analyzed, and the ship itself was largely composed of living tissue. If he accepted the position and became director, Issacs was exactly the sort of man he'd seek to hire.

When he was discharged from the hospital, Okun went home to see his mother. He arrived unannounced early one morning and walked into the house. He found Saylene reading the paper and sipping coffee. She jumped into his arms, and while they were hugging, a man walked out of the bedroom to see what was going on. His name was Peter, and he seemed to have spent the night. Okun looked at his mom and knew by her expression that things had changed around the house. She called in sick and they went out for an all-day lunch. She told him everything that had happened while he was away, how much she liked his haircut, and all about her relationship with her new man. She knew enough not to ask what he'd been up to during the same time, but it was uncomfortable how lopsided the conversation became. It didn't help that Brackish was distracted. He glanced around the restaurant every few minutes like he was expecting someone. The two of them made a plan that Saylene would take a few days off at the end of the month and they'd take a trip together—just the two of them. But it was a journey they would never take.

Every day that Okun was home, he was sure they would be watching him. He developed a habit of glancing over his shoulders when he walked down a street. When he borrowed the car, he spent more time watching the rearview mirror than the road. He was positive the phone was tapped and the

house was bugged. He walked around the neighborhood looking for a van with tinted windows and extra radio antennas.
But search as he might, he could find no shred of evidence
he was under surveillance.

One day he received a piece of mail. Inside there was a
note: "Thought you'd find this amusing. Hope all is well.
Spelman." Enclosed was a newspaper article from an El Paso
newspaper with a headline that read:

Mythical Monsters of Mexico, number of chupacabra
sightings rise after youth tells story.

There was a photograph of Pedro standing in front of the cliffs
where they'd discovered the hidden ship. Okun got a kick out
of the article, but didn't believe the implication of Spelman's
note. *Hope all is well. As if he doesn't know exactly how I'm
spending every minute.*

The attempts he made to reenter his old life proved futile.
He called friends and visited a few of his old professors at
Caltech, but their conversations were strained. He found
himself growing more adept at steering the conversation away
from himself, but as he listened to these people talk about
their lives and concerns, something kept him from nodding.
For some reason, he couldn't enjoy normal people as he once
had. He told himself his distraction was due to being followed around all day. So he devised a plan to flush the spies
around him out of their hiding places.

One afternoon he phoned a television station and asked to
speak with a reporter. He said he had a major news story
concerning extraterrestrial visitors. Of course, the journalist
didn't believe him, so he told her enough to show her he was
serious. And enough to make whoever was listening in on
the conversation very nervous. They made an appointment

for the next morning. Okun hung up the phone and waited on the front porch for the unmarked sedans to start arriving. But no one came. The next morning, he dressed in a suit and drove to the station. When he came through the front doors, there were no federal agents waiting there to arrest him. *I guess they're not watching*. He sat down in the lobby and considered what to do next.

Although he had not gone to the station intending to talk with anyone, he considered going ahead and breaking the story. He could imagine Wells's reaction if he saw the announcement on television. He'd immediately demand that the nurse release him so he could assume the role of Earthly Dictator. He was crazy, but he had a point: didn't the people of earth deserve to know about the visitors? Wasn't it somehow the birthright of every human to know the truth? That's what he'd always been taught. He, Brackish Okun, could end a quarter-century-old conspiracy simply by keeping the appointment he'd made. He could give them names, technical sketches, report numbers, and he could explain the significance of the trinket he was wearing around his neck. The government's public relations teams and CIA disinformation specialists would have a hard time discrediting his story.

But now that it was in his power to do this, he wasn't sure it was the wisest path. Dworkin hadn't thought so. He remembered quite clearly Sam's warning about society disintegrating under the strains of uncertainty and fear. He'd felt the effects himself, having trouble sleeping at night wondering if he really had been *marked* by the Tall One. Breaking the story would certainly cause a panic, and there was no guarantee it would produce any benefits. Politically, it would play right into the hands of those ugly, fascist men who wanted to turn America and the world into an armed camp.

In the end, the question of whether to tell what he knew came down to a decision between two very different approaches to the world. In Okun's mind, it became a choice between Dworkin and Wells.

He stood up, walked out of the lobby, and climbed back into his car. Out of habit, he found himself glancing too often into the mirror. Every time he did this it reminded him that he was free. No one was looking over his shoulder anymore. He was surprised when this didn't make him feel any more at ease than he had since he'd returned home. It just made him feel disconnected. He realized why he had been so distracted, so unable to nod, when he was with his old friends. It wasn't lurking spies. It was that their hopes and dreams and daily problems, everything that was important to them, seemed trivial compared to the task of learning about the alien visitors. The whole time his mother had been describing how she met her boyfriend, Brackish's mind was 185 miles from earth, contemplating the next period of increased radioactivity of the inner Van Allen belt. As he drove home, he told himself, *I know too much to lead a normal life,* and realized how true Dworkin's words about knowing too much had been. He didn't need any CIA spooks to bury him; the knowledge he was carrying around in his head did that on its own. By the time he pulled into the driveway, he'd decided he was going back. He would have gone back even if they weren't offering to make him director. Like his older colleagues, he felt the work in the labs was more important than his personal destiny.

He called Spelman, and said, "I'm ready to come back, but I have a couple of conditions."

"Go ahead, I'm listening."

● ● ●

He spent a month at Edwards Air Force Base working with NASA engineers on the vehicle that would carry him back to the facility beneath Groom Lake. The result was a heavily modified VW van completely covered with a gray material derived from Teflon. A portable power station in the rear cargo area generated a force field of electromagnetic energy strong enough to disrupt the radio reception of the cars he passed on the drive out to the desert. The engineers who helped him build it nicknamed the vehicle the StealthWagon and thought the military might be able to apply the radar-deflecting material they'd designed to the construction of new aircraft.

When he motored up to the X-shaped landing strip out-side of Area 51, he could see evidence of new construction. The shantytown of wooden houses which had once housed the lab's staff had been torn down to make way for the con-struction of a giant sliding door, one that would allow the spaceship below to make a quick exit if the need ever pre-sented itself. He drove the StealthWagon into the hangar and rode the new freight elevator down the six flights to the floor of the lab. Everything looked different. When he came into the long narrow hallway which had, for years, housed the chaos of the stacks, he found it freshly painted and bril-liantly lit. A small work crew was busy organizing the files and entering their catalogue numbers on the lab's new com-puter system. An elevated walkway had been installed down the center of the long room, which Okun planned to make a dust-free research area. As he walked farther along, he found a crew of hard hats excavating space for the new elec-trochemical research unit. He came to the huge concrete bunker that was home to the captured alien spaceship. The room was empty except for a giant crate seventy-by-seventy and twenty feet tall. Stenciled on the outside of this over-

sized wooden box were the words CHEMICAL EXPLO-
SIVES—NO SMOKING. He toured once around the box to
make sure the ship within could not be seen. On his way out
of the bunker, he noticed a doorway that hadn't been there
before and went inside. It was the new medical facility, complete with a glass-enclosed operating room. Although the
workmanship was marvelous, something about the room
gave him the creeps.

The door to the kitchen was locked. After pounding on it to
make himself heard over the noise of the construction crew,
the door was opened by a young man who stared at him in a
slightly demented way. Dr. Issacs, his first hire.

Even before he stepped inside the familiar room, he was
getting an earful from Lenel. "What kind of boss are you,
anyhow? Ever since you took over it's been so darn noisy
down here we can't get any work done." The old man was in
a body cast that went from his underarms to his kneecaps.

"You look like a mummy in a swimsuit," Okun opined.

While Freiling and Cibatutto stepped forward to welcome
Brackish back, Lenel tried to sustain his grouchy demeanor.
"If I do," he snapped, "I've got you to thank for it."

"That's right," Freiling came to Lenel's aid. "We've heard
all about how Dr. Lenel saved you from falling off that cliff."

"Saved me?" Okun asked, flabbergasted. He turned to
Lenel, who was shooting him a look that said *don't you dare
tell*. "Oh right, saved me." He grinned. "By the way, Dr.
Lenel, I haven't had a chance to thank you for that."

"All part of the job," Lenel grumbled.

Owing to the presence of the construction crews, the staff was
prevented from working on the ship for nearly three full
months. During this time, they kept themselves busy with

whatever small projects could be brought into their sleeping quarters or the kitchen. To everyone's dismay, Issacs turned out to be a neat freak and was continually chiding his coworkers to keep the place organized. "You can't teach an old dog new tricks," was the stock reply he received from the trio of senior citizens. But he kept after them, and slowly they began to see his point.

When the last new rooms had been finished and the last unauthorized personnel left the labs, the men descended on the alien spaceship like a pack of starved dogs. They were eager to apply all they had learned from the undamaged craft they'd found in Mexico. For six full months, they rewelded, rewired, rethought, and rebuilt every inch of the ship. After a series of preliminary tests they felt it was time to invite Spelman to Area 51 for a demonstration.

He arrived on a cloudy morning in early July and brought some guests, all of them former members of the now-defunct Project Smudge: Jim "the Bishop" Ostrom, Jenkins, the new chief of Domestic Collections Department, whose men had found Okun sleeping in the desert, and Dr. Insolo from the Science and Technology Directorate. Okun recognized him from Sam's funeral. After a quick lunch, the guests were invited into the concrete bunker to witness an experiment. They gathered on a newly built observation platform while the scientists readied their monitoring equipment. When everything was ready, Okun addressed his visitors.

"Several years ago, my predecessor, Dr. Wells, developed a technique of feeding high-voltage power into the ship's energy system and found he could achieve low levels of performance from the instrumentation within. Partially because the design function which expels energy from this system was incomplete, excess or clogged power generated high temperature levels." He was only at the beginning of his speech, but saw from the blank looks on the faces of his audience there was no point in continuing with the lecture. Instead, he simply said, "Watch this."

He passed out pairs of prismatic goggles, then gave a signal to Freiling, who was standing on the operator's platform of the energy cannon. The old man threw a switch, and the room filled with a shrill buzzing sound as the gun began bombarding the alien ship with power. A loud crack ripped through the vessel and bounced off the concrete walls. Lenel gave an OK sign from the output meter he was watching. Cibatutto directed the visitors' attention to the mirror at the bottom of the ship, where they watched the swirling green cyclone being created by the aqua-box. And, through the special filters of the goggles, they were able to watch the energy being purged from the ship's system. Instead of the spasmodic and undirected waves they had seen before, the energy was now channeled through the arms of the whirling ankh. Four pinpoint beams traveled around the walls of the bunker, searching for another ship to power.

A moment later, the wooden trestles holding the ship off the floor groaned as the weight bearing down on them began to ease. Slowly, like an ancient pterodactyl riding an updraft, the ship lifted into the air. The moment it did so, the scientists abandoned the monitors they were watching and threw their arms in the air, cheering.

"Holy guacamole!" Okun gasped. When a nod wasn't enough to express his excitement, he began bouncing up and down, then turned and grabbed the first body he could find—it happened to be Spelman's—and bounced around with the colonel wrapped in his arms. He leaped from the platform to the floor of the bunker, still bouncing. The ship had lifted two feet above the trestles. He gave Cibatutto five, then bounced over and kissed Lenel on the forehead before the old man could swat him away. When he came to Dr. Issacs, a little of the air went out of his tires.

As calm, cool, and collected as ever, Issacs indicated the heat gauge. "The temperature inside the ship is 160 and climbing," he called out over the screech of the electro-cannon. "It's time to shut down."

Okun turned and waved the cutoff signal. But Freiling remained oblivious, hypnotized by the dark bird floating before him, until Okun ran up next to him, and yelled, "TURN IT OFF!" The old man flipped the kill switch, abruptly bringing the power level down to zero. The saucer crashed down onto the trestles, which cracked and teetered, but, fortunately, did not collapse.

"Gotta work on the landing," Freiling observed, pulling off his goggles, "but I'll be damned if we didn't get her to fly."

"We sure did, Daddy-o!"

"I only wish Sam could've seen this."

Okun smiled sadly. "Me too."

The scientists rejoined their visitors on the observation platform, then repaired immediately to the kitchen. According to the long-established rules of procedure at the top-secret facility, champagne was served.

Somewhere between the uncorking of the bottles and the departure of the visiting dignitaries late that afternoon, there was an important exchange of documents. Okun went first.

As Spelman had requested, he'd prepared a report detailing everything he knew about the aliens up to that point. It ran to over two hundred pages. At the end of it, he tried to answer the question of how great a threat the aliens posed to the world in general and the United States in particular. He found the question nearly impossible to answer. Despite all that had been learned about them, the most basic question of all remained a mystery: What did they want? The possibilities ranged all the way from the hope they were beneficent beings bearing gifts to the fear they had come to invade the planet and take it away from us. Okun took both possibilities seriously. But his gut told him it was bad news, VDJ. They were dealing with an intelligent race with advanced technologies. Their ships were armed, they used other beings as armor, and they had offered no sign of friendship. If Wells had interpreted the vision of the alien planet correctly, they were also dealing with a catastrophic food shortage. Perhaps the encounters were few because these were only scout ships. On the other hand, they had made no sign of being hostile either. Never once had they demonstrated a clearly malicious intent to humans, with the possible exception of the Eau Claire case. They had ample opportunity to torture, maim, or kill any of the people they'd captured. Instead they had been released unharmed, and although many of these people came away from the experience traumatized, an equal number longed for it to happen again.

Then there was Okun's own experience. He recalled how wildly terrified he'd been of being detected by the aliens outside the cave. But looking back on it, they must have known he was there all along. Instead of harming him, the Tall One had given him the ankh, allowing research to continue. It might even turn out they were shy tourists ferried through a time warp in the Van Allen belts for five-day vacations, observing earth from the safety and comfort of their flying fortresses—their version of visiting a safari park. Who knew? He concluded that it was too early for conclusions and called upon the military and intelligence branches of the government to aid in the recovery of more evidence. To this end, he proposed a handful of clever stratagems designed to lure the creatures into traps.

Spelman accepted the report with the promise that it would circulate through the highest levels of the government.

"Including the president?"

"Especially the president."

Okun actually breathed a sigh of relief when he learned that soon this important information would be in the right hands. It was too heavy a responsibility for him to carry around, and he didn't feel right about the CIA and the Army being the only ones to know about it.

"Now we've got something for you."

Dr. Insolo snapped open the locks on an attaché case and pulled out some pieces of paper. "The only reservation any of us had about appointing you director concerned your educational qualifications. Something isn't quite right when the leader of one of the nation's top laboratories doesn't hold a Ph.D. But given the restrictions on your travel, we knew you wouldn't be able to attend classes. So, we took the liberty of transferring your credits from Caltech to the United States Naval Postgraduate School, where I'm a member of the faculty. Hope you don't mind." He held up what looked to Okun like a diploma and read what was printed on it. "Whereas the candidate, Brackish Okun, has exhibited full mastery of the body of knowledge and technologies associated with his field of study, and whereas he has made a unique and original contribution to this field, he is hereby awarded a doctorate of philosophy in Xenoaeronautics."

Spelman was the first to extend his hand. "Congratulations, *Doctor* Okun."

"How utterly cool," Okun enthused, reading over the diploma. When he looked up he was surrounded by the smiling faces of his friends and guests. Without realizing it, they had all begun mirroring the minuscule cranial motion so characteristic of the lab's director. The entire room was nodding.

"The end." Nimziki smirked when he saw those words on the last page of Okun's report. "What does he think this is, a bedtime story?"

"Sometimes he's a little weird." Spelman chuckled.

"What did you think of it?" Nimziki asked, tossing the report onto his desk.

"It's wordy, and parts of it don't make much sense, but the ideas are strong. Overall, I'd say it's a balanced presentation of the evidence. I'm anxious to hear what the president has to say about it."

"Yeah, me too," Nimziki said absently. He wasn't any great fan of President Ford's. When it had been time to appoint a new director of the CIA, Ford had ignored the unanimous recommendation of the intelligence community that Nimziki get the job. He had named one of his longtime political allies to the post instead.

"I especially liked his ideas about how to capture another ship."

"Yeah, I'll have to reread those. Smart."

"And what about his ideas for slowly introducing the truth about the aliens to the public?"

"The stuff about saturating the media with alien stories before breaking the true story. Interesting. I'll have to give it some more thought." Spelman could see Nimziki was tired and distracted by other thoughts. That was understandable. It was almost eleven o'clock at night, and they'd both been at work since early that morning. "I think I'll get out of here and let you go home." Spelman walked to the door, then turned, and said, "Please let me know as soon as you get any reaction from the White House so I can pass it along to our team out at Groom Lake. I'm as anxious as they are. And, Al—" he waited for Nimziki to glance up—"we all did a hell of a good job on this one, didn't we?"

"Yeah, we sure did, Bud. But listen, don't expect an immediate response from the president. You know how they are over there. They want to preserve their plausible deniability option. But the moment I hear anything, on or off the record, I'll let you know."

When Spelman was gone, Nimziki thumbed through the report once more, then walked into the next room and fed it into a paper shredder. He turned out the lights and went home.

This is Mr. Molstad's third book for Centropolis Entertainment. Before writing the novelization of the hit movie *Independence Day*, he was a collaborator on the Hugo-nominated novelization of *StarGate*. After graduating from the University of California, Santa Cruz, he spent several years traveling, teaching, and playing pickup basketball. He lives with his wife Elizabeth in Los Angeles and invites your E-comments at molstad@centropolis.com.